ORDINARY FURIES

Linda Morganstein

Spinsters Ink
2007

Spinsters Ink
P.O. Box 242
Midway, Florida 32343

Printed in the United States of America on acid-free paper
First Edition

Editor: Christi Cassidy
Cover designer: LA Callaghan

ISBN10: 1-883523-83-4
ISBN 13: 978-1-883523-83-1

To Melanie

Acknowledgments

There are many people who helped me to research this book and a few who patiently listened to me wrestle with plotting, drafts and characterization. Thank you. As far as legal issues are concerned, I would especially like to thank Gordon Scott, who graciously spent many hours with me over coffee in Santa Rosa, patiently explaining the intricacies of law. As to the topics of self-defense and martial arts, I am grateful to my advisors and martial arts teachers, all of whom are dedicated to women's empowerment. These include: Sifu David Meyer, Master Deb Hall, Judith Fein, Mr. Herb Cody and Melissa Soalt (a.k.a. "Dr. Ruthless"). I would also like to thank Christine Cassidy for her careful and inspiring editing. To Erica, who helped me become a better person. Most of all, I would like to thank my family, Melanie and Sherman, for putting up with me and my high-maintenance ways.

About the Author

Linda Morganstein is an award-winning writer who grew up in the resort hotels of the Borscht Belt in upstate New York, dropped out of Vassar College and drove a VW van to California, where she lived in Sonoma County for many years. She currently resides in the Twin Cities of Minnesota with her partner and her intrepid dog, Sherman.

PROLOGUE

In the end, Alexis Pope probably had Mrs. Lips to thank for her adventures in criminal investigation, although it would be some time before she contemplated explanations of her new life.

Mrs. Lips wasn't her neighbor's real name. She was a sparrow of a woman with large voluptuous lips that earned her the fantasy title.

Alexis, who preferred to be called Alex, and her husband, Stacy Carlyle, had lived next to Mrs. Lips for three years before he died. They'd barely spoken to her. Worse, really. They'd ridiculed her and her barrel-shaped husband and dumpy children behind their backs.

The Lips were fundamentalists with praise-the-lord bumper stickers on their his-and-hers Cadillacs. A CROSSROADS OF LIFE minibus picked the boy and girl up for religious school. The kids' invented names were Sodom and Gomorrah Junior, for the epic rebellion Alex and Stacy fantasized they'd eventually perpetrate on their parents.

Alex and Stacy had always made up things. The mailman was Postal

Manson, a creepy guy with lunatic eyes. He didn't just deliver mail. He snuck it into the mailboxes, peering around with a serial-killer smirk.

A clerk at the Whole Foods Market was Linda Lovelace-Woodstock, named for her contradictory look: part porn star, part granola Earth Goddess. Interestingly, Linda Lovelace-Woodstock had thin lips. As to that incongruity, Stacy had decided that in a weird twist of fate Mrs. Lips had gotten Linda Lovelace-Woodstock's lips and vice versa.

One night, over a bottle of Anderson Valley Cabernet Sauvignon, Stacy had invented names for everyone in his law firm, including his father, Hunter Carlyle. The head of the firm became Dictator, an aging racehorse overdue to be put out to pasture.

Stacy was the cleverest man Alex had ever met.

No, that wasn't a way for her mind to go. She wouldn't think of him at his most charismatic. She would think of their sins together. Mockery, snobbery, self-delusion. Sins of the ego that made her feel remorseful, taking some of the focus from grief.

Was that a stage of mourning? Remorse? She wasn't sure. She refused to read the book. Screw Kubler-Ross. Hadn't the old broad gone rampaging into death ugly with bitterness? Or was that Georgia O'Keeffe? Not that it mattered.

Whatever the stages were *supposed* to be, Alex had been through several stages of Hell on Earth the past few months, most of them confined to her suburban mansion, a wedding present from Hunter and Bunny, the Carlyle in-laws.

There was the circle of hell of lawyers, followed by the dreadful circle of the press and media. The worst, however, was the circle of well-meaning friends and family, bent on proving to Alex that she had done nothing wrong.

To protect herself while voyaging through the underworld, Alex refused to speak to anyone when it wasn't absolutely necessary.

Two days after Stacy's funeral, Mrs. Lips had appeared at the door with a stack of Tupperware. She rang the bell until Alex answered. Alex, who hadn't eaten in two days, stared at the plastic containers. "Thank you, but no," she said. She was barefoot, wearing a pair of unwashed pajamas and didn't smell very good.

Like an inspired missionary to a starving but resentful country, Mrs.

Lips advanced into the house and set the Tupperware on the table in the hallway. "I want you to eat this," she said. "I'll be back for the empties."

Alex held her hands up to her ears. "Don't talk."

The truth was, she was too hungry not to eat. And it was good, too, even to her diminished taste buds. Beef Stroganoff with egg noodles and buttered vegetables. A breakfast Tupperware filled with yogurt and fruit. Not to mention, as though Mrs. Lips had read her mind, Alex's favorite, carrot cake with cream cheese frosting.

For three entire months, Mrs. Lips appeared, replacing the empties with fresh containers. It was mind-boggling, when you thought about it. After two weeks, Alex had handed Mrs. Lips a key so she didn't have to answer the door.

Later, when Alex was too ashamed not to start cooking for herself again, Mrs. Lips just dropped off fresh bread and cookies.

Then, Mrs. Lips stopped coming. Just like that, she was gone. Had Mrs. Lips decided at last that Alex was going to Hell? The real one? Alex hadn't killed her husband. In all rationality, she was blameless. But what about in God's eyes? Particularly the God of Mrs. Lips.

Around the time Mrs. Lips stopped coming over, Jeffrey started calling again. Jeffrey was Alex's cousin who'd recently moved to the Russian River resort area north of San Francisco with his lover, Max.

When they were little, Alex and Jeffrey spent time together whenever Jeffrey's parents were at war. They'd pack Jeffrey onto the Amtrak and ship him up to Annandale-on-Hudson to stay with Alex and her parents, who never fought. Then his parents would have him shipped home. Back he would go to the public schools in Queens, in whose hallowed halls he'd get beaten up.

After Stacy's funeral, Jeffrey called every day, until she asked him to stop.

"Jeffrey, I love you, but I can't talk."

"It's *me*."

"Not to anyone."

Finally, she hung up on him and then he stopped calling. Jeffrey was very sensitive.

Now, almost six months later, he was trying again. His first words were: "Don't hang up."

"Don't ask me if I'm better," Alex replied.

"I wasn't going to."

"I'm a little better."

"Listen, I have a fantastic new job and I live in this unbelievable fairy-tale cabin—no fairy jokes, please—in the redwoods and Max has his own painting studio in the middle of a meadow. He's painting purple sheep. He says they turn purple at sunset. So he drags me out one day and you know what? They do."

"That's great, Jeffrey."

"You already knew about the move, didn't you?"

"Arlene told me." Arlene was Alex's mother, advice columnist for *SHE*, the premier magazine for professional women. Arlene was a clinical psychologist, but she'd given up practicing therapy years ago after she'd come to admit she had no patience for dealing with people's emotions in person, although she very much liked telling them what to do. Now she lavished her opinions on professional women, who—judging from the volume of letters that poured into *SHE*—ate it all up with big, adoring gulps of gratitude.

Alex's father was Arthur Pope, renowned sculptor and art professor at Bard College. Alex had started calling her parents Arlene and Arthur on her seventh birthday, at their request.

Alex took a deep breath. She'd been trying to breathe through her diaphragm again. Like before, when she knew how to breath properly. Lately, she liked the ache she felt when she contacted her chi, her energy source. Still, although she appeared to be moving past numbness, she didn't know if she was ready for Jeffrey yet. But she didn't hang up on him.

"I'm not going to beat around the bush," Jeffrey said.

"CLICHÉ!" Alex cried.

Then she felt a twisted stab of guilt. She had reacted to Jeffrey like in the old days when they were pals and referred to themselves as the cliché police.

"I want you to drive up here and stay with me," Jeffrey said.

"No," Alex replied.

"I'm managing this amazing restaurant in a resort paradise. Come help. Or forget that. Come up here and vegetate. I'll buy you SpaghettiOs and instant chocolate pudding. You name it. Anything your parents never let you have."

With some remorse, Alex hung up on one of her favorite people in the world. Again. That's what life had come to.

A few days passed, however, and something odd happened. She felt lonely. Not the black hole nothingness of mourning. Just loneliness. So she went out into the yard and flopped onto the stone bench in the herb garden and puked into the lemon thyme. Then she wailed from her core like something from *The Exorcist*.

Which was what she was doing when Mrs. Lips appeared, having traversed the nearly two acres of lawn and landscaping that made up their respective properties. Alex was too busy purging demons to notice until Mrs. Lips was next to her.

Alex looked up, sour-mouthed and puffy, to regard the sparrow face that appeared calm and lacking in judgment as usual. She wiped her mouth with the tissue handed to her by Mrs. Lips. She refrained from asking, *Why did you stop coming?*

Instead she asked, "What's your name?"

She almost fainted when her benefactor said something that sounded remarkably like "Mrs. Lips." Taking her silence for confusion, the woman repeated, "Mrs. Liftz."

Mrs. Lips. Mrs. Liftz. Very good. Clever Stacy.

"Did my husband, Stacy, know your name?"

"Well, yes. I introduced myself just after you moved in."

Why hadn't he told her he knew Mrs. Lips' real name? Before Stacy died, Alex occasionally had a nagging suspicion. She suspected that Stacy had kept some of his best jokes to himself. That he might even have had an imagined name for her.

"Can I sit?" Mrs. Liftz asked.

Alex slid over on the stone bench.

"I had a dream about you," Mrs. Liftz said.

"Oh?" Alex responded. *Oh no* is what she thought. But something odd was happening. The vomit-inducing loneliness was changing into a need for human contact. So she prompted, "A dream?"

Behind Mrs. Liftz, a stand of white birch glowed in the sun, the tender green leaves lit like brilliant paper cutouts. Alex thought of Jeffrey's offer. She didn't need to go to a resort. She lived at a resort.

"You were on a white horse," Mrs. Liftz said, interrupting her reverie, "and you wore a crown and were holding a bow!" She stopped and stared at Alex. When Alex didn't reply, she said, "Revelation. It's a final chapter in the New Testament."

"I know," Alex said. "I took a Bible as Literature course."

"Then you might remember this," Mrs. Liftz said. "'And I saw, and behold, a white horse, and its rider had a bow; and a crown was given to him, and he went out conquering and to conquer.'"

Awkward human silence. But not life silence. Birds sang universal songs; crickets chirped with archetypal meaning. Timeless wind rustled in the trees, blowing the scent of wood smoke from a neighbor's chimney.

Mrs. Liftz grimaced and stood. "I don't want to be intrusive. It's just what I saw. I'm seeing it just as clearly now as I look at you."

Alex stood. She was at least six inches taller than Mrs. Liftz. She hesitated, towering over her neighbor.

"It doesn't make sense," she said finally.

Mrs. Liftz nodded in a manner indicating she understood Alex's statement in its broadest context. In yet another act of generosity, she didn't make any reference to God's mysterious ways.

ONE

Of her proficiencies, Alex could not include a great sense of navigation. She pulled into a Shell station just off the River Road exit in Santa Rosa to get Jeffrey's directions to the Overlook Lodge clarified.

As she turned off the engine of her Lexus, she noticed a couple of Hell's Angels lounging against the ice machine on the sidewalk outside the station, one bald and the other with a gray ponytail. The bald one scratched his crotch.

Alex mentally surrounded herself in an orange cone of light. She swaggered to the entry emanating a don't-mess-with-me attitude.

"Nice jacket," the ponytailed one said, leering.

"Thanks," Alex said, making direct eye contact and checking out vibes. It was okay. The biker dudes were fine. And it *was* a nice jacket. Italian black leather. Stacy had said it made her look like a dyke. Which had inspired some raucous sex between them.

As she entered the store, two actual dykes were leaving. Young ones with nose rings and gelled hair. They leered at her, too.

Well, she must still look pretty good, even after six months of apathetic mourning. She was never sure exactly why, but both men and women tended to melt over her copper-colored hair and blue eyes. Most people who didn't know better thought she was Irish. Religious observation aside, however, her ancestry was pure Ashkenazi Jew.

The clerk at the counter was an Asian drag queen. Bikers, lesbians and a drag queen. If Alex had any doubts she was approaching the Russian River resort area, they were scattered to the winds.

It was November 29th, the Friday after Thanksgiving. She'd spent the holiday anonymously in the Mission District working the food serving line at a shelter for the homeless. She'd refused a dinner invitation from Hunter and Bunny, the persistent Carlyle in-laws. She returned their calls at odd hours when she knew she'd get their answering machine.

It was almost dark by the time she reached the turnoff for the lodge. She'd nearly missed Dearborne Road despite the large sign for the Overlook Lodge just at its base. It wasn't more than half a mile to the steep driveway of the resort.

She climbed the rise to a clearing dominated by a sprawling brown-shingled lodge with a vast front porch and immense windows. Alex climbed out of her car and headed toward the blazing lights.

The lobby of the Overlook was an oasis of honey-colored wood with a jazzy art deco bar and cozy seating areas, including a grouping facing an enormous stone fireplace. Rustic comfort and contemporary chic, the place seemed ultra-charming yet calculated.

"Can I help you?" a woman asked from the reception desk. She was a type, Alex noted. When they worked in restaurants or hotels, they were the sexy and efficient hostesses or front desk clerks. The woman's perfect dark brown hair accented large limpid brown eyes.

"I'm looking for Jeffrey Rosen. I'm—"

"Jeffrey's cousin Alex, I know. I'm Julie."

The phone rang.

Julie picked it up. "Overlook Lodge. Can I help you?"

When it appeared the calling party was going to blab at length, she rolled her eyes at Alex and pointed to the dining room.

"Alex!"

Jeffrey sashayed over in his Jeffrey way, pansy crossed with eternal host. He flashed his dimpled smile. Jeffrey described himself as standard-issue gay man. Attractive, toned and clean-cut. Unlike Alex, Jeffrey was not red-headed. Actually, he was a bit sensitive about how boring his dishwater-brown hair was and he tended to wear it very short, in a Sargeant-Nelly crew cut, as he called it.

Alex put her arms around her cousin. She and Jeffrey were both five-seven, so their shoulders touched. It wasn't much of a hug, but she hadn't had much bodily contact for a while. The touch caused a complex explosion in her middle.

"You okay?" Jeffrey asked.

"Lately, I've been thinking I might someday see the light at the end of the tunnel." She paused. "You're supposed to say cliché."

"I wasn't sure if I was allowed."

"Please, don't treat me with kid gloves."

Jeffrey thrust his hips to one side and threw his hands in the air. "Cliché!"

They both grinned.

"You look amazingly good," he said.

"You mean for someone who's been hibernating and a slug for months?"

"I mean as always." He glanced up and down at her, pretending to make an objective appraisal. "You really don't know how sexy and alluring you are, do you? You have a vibe—that's the best way I can describe it. Maybe you're so hot because you're not ever trying and you seem not to care."

"I don't know what you're talking about. I care what people think about me."

"Forget it. I love the way you are. It's like the goddess Diana crossed with Ava Gardner—she was a lot smarter than most people gave her credit for, you know."

"Honey, you're getting too gay-boy weird for me." Alex looked around the dining room. Like the lobby, it was chic and comfortable, with a color scheme dominated by forest green, rose and pale cream. "Let's change the topic."

"What do you think of this place? The renovation cost a fortune,"

Jeffrey mock-whispered. He glanced around nervously. "Listen, we actually have a busy night coming up, with customers and everything. I wish I had time to visit."

"I'm pretty tired anyway," Alex said.

"Ask Julie for directions. And tell her I need her. She's usually the dinner hostess, but she does the front desk when she has to." Jeffrey wiped a bead of sweat from his brow. "We're short of staff. Budget issues." He stopped. "But we don't need to be talking about that now."

"I meant it when I said I'd help," she said. "You know. Miss College Dropout. I was the menial job queen."

"Don't worry. We have things for you to do." He smiled fondly at her. "The lodge is closed for dinners on Sundays. Can you come eat at my place? Of course you can. What else would you be up to?"

"Jeffrey!"

A tall, muscular boy of about eighteen, a linebacker of a boy, came running up, waving a spoon. "I can't find the new spoons."

"I told you to look in the storage closet."

"I did."

Jeffrey turned to Alex. "This is Julie's son, Wesley. Best bus person on the planet."

"Julie the hostess?" Alex asked. The woman did not look even remotely old enough to have a teenaged son.

"I'm eighteen. She had me when she was sixteen. You can do the math." Wesley's tone implied he'd explained this many times before, but he didn't sound nasty. In fact, he had an unusually gentle and sweet quality, particularly for his age and in contrast to his hulking appearance. Wesley turned back to Jeffrey. "I looked *everywhere* for those spoons."

"Oh, my God," Jeffrey wailed. "I swear that order was put in a month ago."

"See you later, Jeffrey," Alex said, but he was too busy to listen, so she slipped away.

After returning to her car, she followed a narrow private road until she reached another brown-shingled lodge. This one had not been renovated. Even in the dark, lit by a scattering of porch lights and pole lamps, the place radiated funky.

She was searching in her trunk, sweeping its darkness with a flashlight, looking for the box of See's candy she'd brought as a thank-you gift, when someone spoke. "Alexis Pope?"

Alex spun around, raising the flashlight. Just as quickly, an arm flew out and grabbed her wrist.

"Whoa, girl! I'm harmless! Jack Campbell, the owner."

"Oh, sorry," she said.

"Pretty amazing reflexes you have," Jack said. "You're a fighter."

In her experience, men often made comments like that with condescension or sexual innuendo. But she detected neither in Jack Campbell's look. What she saw was a sturdy, balding man with a kind face and amused eyes. "I do have good reaction time," she admitted. She really didn't want to go into any details. "So do you." From his responding expression, Alex got the feeling that Jack didn't want to dwell on defensive reactions either.

"Come on in and meet Marge, before she begins to think I'm out here flirting," Jack said. He flushed. "Just kidding, Alexis."

"It's fine." Alex retrieved the box of See's chocolates and closed the trunk. "Call me Alex."

The house smelled of roasted chicken, apple pie and wood smoke.

"I'm in the kitchen!" a woman's voice called.

They passed through the shabby living room, followed by two leaping Pugs determined to be adored. They snorted and panted and licked at Alex's ankles.

Alex was charmed by the lack of pretension, by the orange plaid sofa, the electric blue La-Z-Boy with a spot worn by backsides, the speckled shag carpet. By terrible art in terrible frames, the kind of art her renowned sculptor father didn't even acknowledge.

The kitchen was large and cluttered. "Welcome," Marge said, wiping her flour-dusted hands on a worn denim apron. She was a small woman with thick gray hair framing a pleasant face.

"Thank you," Alex said. She held out the box of See's chocolates. "I brought these for you." Much to her dismay, her voice trembled, but the Campbells paid no obvious attention. Marge accepted the box with quiet dignity and reserve, which led Alex to suspect that Jeffrey had told them some things about her situation.

"Do you drink wine?" Jack asked. He pointed to the large open jug on the kitchen island.

"Yes, thank you."

Alex thought of Stacy. He'd have drank a few token sips of the cheap swill then made jokes about it when they arrived home. Would she have joined in? Probably.

Jack filled a large glass to the very top.

On second entry into the living room, Alex noticed two walls blanketed in photographs. Portraits, school pictures, club pictures, picnics, weddings, resort pictures. Two walls of family and hotel history. Growing up in the Pope home, there had been no amateur photographs on walls. Arthur and Arlene thought it was tacky.

"This is our son, Chris," Jack said, pointing to a high-school graduation photo of a boy with smooth skin and dark eyes.

"He gets his dark features from my mother," Marge explained. "She was French-Canadian."

"Did you meet Chris at the lodge?" Jack asked.

"He's not there," Marge said. "Remember? He's in San Francisco tonight. Some kind of concert."

"On a Saturday night?" Jack said lightly. "I thought we were short of help. Maybe I should go over." He turned to Alex. "Chris is taking over the business. He and his partners did all the renovations. He usually runs things when we aren't there."

"If they need us, you know they'll call," Marge said.

"Is that you?" Alex said, pointing to a wedding photograph.

"Yes," Marge said. "Look at us. Nineteen sixty-seven. Those clothes."

"And this?" Alex asked. "Isn't this the Overlook?"

"When it was first built," Marge said. "By my grandparents. See? It was quite splendid."

"Before we took over and ran it into the ground," Jack said.

"Jack! It wasn't our fault. It was the times. We couldn't help the changes in this area, and the floods, and the—"

"I know, I know," Jack interrupted.

"Is that your son now?" Alex asked, steering the topic away from this obvious sore point.

The photo showed a man in a black polo and beige hiking shorts, his arm around a rail-thin woman who could have been strutting on a runway.

"Yes, and his fiancée, Leslie." Jack gestured at her previously full glass, which she'd drained. "More wine?"

"Maybe she needs to eat," Marge said.

"I didn't expect you to cook for me." Alex's words were slurred. She hadn't eaten since the dry bagel she'd had that morning. The wine had raced to her brain through her empty stomach.

Jack and Marge looked aghast.

"Of course you'd be hungry," Jack said.

All of a sudden Alex realized she wouldn't hold up through a normal dinner with normal strangers, however seductively comforting they were.

Jack and Marge glanced at each other.

"Let me put it in some Tupperware," Marge said.

The Campbells insisted she not drive her car, even up the driveway to the garage. Jack drove it to a spot in front of the two-story structure, and then retrieved her from the orange plaid couch. She tottered beside him, stubbornly gripping her glass, while he clutched the stack of Tupperware.

When they reached the garage, they climbed an outside flight of stairs to the granny unit on the second floor. When Jack flicked on the light, Alex sighed. The room was rustic yet charming, like the renovated lodge.

"It's just this kitchen/living area and the bedroom back there," Jack said. "Chris had it renovated for himself. Then he and Leslie got engaged. Now they have a place in town. They think this is small for two people."

"It's wonderful," she said.

"Should we get your bags then?" Jack asked.

"I'll get them later," she said. "Thanks so much. You've done enough." As soon as he shut the door behind him and she could hear him clumping down the stairs, she tore into the Tupperware.

TWO

At first, it seemed she was being attacked in her sleep, her head bludgeoned with a heavy fist. But when she opened her crusty, swollen eyes, she realized someone was pounding on the door. She stumbled across the Oriental carpet, her stomach roiling. She was wearing the same clothes from last night, now rumpled and smelly.

"Beautiful day!" Jack roared. His smile froze. He glanced over to the couch where it was obvious she'd slept, wrapped in an old coat she'd found hanging in the front closet. He cleared his throat and gave her shoulder a shake. "No matter how strong a person thinks they are, there are some things that can break them. The strongest sometimes fall the hardest."

Good thing Jeffrey wasn't around. It was a cliché worthy of the cliché police. But looking into this earnest man's face, Alex felt her heart melting. And now look, she was thinking in clichés.

"Put some work clothes on and meet me at the house for breakfast. I have plans for you, young lady."

When he left, Alex went down to the Lexus. In the trunk were two large suitcases. In one suitcase were the things from her marriage days and in the other was her old stuff from pre-marriage that she'd hidden in the attic of their suburban mansion.

Nothing wrong with the post-marriage clothes. It wasn't like she'd become Martha Stewart. But every item bought since her wedding had been only the best, from the Ralph Lauren underwear on up.

The clothes from the old days before her marriage came from secondhand stores and thrift shops, from Target and the Reebok outlet. She'd dressed that way at Mills College and the same after she'd dropped out, with only one semester left before graduation.

Dressed that way until she and Stacy got together and started attending his family and work functions. Then, he'd suggested, as though it was all a silly game, that she pick up a few "nice girl" things.

Now the whole shebang was represented in the trunk of her car. The only things she was lacking were the expensive Bohemian ensembles of childhood, and she'd have probably brought those too, if she could have gotten hold of them.

Why not bring along all the baggage of the past?

"Did you sleep well?" Marge asked, slipping a piece of freshly baked asparagus quiche next to the Canadian bacon on Alex's plate. "That's a new mattress on the bed. Top of the line. Chris just bought it three months before he moved out."

Alex glanced at Jack, who winked at her.

"It was very comfortable," Alex said. "I slept great." She hesitated, staring at the perfect, steaming quiche. Her stomach growled. She dug into the heaping plate of food with gusto. When she could speak again, she said, "Thanks again for letting me come here."

"You're a welcome addition," Marge said. "Another piece of quiche?"

"Yes, please."

"We're going to miss it here very much." Marge sighed.

Alex lowered her fork. "Are you going somewhere?"

"Didn't Jeffrey tell you?" Seeing Alex's blank look, Marge explained,

"We're retiring. Chris made the arrangements." She glanced at Jack. "When Jack and I go to Florida, then Chris gets this house. He and Leslie will raise a family here. My parents did it for us. Now we'll do it for our son."

"Her parents died in Florida. One, then the other one six months later. Funny how that happens," Jack said, busying himself with cutting a piece of bacon into little bits.

They were interrupted by a woman's voice calling hello from the living room, then by the woman herself. "What a feast," she said, eyeing the table.

"Sit down," Marge said. "Would you like some quiche?"

"Any meat in it?" the woman asked.

"No meat, but eggs, milk and cheese."

"That's cool. I've decided not to be vegan anymore." The woman glanced at Alex. "I'm Ivy. You must be Alex."

"Yes," Alex said. Obviously, everyone at the place had been alerted to her arrival. She couldn't help staring.

Ivy had platinum hair spiked with pink tinges, several rings in her nose and a map of tattoos on her arms, a twisting mass of ivy vines creeping from her wrists to her shoulders. Her clothes were a combination of airy fairy and rugged mountain woman, including a silky Indonesian blouse and a mighty pair of scuffed Red Wing boots.

After Ivy had polished off a large piece of quiche, she stood. "You're with me this morning," she announced to Alex. "Let's roll."

"I have to fix a kitchen pipe plus look at a water heater." They were in Ivy's funky green Toyota pickup, just passing the main lodge. In daylight, the Overlook was even more striking. It spread across a lovely, isolated-feeling clearing, ringed by towering redwood trees, against a backdrop of tree-studded hills.

"I'm not really into plumbing," Alex said.

"Get into it. This is the life here. We live under Mister Jack Campbell's creed: We're a team-slash-family and the more everyone knows about all the jobs, the better the team/family works." Ivy's words could have been mocking, but they were said with fondness and a touch of mock impatience.

"Do you have a job title?" Alex asked.

"Head of housekeeping. I used to do more. I worked in the restaurant and was a bellhop." Ivy shrugged. "Until Chris came back. Now I'm not welcome working with the guests. Can you believe it? Like who cares about a few nose rings and tattoos these days?"

Some of Stacy's law partners would care, Alex thought. Some of their neighbors in San Ramon would care. From the look of the renovations at the Overlook, those were the kinds of guests Chris Campbell and his partners were trying to attract. But she didn't think it was really necessary to point that out to Ivy.

"How long have you been here?" she asked.

"A million years."

"That's a long time."

"Actually, since I was eighteen or so. Let me see, so that's six years. Chris came back about a year and a half ago."

Ivy was driving very slowly. Her vehicle speed was in inverse relation to her conversational speed.

"My grandfather sent me here after I got out of rehab, which is another story. Ernie Lightfoot, my granddad, is an old pal of Jack's. They have some kind of history together, but they won't talk about it. From the family rumor mill, I guess it's creepy Vietnam memories. Anyway, I was *really* a punk when I first got here." They had slowed almost to a crawl. "Everyone here has a story." Ivy glanced at Alex. "I'm sure you do."

Alex flushed, aware of the contorted look on her face.

Blessedly, Ivy didn't pursue that line of discussion. She sighed. "All gathered under Jack Campbell. He hires people and they enter the Campbell's Benign Kingdom. Before Chris came back, that is. Now, who knows?"

They were winding up a curved road lined with cottages. As they crept along, Ivy waved to a couple of women outside one of the cottages.

"That's Mrs. Juarez and her daughter Teresa. Practically the entire Juarez family works or has worked for the Campbells. Jack's helped some of the kids get started in college. That's supposed to be a secret. Don't tell him I told you." Ivy smiled. "I love that man. And he's a Republican. I don't care."

• • •

"Turn it harder."

"Urrrr!" Alex growled, giving the wrench a mighty tug.

"What a woman," Ivy crowed.

Alex crawled out from beneath the sink holding a segment of pipe. "I have to warn you, I'm better at tearing things out than reinstalling them."

"I'll guide you through it," Ivy said.

They were in the Shed. The cutely self-effacing name contradicted the appearance of the elaborately renovated structure behind the pool area. Its ballroom-sized main room was, according to Ivy, used for weddings and other special events.

Before Alex could contort herself back into the cabinet, the Juarez women barged in with flushed faces. They engaged in a heated conversation in Spanish with Ivy. The daughter, Teresa, was trembling.

"Let's go," Ivy said grimly.

The four of them trooped through the gardens, an expanse of raised beds planted with herbs and winter greens. They headed to the most remote cottage on the property.

The place was a shambles: bed stripped of its linens, lamps knocked over, tissues, brochures, pens and everything that had once lined the desks and nightstands thrown to the floor.

"Me, I found one wrecked just like this last month," Mrs. Juarez said, putting her arm around her daughter.

"Did the people who checked out do it?" Alex asked. She had to suppress a smile, imagining some gray-haired stockbroker and his wife ransacking the room in a burst of unleashed primal fury.

Mrs. Juarez shook her head vehemently. "We get very nice people here. And this is the same as last time. One time? Maybe. Two times? It's someone sneaking in."

Teresa let out a tiny moan.

Mrs. Juarez tightened her grip around her daughter's shoulder and crooned to her in Spanish. She turned to Alex, blushing. "Someone masturbated onto the sheets."

"Have you told the Campbells?" Alex asked.

"We told Mr. Chris about the first time."

"Let's go back to the lodge and report this new one," Alex said.

"Oh, we can't leave now," Mrs. Juarez exclaimed. "Too much work. No time." She hustled up to the cart just outside the door and began pushing it into the disastrous cottage. Teresa followed her.

"We should go tell the Campbells," Alex said. She was surprised by the veiled look on Ivy's face.

"I don't think we should bother Jack or Marge with this. They need to let go of this place and it's hard enough as it is."

"Then Chris?"

Ivy's look hardened. "I'll tell you this, he won't listen to me. Maybe you should go. You're new. No past history."

Something was obviously screwy at the Overlook. Alex was going to have to decide right here and now whether she was going to jump in regardless of the consequences. Damn. Why was it peace seemed to elude her?

Alex strode back to the lodge in her don't-mess-with-me mode, aware of her surroundings, alert to potential dangers, but it felt ridiculous. The whole place was radiating charm and security. A pretty little wonderland.

In the lobby, she recognized Chris from the family photos at the Campbell home. He was wearing a rose-colored long-sleeved cashmere polo and khakis.

"Can I help you?"

"I'm Alex Pope," she said.

They all seemed to know who she was. She got the expected response. A flicker of recognition. *Oh, her! The one with the dead husband.*

She couldn't help herself. "You know, the one with the dead husband," she said. What'd triggered that? She had to admit Chris Campbell reminded her a little of Stacy. If he were anything like Stacy, he'd appreciate the dark humor.

Chris didn't disappoint her. He gave her a tiny ironic smile. "That's you," he deadpanned. "The one with the dead husband." He held his hand out.

She took his hand and shook it.

Chris nodded at her sweatshirt. "You went to Mills?"

"Yes. How about you?"

Chris shrugged with faux modesty. "Undergraduate degree from UCLA. M.B.A. from Stanford. What was your major?"

"Journalism, with a minor in psychology. But I dropped out. One semester short of graduation."

"Jeffrey told me that you're Arthur and Arlene Pope's daughter." He gave her a knowing look. "Those are some footsteps to follow in."

"I decided not to try," Alex said, surprised at her candor. "I love *your* parents, by the way," she added.

A complicated look passed over Chris's face, which he quickly hid with a thin smile.

Their hands were still entwined when the fashion model from the Campbell photos marched up. Leslie, that was her name.

"Chris?" Leslie said, eyeing the handholding.

Chris removed his hand from Alex's. "This is Alex," he said. Seeing his fiancée's blank look, he added, "The one with the dead husband."

Leslie looked horrified. Alex hid a smile, then changed the subject. "I recognized you both from the photo wall," she said.

"My mother and father subjected you to the endless gallery of amateur photography already?" Chris asked.

"I enjoyed it." Before either of them could respond, Alex turned the conversation to the ransacking incident.

"Damn," Chris said. "Was there anyone else around?"

"Guests?" Alex asked.

Chris nodded.

"No."

"Damn," Chris repeated. He wrung his hands like an actor in a melodrama.

"Do you think we should call the sheriff?" Leslie asked.

"Leslie!" Chris barked. He wagged a finger at the two women. "It's probably dumb kids on a prank. It's only happened twice and we're trying to build a business. This would be pretty horrendous publicity, wouldn't it?"

Leslie seemed inclined not to argue and Alex wasn't sure it was her place to even try. Besides, she already beginning to feel too involved.

THREE

"Are you sure you're up for this?" Jeffrey asked.

It was late afternoon and it had already been, needless to say, a weird and busy day. They were in the empty dining room.

"Absolutely." Alex was feeling possessed of an astonishing energy, like her former dynamo self.

Jeffrey shrugged. "I'm going to believe you." He handed her a white coat. "Maybe I should explain a few things before—"

"Jeffrey, you bastard!" A beefy man in chef's garb, including toque towering on his head, rumbled toward them. The glassware on the tables shook. "Why do we even put things on the menu if you and your pathetic dining staff can't get people to try them?"

The chef came up so close that Alex could smell garlic on his breath. Both she and Jeffrey took a step back.

"This is Mark Heller, our executive chef," Jeffrey said.

"No one is ordering the persimmon-glazed rabbit," Mark bellowed.

"We've sold maybe three sweetbread appetizers. Why is the whole fucking restaurant ordering grilled steak and broiled sea bass?"

"Mark, I adore your cooking and I idolize you," Jeffrey whined. "But—"

"Cut out the fucking whining," Mark interrupted, with exaggerated disgust. "But *what*?"

"But some things are maybe too adventurous, especially at a rustic lodge, no matter how chic it is. I think we're confusing people. So they're sticking to basics."

"Screw basics," Mark bellowed. "You should be *pushing* the specials. But you're a pussy letting yuppies and socialite assholes walk all over you."

Alex remembered witnessing Jeffrey's father berate Jeffrey. She'd fantasized how she'd fly into action, knocking her uncle's block off. Now it was all she could do not to knock Mark's block off. And she could if she wanted to.

Jeffrey glanced at her with a don't-interfere look.

He was probably right. He was an adult, let him take care of it his way.

"I'll speak to the waiters," he said to Mark.

Mark nodded, his point taken. In a split second, his demeanor changed completely. He smiled at Alex with disarming charm. "And who's this lovely young lady?"

Alex glared at the chef while he did his macho inspection of her, running his eyes from her neck to her groin.

Mark was maybe five-nine and strongly built. A man who would go to fat if he wasn't careful. Large cleft chin, a big nose. Attractive, Alex thought, if you liked men who thought they owned the world. She glanced at Jeffrey, who had a sickening look of adoration on his face, as though he was in the presence of God or Robert DeNiro. Too bad he wasted his infatuations on jerks.

"This is my cousin Alex," Jeffrey said.

"The one who's going to work in the kitchen?" Mark asked.

"The very one," Jeffrey said.

"Does she know anything?" he asked.

"I'm here in this room," Alex said. "I know how to speak."

Mark hesitated, then broke out in a loud bark resembling a laugh. "Okay. Okay. Do you know anything?"

"I've done a lot of catering, a little regular restaurant work. Mostly prep and waiting tables."

Mark shrugged. "Good enough. Half the Juarez family is sick with the flu." He stabbed his finger at the cook's coat Alex was clutching. "Put that on. We've got things to do." Now that his tantrum was over, he was becoming increasingly jovial and sweet. "Glad to have you aboard, Alex," he said, gesturing for her to come along.

"Wait," Jeffrey intervened. "Let me introduce her to the dining staff, then I'll send her in." As soon as Mark had gone, Jeffrey held up his hand. "No comments, *please*. He's right. I should be pushing the specials. I'm being a weenie."

"He shouldn't talk to you like that," Alex said.

"Alex, this is an old topic."

"It's a *vintage* topic," she said, squeezing his forearm affectionately.

"Look, here they are." Jeffrey gestured to the entry. "Come meet the waitrons."

Alex went through the introductions with the two adorable waitrons. Dean, an adorable slight man with short ultra-styled hair, and Roxanne, an adorable slight woman with short ultra-styled hair. Each felt compelled to provide her with biographies.

Dean was a gay boy in his early twenties who'd waited tables in the Hamptons until getting the California urge. Roxanne was a local woman, late twenties, single, with a five-year-old named Harmony, currently being babysat by Roxanne's mother, a telephone psychic named Francine.

"My mother predicts a very busy holiday season," Roxanne informed Alex. "She sees some kind of huge publicity coming very soon."

Before Alex could comment, Jeffrey interrupted. "I think Mark is waiting for you. He hates to wait."

Screw Mark, Alex thought. But she took off for the kitchen at a brisk pace.

Once she arrived, Mark led her to a pointy-featured woman wearing thick black-framed glasses that magnified intelligent blue eyes. Her hair was so blond it was almost white, pulled back in a ponytail. She was introduced as Astrid Sorenson, former college professor turned sous chef.

Originally from Stockholm.

"Nice to meet you," Astrid said. She was removing the tops from a large pile of carrots.

"Oh, my God!" Mark turned to Alex. "What do these look like?" he asked, pointing to a cutting board.

"Is this a trick question?" Alex asked.

"No, it's a very, very simple question. *Answer!*"

Alex froze. Then she replied, "You're going to have to ask in a more civilized tone."

She watched Mark's already red face grow even more florid. But she just kept looking him right in the eye.

A tight smile formed on the chef's face. "All right," he said in a relatively civil tone. "Would you, Alex, please identify the items on this cutting board."

She looked over the items. "I believe they're carrots."

"Thank you," Mark said. "And would you say that they are baby carrots with tops?"

"No," she replied. "I would have to say those are full-grown carrots with tops."

Mark turned to Astrid. "Why the fuck did you let them deliver big carrots? The menu calls for roasted baby root vegetables. I thought I could trust you."

Astrid turned a level gaze to Mark. Good for her, Alex thought.

"They didn't have any babies. So, it was big carrots or no carrots."

"Jesus! What are we going to do?"

"Mark, Mark," Astrid said in a soothing tone. "We'll just cut them up. The big ones always taste better anyway."

"The menu calls for roasted baby root vegetables," Mark repeated, but he appeared to be wavering.

Astrid raised an eyebrow. "It's all going to be so incredible, no one will care. And if some fool does, forget about him. Philistine." She raised her hands in front of her in a meditative gesture. "Chill, dude. Take a deep breath and chill out." Her Swedish-accented kitchen slang was hard to resist.

"You're right." Mark grinned at his sous chef. "You know I can't do without you." He turned to Alex. "Okay, you're cutting carrots. Astrid will show you. I want them perfect."

After he had stomped off, Astrid demonstrated the perfect cut and watched like a hawk while Alex practiced.

"I'm going to leave you here," she said, "while I try to locate the lost caviar for the oyster appetizer. If I'm not back in fifteen minutes, assume the worst. That the caviar is missing and I've strung myself up in the walk-in."

"Who do you want to discover you?" Alex asked.

"It would have to be Mark, of course," Astrid said. "I will have left him a note, written in goose blood. Natural Sonoma goose blood. We always try to use fresh, local ingredients." She peered through her thick glasses at Alex. "He's a master, you know. I've never met anyone able to put together flavors and visual beauty yet still have it all seem simple and comforting. I can tolerate the rest to be in the presence of such genius."

Alex nodded. There really wasn't anything to say. She wasn't in the mood to get into anything too deep about behavioral excuses for geniuses. Besides, this was a restaurant kitchen. The rules were different in kitchens.

An hour later, she had thrown away a pile of reject carrots and finally made a pile of perfect spears when Mark reappeared.

"Good," he grunted.

She felt pleased at his compliment and was annoyed at herself for the response. *Oh, well, we're all just human*, she reminded herself.

"Now go help Jean," he ordered, pointing to the pastry station. "She's in the weeds, as usual." He left her to go over by herself.

"Jean, I heard you were in the weeds," she said to the pastry chef.

"It's easy to get behind when the menu is so demanding," Jean replied, shrugging. She pointed to a large tray of chocolate truffles. "Roll those in cocoa and sprinkle them with edible gold leaf."

"Pretty fancy."

"It's our signature," Jean said. "Each diner gets one at the end of a meal. Guests get them on their pillows at night."

Pretty expensive, Alex thought.

Jean was a slow-moving woman with odd, jerky movements. She reminded Alex of a puppet pulled by invisible strings. They worked silently for almost twenty minutes.

Finally, to make conversation, Alex nodded her head in Mark's direction. "He's something else, isn't he?"

Jean manufactured a weird, marionette smile. "Yes, he is, isn't he?" she replied.

"Astrid says he's a genius. Has she worked with him long?"

"A few years. She's been with him at three restaurants in San Francisco."

"Three restaurants in a few years? He moves around a lot, doesn't he?"

"For one reason or another."

"And how did you hook up with him?" Alex asked.

For the first time, Alex saw a slight spark in Jean. A brief fluttering of the eyes.

"He's my husband," Jean answered.

As the night continued, the pace picked up. Alex was pulling her weight and feeling good about the hurried thanks she got as she hustled around.

Mark became the absolute center of their world. Between shouting orders, he carried on a running banter, cheering on his troops and happily complaining.

Despite the adult vegetables and general chaos, the waiters reported widespread ecstasy among the diners. Four customers made a point of complimenting Mark on his braised rabbit served over roasted garlic polenta.

Just as the last seating was finishing up, Jeffrey came running in, waving a newspaper. "Oh, Christ, you won't believe it! We've been reviewed in the magazine section of the Sunday *Chronicle!*" Apparently, a diner had brought in the early Saturday-night edition of the Sunday paper.

A collective gasp blew out among the kitchen crew.

"How many stars?" Astrid asked.

"Two and a half for food. Three and a half for service. Four for ambience." Jeffrey threw the magazine onto the stainless steel counter. "Two and a half for food. Screw them," he said, but without much rancor. He and everyone else knew that for a new spot located in the sticks, two and a half stars for food was pretty damned good.

Mark grabbed up the newspaper section. He read aloud the praises of his skills and the magnificence of his food. It was a Mark Heller love note. He paused. It was time for the desserts. "The desserts, while delicious, are perhaps the only thing not up to standard. They do not have the level of sophistication and rustic playfulness that the rest of the menu accomplishes with such style and wit. Still, we enjoyed them very much, particularly—" He broke off here, glaring at Jean. "That's why the two and a half, because of *you*."

For her part, Jean maintained her distant, artificial look.

"*You*," he repeated. "And you don't listen when I tell you how to improve."

Alex felt grateful as Roxanne jumped in, clearly trying to divert the ugly barrage. "I told you. My mother predicted this. Read the rest."

Mark finished the dessert comments and read the glowing last paragraph. He glanced up, his look both triumphant and panicky. "You know what this means?"

Just then, Julie rushed in. "What's going on? The phone is ringing off the hook. We have reservations booked for two weeks."

"Oh, thank you, thank you, restaurant gods," Jeffrey called out.

But Alex, who'd worked in restaurants, understood Mark's seemingly ambivalent reaction to the review. The gods had just bestowed both a blessing and a curse.

FOUR

Alex gunned the accelerator of her Lexus, forcing it up a steep hill just outside Monte Rio. She navigated the twisting, narrow road, her headlights illuminating ribbons of fog that snaked among the dense foliage that lined Wyman's Rise Lane. She pulled up to a cottage draped with vines, set in a garden of hardy primrose blooming in the mild winter chill. Like the Overlook, the cottage was surrounded with towering redwood trees, giving the place the same enchanted yet claustrophobic feel that seemed to characterize much of the Russian River area.

Jeffrey greeted her at the door, holding two glasses of red wine. "Is this too much or what?" he said, gesturing at the fantasy setting. Without waiting for an answer, he stepped back. As she entered, he handed her a glass. "It's a private reserve I had to kill someone to get." He sipped and sighed. "Even if I get twenty to life, it'll have been worth it."

Alex took a sip.

"Well?" he asked.

She smiled apologetically. "You know I'm not that much of a wine expert."

"I thought Stacy educated you—" Jeffrey stopped abruptly. "Oh, my God, I'm sorry."

"It's not like you can't mention him." Alex brushed past her cousin, settling in a soft leather club chair by the crackling fire in the stone fireplace.

Before Jeffrey could reply, a voice called, "Alex, Alex, Alex." Max came out of the kitchen wearing an apron dusted with flour. He was a tall, thin man with a trim graying beard and very bushy eyebrows. Alex burst out laughing.

"What's up?" Max asked. "You have something against men in aprons?"

"Max, come on, that apron is patterned with *pansies*."

"It's an ironic statement," Max explained with exaggerated dignity.

Jeffrey sighed. "Artists and their ironic statements."

"Bugger off," Max shot back.

"I can see you two are as close as ever," Alex commented.

"Closer." Max gestured toward the far wall of the living room. "Jeffrey, show off my latest purple sheep and I'll get the appetizers."

They dutifully studied the large canvas of dazzling purple sheep dominating the wall of the small room. Her father would have approved of the painting. He would have approved of Max, too. With good reason.

"He's so much like my father," she said.

"For the entire four years that Max and I have been together, you say that every time you see him."

"It's so striking."

"At least if I'm going to be Freudian, I didn't pick my own father." He shivered. "Ugh."

"And my father is a better choice?"

"Anyway, who's talking? You're glomming onto Jack and Marge, the Ward and June Cleaver of Northern California. Talk about parent fixations."

"At least they're normal, nice people. *My* father—"

Jeffrey peered around the room dramatically. "I hear things," he warbled, "I hear voices repeating things. Boring, boring things about the past."

"Déjà vu voices," Alex said, grinning. "Worse than clichés."

"No déjà vu allowed," Max said, entering the room with a tray of crudités. "Live life for the moment."

"Cliché!" Alex and Jeffrey cried in unison.

Max sighed. "Eat my appetizers," he ordered, setting down an elaborate array of world cuisine dishes accompanied by small bowls of dipping sauce.

Alex picked up a tiny empanada and bit into it, then sighed. "I thought my taste buds had died."

"I can think of any number of body organs I'd rather have pass away," Max said with horror.

The purple sheep admired, the appetizers consumed, they landed at the dining room table, where Max served a Thai-themed meal involving spicy meats and vegetables accompanied by steaming jasmine rice.

"Max, you're incredible." Alex moaned, finishing off a coconut-crusted shrimp.

"Good enough to be a chef?" he prompted.

"Absolutely."

"Good," Max said. "If the Overlook loses its prima donna, I'll take the job."

"Don't start," Jeffrey warned.

"Start what?" Max asked.

"Can't you just lay off with your comments about Mark?"

"I would if I thought he was reforming. That was the deal. But he isn't reforming."

"He's one of the most creative chefs working today and we're lucky to have him in what some might consider a minor operation relative to his skills and talent," Jeffrey said.

Max placed his chopsticks in his bowl and wiped his hands on his napkin. "Alex, ask him why a man of such magnitude has consented to take such a lowly position."

Jeffrey frowned at Alex, shaking his head.

"I found this fascinating Web site the other day. It's devoted to exposing the serial bully." Max waved his hand at Jeffrey's look of protest.

"Serial bullies can be quite charming and talented, but they pollute their environment with manipulation and deception in order to control and gain power."

"You don't blather on and on about what an ass and psychopath Picasso was. Or how about your great Jackson Pollack?" Jeffrey said. "Mark is not some hack office manager pushing around secretaries and mailroom clerks. Give him a little space to create like you do your idols."

"I wish it were that simple." Max sighed. "Alex, you know Jeffrey is drawn to abusive men. I just want him to be more aware and careful, so he doesn't get hurt."

"I won't get hurt," Jeffrey insisted.

"You worked with battered women, didn't you?" Max asked her.

"Max, you're asking questions you know the answer to," she replied.

"I'm trying to make a point. You taught self-defense to battered women who lived with abusive men."

"I did," she answered.

"Who do bullies prey on?" he asked.

Alex took a deep breath. "Max, I'm sorry. I won't answer any more leading questions."

"Bullies prey on the weak," he concluded.

"I can't take it!" Jeffrey said. "I wasn't planning on an evening of *Who's Afraid of Virginia Woolf.*"

Suddenly, Alex twisted her expression, transforming it into an impersonation of Sandy Dennis, including the awful buck-toothed grimace. She giggled nervously in a perfect Sandy Dennis manner. Both Max and Jeffrey burst into shocked and delighted laughter.

"Can you do Liz?" Max challenged.

"I can do better than that." She rearranged her features into Richard Burton and sang, "Who's afraid of Virginia Woolf, Virginia Woolf, Virginia Woolf." Then she became Elizabeth Taylor. "I am, George, I am."

Max and Jeffrey applauded.

"That was incredible," Jeffrey said. "I thought only gay men had the entire script memorized."

"Don't be homoelitist," Alex said. "Stacy and I had the video. We watched it at least once a month."

"Maybe you both were gay men in your last lives. Let me hear your Barbra Streisand."

"Jeffrey, that's *so* stereotyped," Alex protested.

"Don't squirm out of this with political correctness," he replied.

Alex took a deep breath, then belted out a full minute of "Second Hand Rose." Another round of applause.

"Would you believe she was a serious child?" Jeffrey said to Max. He turned to Alex. "When did the diva side turn up?"

"When I dropped out of college," Alex said. "You were still in New York. I know Arlene told you about all this. The terrible boyfriend. The terrible drugs and alcohol." She smiled. "I never told her about the karaoke. I believed she and Arthur would be more horrified by that than the boyfriend or the drugs and alcohol." She shrugged. "Anyway, it was only a phase."

"You know what?" Jeffrey asked. "For a long time, I thought you were perfect. You did everything right. The right clubs, the right societies."

"And then years spent proving I was imperfect."

Max chuckled. "Child of famous parents syndrome. How are the king and queen?"

"The same." Alex sighed. "Arthur's having a big show in Manhattan next year. He's chipping away at a granite piece called *Dementia*. He sent me an in-progress photo."

"I'd love to see it," Max said reverentially. "What's it like?"

Alex flushed. "It looks like a body part. I used to have nightmares featuring his sculptures. They all looked like dismembered body parts to me."

"Oh, my," Max said, "what would Dr. Joyce Brothers make of that?"

"Don't ever let Arlene hear you call her that, not even in jest. She takes her advice column very seriously. It's in a magazine for very accomplished professional women."

"Which, to get back to the personal, was the way I always thought you'd turn out," Jeffrey said. "I comforted myself with the thought that you had to have some kind of hidden dark side. And you demonstrated that." He laughed affectionately. "Marrying Stacy. That got you out of the loose crowd."

"Actually, it was the martial arts at first. I got my black belt in a pretty tough school. Marrying Stacy—" She paused, a vague panic invading her middle. "Maybe we can go on to another topic."

With that suggestion, the conversation turned mellow. Alex left late, feeling content. It was nice. Human contact again. It wasn't until she was driving down River Road that the pain returned. She had to pull onto the shoulder and cry for ten minutes before she was able to drive back to the Overlook.

But it was okay, really. She realized it was going to be a long climb back to where having fun didn't make her feel remorseful.

The nightmares were back that night. In her dreams, she was being attacked from all sides. She couldn't defend herself, her limbs wouldn't work, her martial arts training wouldn't kick in. And, in her state of paralysis, a voice was saying, "You deserve this." Thank heavens for the pounding on the door. Seven a.m. Not much brainwork to figure out who it might be.

"I've got errands in town. Thought I'd invite you to breakfast and show you around."

Alex pushed her hair back from her face. "Half an hour?"

"See you then," Jack said, looking pleased.

So, freshly showered, in her jeans and Mills College sweatshirt, she bounced down River Road in Jack's big black Dodge pickup toward Guerneville. The morning was clear and bright.

"Rains are a bit late this year," Jack commented. "Doesn't mean anything. We could have a deluge anytime."

"It floods a lot up here. Or used to. Didn't they come up with solutions?"

Jack pointed to a house built on stilts. "That's one of the supposed solutions. Raise the flood-prone dwellings up above flood levels. Then there's the dam and the increased water use to the north."

They had just reached the town. Jack pointed to the main street. "See there? In the floods of nineteen eighty-six, the river crested at nearly forty-nine feet, seventeen feet above flood level. Everything you see here was under water."

"Terrible. Terrible and awesome."

"No kidding. They said it'd never happen again, then it came up forty-nine feet again in nineteen ninety-five." Jack shook his head. "They make promises, but the water always rises."

Main Street consisted of bars, restaurants, a pharmacy, realty offices and stores selling books, stationery and office supplies, tackle and guns, jewelry and a couple of places with the required tourist souvenirs.

"Ever been here?" Jack asked.

"No," she said. "Mostly to the Napa Valley."

"Because Napa's classy and refined. See what my son is up against? Him and the others that want to see this area become the next Napa Valley." He shook his head. "This was a hot spot, many years ago. Even Marge's parents, they did a good business, all through the late 'forties and 'fifties. But times changed. By the time Marge and I took over in 'sixty-eight, this was a town of hippies, bikers and struggling old-timers. No one was vacationing here anymore. It wasn't until the gays came in that we saw prosperity again. That was fine until the 'eighties, when AIDS and that big 'eighty-six flood wiped things out again."

They had reached the middle of town.

"I thought we'd go to Stumps," Jack said. "It's been around since the 'forties. But there's a coffeehouse back there where we could go to if you want. Picasso's. You could have a latte and a scone."

"No," she said. "Stumps sounds good."

The diner was hopping. They snagged a recently deserted booth. An older waitress in a pink uniform came over. On her breast, a nametag read HAZEL.

"Cheating on your wife?" Hazel asked, pouring coffee.

"Don't tell."

"Lips are sealed," Hazel shot back. "I know you don't need a menu, Romeo. What about you, honey?"

"I'll have a couple of pancakes, two fried eggs and bacon. Maybe a small side of hash browns," Alex said.

Hazel whistled and marched away.

"She likes good eaters," Jack said.

A man wearing a SRJC WRESTLING jacket approached them. He was balding and had a small paunch, but he moved with the grace of a former athlete. "Hey," he said.

"Hey," Jack replied.

"Cheating on your wife?" the man asked, nodding at Alex.

"Don't tell."

"Mum's the word."

"This is my good friend, Bill Hanson," Jack said to Alex. "He's one of the best junior college wrestling coaches in the country."

Bill Hanson shrugged modestly. "How's Wesley?"

"He's all right." Jack's tone was cautious.

Bill glanced at Alex. "I was Wesley's coach at Santa Rosa Junior College. Biggest, most graceful boy I've ever coached at this level. Until he dropped out."

"He'll be back," Jack said. "It's only for the semester, until everything settles down."

"I'll tell you when everything'll settle down. When he gets himself a new mother. Short of that, then a scholarship at some university good and far from here."

"Bill," Jack said.

"Okay." Bill turned away.

Hazel swept upon them, juggling a million plates and bottles. She swept it all across the table, ending with a bottle of hot sauce.

"Thank you," Alex said, taking in the greasy odor of the eggs and steamy heat of the pancakes.

Jack laughed. "Now we'll see what kind of woman you are."

Alex poured a thick stream of syrup over her pancakes. "Don't underestimate me."

"Never." Jack took a bite of his steak. He glanced over to the counter where Bill Hanson was sitting, then pointed his fork at her. "This *isn't* gossip. It's informative. Bill Hanson was beating around the bush."

Cliché, Alex thought.

"Julie got arrested for drunk driving last June. Wound up with a six-month suspension of license. Wesley left school for the fall semester. Drives her around. Including to work. Since he's out of school, we put him on extra shifts, so at least they can both be working at the same time."

"That was good of you."

Jack frowned. "Survival is teamwork."

Before she could respond a slick man with gelled hair marched up to the booth. "Cheating on your wife?"

"Don't tell."

"Cat's got my tongue." He slapped Jack on the back. "You get in touch with that buddy of mine down in Boynton Beach?"

Jack was cleaning his plate with a folded piece of toast. He snared a bit of egg with it, then some ketchup and the last bit of steak. But he didn't raise it to his mouth. "Chris's making all the arrangements." He turned to Alex. "This is Fred Gurkey, realtor here in town."

"And who is this attractive young lady?" Fred asked.

"She's helping out in the restaurant. Alex."

Alex was grateful to Jack for making the explanation short and simple.

"Heard good things about that new restaurant Chris made up there." Fred poked Jack's shoulder. "Nobody we know can afford to eat there, but you make big bucks with tourists, don't you?"

"That's what my son and his partners tell me."

Fred Gurkey stood silent, fidgeting.

Jack glanced up at him. "Something you want to say?"

"No." Fred looked at his watch. "Gotta go."

Jack watched the realtor rush away. "Got some kind of bug up his butt." He dropped the toast he'd been obsessively wiping around his plate. "Running a resort is for fools and workaholics. But Marge and I love it." He hesitated. "I guess you know what it's like to try and start a new life."

She found herself saying, "You know my husband died."

Jack nodded.

"Do you know how? It was on the news."

Jack cleared his throat. "Either missed it or don't remember."

"I met my husband when I was fumbling around in my life. I was on a catering job. A big event for one of the most respected law firms in the Bay Area. The head lawyer was Stacy's father. Stacy was in the same firm. We got to talking. It was an instant attraction. Plus, I believed if we got together, my life would be cast under the same charmed spell he seemed to live under." She paused.

Jack didn't speak, just nodded.

"He had a terrible accident. I blame one person. Me."

Jack grabbed the bill. "Let's go," he said.

It wasn't until they were rolling down River Road, headed back to the Overlook that Jack spoke again. They had just driven through one of the darker thickets of redwood, then passed into the blinding sunlight. Jack adjusted his visor.

"I don't know what you did. But I can tell. You didn't mean anything wrong." He cleared his throat. "Blame is a poison. Don't do that to yourself."

A tear rolled down Alex's cheek. She swiped at it, staring out the passenger window.

FIVE

True to Francine's psychic predictions, the crowds swarmed to the Overlook. They came clutching Sunday *Chronicle* reviews in their fists. It was a frightening invasion of spoiled people with heavy expectations.

Alex was doing okay. She was surrounded in her orange cone of light and she was inwardly chanting, *Everyone has a Higher Self.*

The third day after the review, she spent a few hours assisting with check-in and performing slavish butt-kissing. Next, she reported to the dining room, ready to take on a busy evening.

Jeffrey came rushing up to her. "Where's Julie?"

"I have no idea."

"Can you look around?" He rushed off.

Alex went into the kitchen, which was a scene of barely contained pandemonium. Out from the pack of maniacal workers, Astrid came rushing up to her. "Where's Mark?" she asked. "This sauce has broken. Can you look for him?"

"Okay," Alex said. What she should do was walk around for a few minutes and then report nothing. But she didn't. Her trouble radar was activated. It was pushing her to investigate, pointing to the dim hall behind the kitchen. Damn. What was it going to take to cure her from her attraction to trouble? Wasn't a dead husband enough?

As she passed the freezer and the dry goods storage, she could hear muffled moans coming from the janitorial closet at the end of the hall. Sighing deeply, she pushed the door open.

"What the hell!" Mark yelled.

His checked chef pants were down around his ankles. Julie's dress was up around her waist. To top it off, they were both glaring at her as though she were invading their privacy. Who knew? Maybe she was. She was about to make a sardonic remark when she heard footsteps.

Wesley was coming down the hall.

Alex slammed the door.

"Have you seen my mom?" Wesley called.

Alex ran up the hall. "Nobody down here."

An unspoken conversation telegraphed back and forth between them.

"It's useless to be down here," Alex said finally.

"Useless," Wesley repeated, meeting her gaze.

Alex hoped the two in the closet had enough common sense, or at least a sense of self-preservation, to remain hidden until the hallway was empty.

Thank God no one had the flu. All hands were on deck that night, including Mrs. Juarez, who, it turned out, was a pretty mean prep person.

"I teach all my children to cook," she announced. "But me, I am the best. *I* should be a chef."

"Oh, no," Mark moaned. "Just what I need. Another rival." But he was clearly impressed by Mrs. Juarez's skills. "I'm going to steal this woman," he announced. "She's too good a prep cook to be a maid."

"Head maid," Mrs. Juarez corrected. "I make good money."

"You steal her and I'll kill you," called Ivy, who was passing through the kitchen.

"Stand in line," Mark called back jovially.

With the kitchen fairly well staffed, Alex was sent to the front of the house to help. Jeffrey approached her, looking ingratiating. "I'm holding you to your promise. The one about doing anything."

"What?" Alex said.

"Lap-dancing. Do you have a g-string?"

"That's very funny. What do you really want me to do?"

"Help Julie with the clients from hell tonight."

"And?"

He averted his eyes. "Do you have a sexy but classy dress?"

"Lucky for you, I brought a large selection of my wardrobe, including one sexy but classy dress."

"You're saving me. I love you."

"That's not unconditional love," she said.

"I don't believe in unconditional love," he replied.

"Neither do I." She sighed. "Not anymore."

"Vah-voom!" Julie greeted her, when she returned to the lodge, entering the lobby in her Italian high heels.

The spiked heels were an afterthought. She'd worn them maybe once in the two years she'd had them and had to soak her ankles in ice for two days as a result. What the hell. Might as well go for broke.

Clearly, Julie was going to deal with the earlier janitor's closet sex scandal with a huge case of denial. She maintained a friendly, blank look as she looked over Alex's outfit.

"Wow," Wesley said. He was coming from the bar, on his way to the kitchen, carrying a bottle of Calvados requested by Mark.

"Wesley, put your eyes back in your head," Julie chided. "She's old enough to be your mother."

"Ah, you're just jealous. You like *all* the attention."

Julie's smile tightened, a subtle freeze.

Wesley's face fell. "I was kidding."

"You only kid like that when you're mad at me," Julie said. She stroked the lace on her dress, above her left breast. "Are you mad at me, honey?"

Wesley glared at his mother.

"My feet hurt," Alex said. They looked at her. She shrugged. "I will do this only if I can complain about my feet and my bra straps all night. That's what I do when I wear this kind of getup. It's kind of a symbolic joke." She hesitated. "A joke I used to have with my husband."

"Well, you look stunning," Julie said. "And thanks for the help. It's going to be a zoo."

The people came early for their reservations, late for their reservations and without reservations. Alex passed out drinks, mingled and generally kowtowed to the spoiled guests. Everything was good. Until nearly nine, when a party of four arrived, already complaining as they pushed through the door. Four swollen egos on legs.

"Your Web site directions from the East Bay suck," said one of the two males in the party. He was a well-built man who would have been handsome if his face wasn't so contorted with anger.

"Welcome," Alex said with the forgiving tone she imagined Mother Teresa would have used for evil people. "Can I get you a complimentary drink?" She brightened the orange cone of light surrounding her.

"We want to be seated," he said.

"I'm afraid we won't be able to seat you for half an hour."

"Half an hour?" one of the women asked with the kind of horror usually reserved for life-threatening events.

Have you ever not had enough food? Have you had someone die a terrible death in the recent past? Do you understand how unimportant waiting half an hour is, in the big scheme of things? Alex thought. *Chill, girl,* she told herself.

"I told you not to trust that damned review," the second man muttered. "Every time we go to some newly reviewed place, it's all hype."

The first man stared at Alex's cleavage, sending her nerves tingling. She felt her muscles tightening.

"What if I was Steven Spielberg?" he said, addressing her breasts. "I don't think Spielberg would be waiting half an hour for a table, would he?" He took a card from his pocket. "Take a look at who I am."

Alex reached for the card, barely touching it. She let it flutter to the ground, then speared it with her high heel. "I can offer you complimentary cocktails. There's a lovely empty couch by the fireplace. Let me go and reserve it for you before someone takes it. Oops." She removed the business card from her heel and stuck it into her cleavage, then turned her back. Someone clapped a hand onto her shoulder. A tight, hostile grip.

In a matter of seconds, the man was lying on the floor facedown. Alex gripped his arm behind his back, trapping him in a helpless position. With a quick snap, she could have broken his arm. His mouth was open, but he didn't make a sound. The rest of his party was staring, all too bewildered to speak. Of course by now the entire room was watching, including Julie and Wesley, who'd been on his way to the bar again, and, heading over, wringing his hands, Chris Campbell.

Alex let go of the man's arm and took her knee off his back.

The guest staggered to his feet. Once standing, he broke out into a grin. "Nice move," he said sincerely.

It was too bad, but some men just needed to be taken down in order to mellow out. It wasn't pretty, but what could you do?

The subdued intimidator held out his hand. "Gordon Blakely. This is my wife, Rita, and our friends Bob and Diane Porter."

By now, Chris Campbell was simpering to the group.

"This must be the boss," Gordon Blakely said, clearly amused. "Ready to kiss ass so we won't sue." He put his hand to his chin. "A complimentary evening including seating *right now* would help. Perhaps two gift certificates for a nice weekend would clinch it."

"Done." Chris exhaled. "Our pleasure."

When the foursome had shuffled off, Julie came rushing up. "That was awesome."

Wesley wasn't far behind. "A ninja warrior queen. You are becoming my idea of the perfect woman."

"I only wish," Alex replied.

Just before she left that night, Alex was headed down the secluded hallway to the restroom when she sensed someone behind her. She was about to whip around when a voice called, quietly and urgently, "It's

Wesley."

Alex turned to find the hulking boy coming down the dim corridor with his palms raised in a defensive gesture.

As he approached, his features twisted into a pained grin. "I'll bet you could hurt me pretty bad, couldn't you?"

"I suppose I could," she replied. "What's up?"

"I know what was going on," he said. "In the closet, this afternoon." His face took on a complex look, both disgusted and embarrassed, yet also protective. "She told me, as if I couldn't have guessed. She has to confess, then she feels even worse, like she's messing me up." He shrugged.

"You're a good kid," Alex said. She really meant it, in the best sense. There was something about the boy, something that was strong and good and would survive.

"You know why I followed you." It was a statement.

"Pretty sure," she said.

Wesley came up close to her. "Don't tell anyone about my mother and Mark," he whispered. "Not even Jeffrey, even if he is your cousin." She opened her mouth, but before she could speak, his face fell apart and he started crying. "I don't know what it is with her," he sputtered. "She has to go to the edge and he's just as bad. But they had their thrill. Everything will be normal again. If it doesn't go back to normal, you can report it if you want."

Put that way, she found it hard not to agree to silence. Although she wondered what the "normal" was that they were going back to.

SIX

Needless to say, Alex was not assigned to hostess duties anymore. Jack and Marge insisted on working extra hours greeting guests. It was nice to have them around. They might not be business geniuses, but they were natural hosts, people their son could learn from, if he weren't so arrogant. Chris and his fiancée were not exactly the warmest duo in the world, which inspired the guests to react in kind, resorting to their worst bad rich-people behaviors.

The night after her hostess fiasco, Alex was back in the bustling kitchen doing prep and enduring a barrage of teasing about her taking out the guest.

Ivy Lightfoot had been dragged in to help Jean with the desserts, although she was not shy in criticizing the gold-leaf truffles as elitist excess, and loud enough for the entire kitchen to hear. This inspired a heated political discussion among the entire kitchen staff, all except Jean, who was her usual withdrawn self. Even Astrid felt compelled to make comparisons between Scandinavia and the United States.

Early on in the evening, Alex had noticed Roxanne was not her usual effervescent self. The next time the waitress came into the kitchen, Alex approached her. "Are you okay?" she asked. She liked Roxanne. No matter how crazy it got, Roxanne pumped everyone up with her upbeat chatter, a weird blend of raucous street humor and New Age inspirational clichés.

"I almost didn't come," Roxanne said. "My mother predicted trouble tonight."

"Is she always accurate in her predictions?" Alex asked with as diplomatic a tone as she could muster. She wasn't a complete skeptic when it came to the paranormal, but Roxanne's mother, Francine, was a *telephone* psychic, for God's sake.

Roxanne shrugged. "Not a hundred percent. A lot of it is in the interpretation. Anyway, I had to come. I need the money."

"What's with the bullshitting?" Mark had roared over at them from his station. "Roxanne, pick up. Plates are getting cold. And you, Ninja Queen, where's my parsley?"

Despite Francine's prediction, it was a fine night. Busy, but fine. Near the end of the evening, Alex, done with her kitchen work, was pitching in clearing the dining room. She looked up to find Julie wobbling in, obviously smashed.

"I hate depending on him," Julie whined to no one in particular. "I hate not having my damned driving license and having my kid lug me around everywhere. I'm like a fucking errand, excuse my language."

Wesley, setting a nearby table for the next day's brunch, looked like he wanted to fall into a hole. The rest of the staff pretended they were temporarily deaf.

Roxanne was the first to leave. Not ten minutes had passed when she came running back in. She burst into the dining room, where the rest of the group was lingering over the staff meal. "Some jerk just exposed himself to me in the parking lot," she cried.

Marge stood and rushed toward her. "Are you all right? Did he hurt you?"

"I'm fine," Roxanne said. "No, I'm not fine. I'm pissed. The bastard."

"I'm calling the sheriff," Jack said.

Chris came up next to his father. "Wait a minute. Don't we want to find out what happened first?"

"We just heard what happened. A pervert exposed himself to one of my staff."

"Our staff," Chris said. "Maybe it wasn't anything. A joke."

"Chris!" Roxanne exploded. "Some asshole in a ski mask was masturbating in front of my car headlights. Is that your idea of a joke?"

"I just wasn't sure we wanted to get the sheriff involved . . ." Chris trailed off.

Jack looked suspiciously at his son. "Is this the first time this has happened?"

"This is the first time for this particular event," Chris said.

"What else?"

Chris described the ransacking of the two guest cottages.

"How long has this been going on?" Jack asked.

"Two months."

"Two months!" Jack roared. "Marge, call the sheriff."

"He just wanted to protect the business," Marge said.

"Mom, don't get in the middle," Chris said. "Okay, it was stupid. But I *was* just trying to protect the business."

When the sheriff arrived thirty minutes later, he handed each of them a card from the Guerneville substation of the Sonoma County Sheriff's Department. His name was Deputy Peter Szabo. "Pronounced 'zay-bo,'" he informed everyone.

Jeffrey, despite the upsets of the evening, gave Alex a veiled look that said, "Isn't he cute in his uniform?"

And he was. Alex noted Deputy Szabo's dark blond Slavic look, including high cheekbones and blue eyes. Not that she was interested. The last thing she could imagine these days was sexual attraction. She got a flash of Mark and Julie going at it in the janitor's closet and shuddered.

Deputy Szabo conducted a very earnest round of questions and promised he would be getting back to them quickly.

• • •

When she got back to her place, she found a message on the answering machine. It was from Arlene.

"Call me," her mother said. "No matter how late you get in."

"Oh, no," Alex whispered. She punched in her parents' number, fingers trembling. *You can't take another tragedy,* a voice in her head said. *You'll really lose it this time.*

"Alex?" a sleepy voice said. "Are you all right?"

"I'm fine. What happened? Are you and Dad okay?"

There was a brief silence, then her mother's ironic chuckle. "Dad. I haven't heard you use that word since you were six years old."

"Seven," Alex corrected. No use mentioning it was at their request. Her panic was transforming into the exasperation she mostly felt when she talked to Arlene. "You don't sound like there's an emergency," she said.

"As you know, I'm not much for the paranormal, although I know that recently there has been some evidence . . ."

"Arlene, it's late and I'm still breaking down the adrenalin that flooded my system after getting your message."

"I was worried about you," Arlene confessed. "You know normally I try to stay out of your way when you make decisions, but I haven't felt good about your going up to that resort. In fact, I had bad feelings about it. Tonight I went to bed and had a terrible dream that you were being attacked by a brute in a dark room. I got up and called immediately." She sighed. "There you have it. Old woman's superstition. What's become of me? I am terrified of any signs of, you know—" She broke off. Alex knew her mother was obsessed with even the remotest possibility of Alzheimer's, although no one in the family had ever had it.

Now that Arlene's self-absorption was returning, it was easier for Alex to restore a sense of calm. At any moment, Arlene would offer some words of opinion that made little sense, to Alex, anyway. Words that contradicted Arlene's belief that she didn't encroach on Alex's life.

"Everything's fine here," Alex lied. "Don't worry, you're not growing irrational. You and Arthur will be clear-headed if you live to be a hundred. I'll call you around the holidays. Tell Arthur congratulations on his show and how much I like his new piece."

She hung up the phone and dropped onto the couch. She, for one, had had enough of Great Mother intuitions and psychic revelations for one night. But she had to agree with Arlene on one point. Something was wrong at the Overlook.

SEVEN

A few days later, Jack held a staff meeting. "It looks like my whole team is here," he said. Everyone was seated on chairs pulled into the center of the dining room to make a large circle. "I'm going to get straight to the point. Marge and I have decided not to go to Florida." He looked over at Chris.

"You're announcing this in public before we've talked as a family?" Chris's face looked ashen.

"This is our family too," Jack said, waving around the room to encompass them all.

Chris stared at his father. "Since you seem to think that all of us in this room are somehow equal in terms of family status," he said, "I'll say my piece right here."

Jack nodded, his face calm.

"I won't go on about broken promises," Chris said. "What I will say is that this place would be closed right now if I hadn't come back, and then where would your so-called extended family be?"

"I don't like leaving my resort knowing some pervert is attacking women here," Jack explained. "It's just not a good time to ditch something Marge and I love dearly."

"That's an *excuse*." Chris raised a fist and pumped the air, the gesture of an angry little boy. "This isn't fair. *Please* wait and discuss this with me in private."

A snorting laugh rang out. Everyone turned to Mark Heller. "Spare me. *This* was the point of the meeting? I have work to do." He stood up and glanced around at the hostile faces. "What?" he asked belligerently. "Just because I don't want to get involved in some hokey version of *Ordinary People*? Chris, be a man. This place was a dump ready for bankruptcy when we got here. Lay down the law."

Mark turned to Jack and shrugged. "Sorry, dude. Reality check, know what I mean? You don't know shit about business."

"Leave him alone!" It was Ivy Lightfoot. She jumped up from her chair and pointed an accusing finger at the chef. "You are a mean and heartless man." The twisting ivy tattoos on her arms darkened with an angry flush.

Mark glared at her. "The last thing I need is insults from a vegetarian sideshow freak."

"Enough," Jack said. His look suggested defeat. "Chris and Mark are right. I *was* running this place into the ground. I'm not asking to head the battalion, I'm only asking to stay on with the troops."

"Dad." Chris's face was going from pale to a mottled reddish-purple. "Let's wait on this. Okay?"

Now Jeffrey stood up. "We're all exhausted from the craziness lately," he said. He turned to the Campbells. "We're all honored that you consider us family, but this is an issue for the three of you to decide."

After a brief pause, Jack nodded, followed by Chris.

"Is the bullshitting over?" Mark called out. "I have important things to do."

"Wait." Everyone turned to Alex, who was also standing now. She took a deep breath. "I have an offer." She glanced around the room. "I can teach the women here self-defense."

"I'll bet you can," Wesley called out. "She's a destructive force."

There were a few appreciative giggles.

Alex smiled. "I've had a lot of martial arts training. But the offer isn't about that. Any woman can learn to defend herself. This isn't ninja stuff. It's basic survival skills."

"What are we talking about here?" Chris asked impatiently. "The last thing I want is somebody trying to fight back and getting hurt."

"I don't have time to go into it all, Chris," Alex responded, "but there's a bunch of research and statistics out there supporting fighting back, once you know how. First, it works. Second, it's good for morale. But, most of all, helplessness sucks."

There was another smattering of giggles among the staff.

"We don't have the money or the time to fool around with weeks of training," Chris said.

"I was thinking a one-day seminar," Alex interjected quickly. "I've done them. It's enough to get some basic skills and attitudes wired into the body. And there's no charge. It's the least I can do. You've taken me in. I want to repay."

"I think your offer is excellent," Jack broke in. "I'd be willing to have all the women who want to attend be allowed to go, with pay."

"Of course you would," Chris bellowed. "Give, give. Jack Campbell's motto."

"I can't deal with this garbage," Mark grumbled. He stomped toward the kitchen. "Fuck self-defense," he said, pushing through the swinging doors.

"I'm not convinced," Chris said.

"I agree," Leslie added. "I can't see the point."

Alex felt her stomach sinking. Everyone was staring at her. Their looks ranged from enthusiastic to hostile to confused.

"Didn't you listen to what Alex said?" Roxanne didn't hesitate to jump in. "I'm the one who was attacked. I want to learn to protect myself."

"You weren't attacked," Ivy threw out. "Some guy just exposed himself to you. Big deal. I've lived on the streets. That was an everyday kind of thing you just ignored."

"It was an invasion of my person, even if I wasn't touched," Roxanne retorted. She turned to Alex. "Isn't that true?"

"These are the issues we'll be getting into, if I give the seminar," she said. "That's part of why this class is so important." She paused, grinning. "Plus, you'll learn how to kick butt."

This got a laugh from some, and at least a reluctant smile from some of the others.

"I don't believe in violence," Ivy protested. "Not any kind. Who said women should kick butt anyway? It makes them as bad as men, as far as I'm concerned."

"That's unbelievably naïve," Roxanne shot back.

Alex raised her hand. "It's okay." She was on familiar territory now. "This is another one of the important issues we'll deal with."

She waited now. She tried to keep quiet, let it happen without seeming desperate to have them agree. She wasn't exactly sure why she wanted to teach these women so badly, but there it was.

Finally, Chris spoke up. "All right. If it's free. But no one gets paid to go. It's strictly volunteer."

Alex glanced at Jack, who shrugged.

"How about next Monday?" she asked. That would give her time to get down to San Francisco and talk to Sarge.

Sarge's golden retrievers greeted Alex like a long-lost relative. Their names were Alecto, Tisiphone and Magaera, after the mythological avenging Furies who hunted and punished murderers. The names were a laugh, since the dogs were slavish love bugs. Their nicknames were Allie, Tissie and Maggie.

As soon as she walked into the Victorian flat on Chattanooga Street, they were all over her, attempting to kiss her face, whining at her arrival, their eyes gleaming with soft, wet passion.

"Off!" Sarge called to them. But her voice carried no conviction. When it came to her "kids," she lost all of her formidable authority. "Let's go, let's go," she called, herding the manic trio to the back of the railroad flat. "I'll be right back," she called. "I'll put them in the yard."

Alex went into the living room. Sun streamed through the tall windows. The place was classic—white plaster walls, dark wood moldings and fireplace, hardwood floors. Sarge, she knew, had bought the flat with her ex-husband, long before the divorce.

"It is a great place, isn't it?" someone said, smiling at Alex from the couch. It was a young woman in jeans and a Giants baseball shirt. She had crooked teeth, a stubby nose and a very bad haircut, but her overall persona radiated a pleasant magnetism.

"This is Tracy Sawyer," Sarge said, coming into the room. "She's going to train to be an instructor."

Alex, watching Sarge enter, admired the sinewy tightness of Sarge's middle-aged body. Sarge was a small, concentrated bundle of energy, from her tiny feet to her hair, a mass of graying, dynamic curls. Despite the chill in the typically San Francisco drafty flat, Sarge was wearing latex workout tights and a stretchy latex top, their thin layers revealing her muscled legs and arms.

"And this is Alex Pope," she said to Tracy. "Former instructor, one of my best."

"I'm nervous," Tracy confessed. "But something happened to a friend of mine. She was attacked in the middle of the day on Valencia Street. She lost a front tooth and can't afford a new one. Worse, she feels like a victim. Me, I feel so angry. Alex, why did you start teaching?"

Alex hesitated. Then she said, "I had a friend I used to do catering with. She was raped and beaten one night after a job, then in the hospital for two months. I saw a segment on Sarge and her school on *Bay Area Personalities*." She smiled at Sarge. "I already was training in martial arts, but I saw this was different. Sarge turned these regular women with no training into confident warriors."

Sarge's real name was Naomi Goldstein. Besides having a black belt in a form of Okinawan karate, she'd studied the Israeli Krav Maga self-defense system on a kibbutz. She was the toughest woman Alex knew, including a few champion boxers and a forward on a Spanish women's basketball team who was six-five.

"Speaking of confident warriors, I just made a video." Sarge jumped up and went to the pine entertainment center against the wall. She came back with a video, handing it to Alex. "It was a blast. Here, keep it."

Alex tucked the video into her leather backpack. "It's natural to be nervous," she said to Tracy. "And to be honest with you, you will be teaching all kinds of women, some of them with some pretty horrible stories. But believe me, it's worth it."

Tracy stood. "I'll let you two get on with your day. Thanks, Sarge, for seeing me on a Sunday. I feel better. Thanks to you, too, Alex, and nice meeting you."

"I'm feeling a little nervous myself," Alex admitted after Tracy had gone. "We've been mostly out of touch since my marriage and I have ulterior motives for coming today."

"I'm sorry, Alex. I called several times after the funeral and left messages on your machine."

"I was hiding."

"I should have persisted," Sarge said. "I just dropped it."

Alex smiled. "Maybe I can use this undeserved guilt of yours for a bit of blackmail."

Sarge threw up her hands in mock agony. "What do you want? You can have it!"

"Equipment." Before Sarge could speak, she added quickly, "To borrow, of course."

"You want to teach again? Far out."

"I'm going to teach a group of women working at a resort. Some guy is exposing himself on the property and it's not clear if it's going to get any worse."

"That's bad enough. You know my philosophy," Sarge said, shaking her head. "This is training and knowledge all women should have. Of course you can borrow equipment."

"I appreciate it."

Sarge shrugged. "No problem."

"I'm a little out of practice."

"It'll come back fast. Anyway, you know this. We teach material that triggers instinctive reactions. Women learn they're worth something and how to use what opportunities they have at the moment to defend themselves." Sarge winked at her. "Watch the video. It'll inspire you. How many sessions are you teaching?"

"Just a day seminar."

Sarge frowned. "Better if it was more."

"You'd have all women be superheroes if you could."

"Anything wrong with that?"

Alex grinned. "No."

Sarge sprang from the couch. "In fact, I think I have something even better to lend you." She went to the doorway and called down the hall, "Uli!"

A door slammed at the far end of the hall and in moments Uli appeared, wearing a pair of striped silk pajama shorts, his gorgeous rippled abdomen and swelled biceps exposed. He usually wore his golden mane in a ponytail, but this morning it was loose, accenting the Greek God look.

"Alex!" Uli glanced down at his outfit, or lack of it. "Sorry. I was up late, reading. Still in bed, obviously."

Uli, despite the male bimbo look, was not only a black belt in kenpo but also did some kind of obscure and brainy computer work. He and Sarge worked at the self-defense school together, in addition to the personal relationship that had developed after Sarge's divorce.

"I'm lending you to Alex," Sarge announced. "She needs a padded assailant."

"Absolutely," Uli said. "Tell me when."

"You're both great." Alex sighed.

On the way back, Alex glanced at the seat next to her in the Lexus. On it was a pile of videos. Enough for every woman at the Overlook. Alex had paid for them herself.

Now she was going to have to deal with the panic in her stomach. After all this convincing of others, she wasn't really sure if she could pull it off. She wasn't sure if she was ready to preach about inner strength again, when her own was only just beginning to return.

EIGHT

On Monday morning, all the Overlook women showed up at the Shed, the renovated structure behind the main lodge. In the ballroom-sized main room, there was Roxanne, Leslie, Julie, Marge, Jean, Astrid, Ivy and the Juarez women, including Mrs. Juarez and Teresa. Three part-timers came. One of them was Teresa's sister, 16-year-old Maria, a high-school soccer star bursting with enthusiasm.

Alex sat everyone in a circle and stood in its middle.

"Welcome, ladies," she said. Her voice sounded steady to her own ear, but she was quivering inside. The last time she'd run a class was in a battered women's shelter two weeks before Stacy's death. Right after the marriage, Stacy had made a few jokes about her teaching self-defense, but she had cut him off. It was practically the only thing she couldn't joke about. Now she felt the thrill, despite her nerves, of teaching women to feel strong in themselves. "I want to start by talking about fighting back if you're attacked. Ivy, we already know you have some objections. Feel okay about saying more about them?"

Ivy shrugged. "Violence perpetuates violence."

"Give me a break!" Roxanne exploded. She turned to Ivy. "If you had kids, you'd understand. My little girl, Harmony—you've taken care of her. What if someone was attacking *her*? Would you just watch?"

Ivy frowned. "No."

"Then what's the difference if you have to defend yourself? Are you worth less than that?"

"No," Ivy said. "But I still don't like this attitude about kicking butt."

"Hey, sister," Maria Juarez, the high-school athlete, crowed. "You are like, so *retro*. Man, that's like Woodstock and peace signs. What world you been living in lately? Haven't you ever watched *Buffy the Vampire Slayer*?"

"Okay, okay," Alex said. "For now, let's assume there might be occasion for a woman to defend herself, whether she's enthusiastic about it or not. Does anyone have any fears about fighting back?"

A sea of hands went up, waving furiously.

Alex grinned. "Let's just call them out." She knew what to expect.

"I'll freeze."

"I can't overpower a big man."

"I don't want to be hurt."

"I'll only make him angrier."

"These concerns are what most women express," Alex explained. "But women do fight back and they do it successfully." She paused for effect. "You don't have to be big or strong or even a believer. Just go through the process with me."

Her inner anxiety was down a few notches. She liked standing up in front of these women whom she'd grown fond of. "Look at me. Look at my body." She withered, head sinking, chin tucked in, eyes averted and shoulders hunched.

"You look weak and apologetic," Sally, one of the part-time desk clerks, observed.

"Now?" Alex adopted her don't-mess-with-me posture.

"Watch out, mama!" Maria yelled. The rest of the women laughed.

"Stand," Alex commanded. When they had, their expressions ranging from wary to amused, she said, "From now on, I want you to think of this body of yours as a set of tools powered by this." She pointed to her head. "Your mind, your attitude. I want you to imagine the powerful attitude traveling to here." She pointed to the center of her body. "This is your center of balance and strength, also your anger center." Alex pointed to her hips. "These are part of your power. In this class, you will learn to use your tools, the parts of your body, energized from this center of strength. You won't have time to think; your adrenalin will be pumping. You will react."

"Way cool," Maria said. Ivy frowned at her.

"Aggressors and predators are bullies who seek people they can intimidate," Alex said. "Don't be easy victims." She began walking, lightly balanced, her center of gravity lowered. "Be aware of your surroundings and your own stance as you go through the world, and you can often prevent any bad encounters before they happen. I'd like you to stand and walk. Feel like you have an anchor of strength in your middle and radar for what is going on around you. Don't let anyone come into what you feel is your personal space. Move away in a confident manner."

Alex watched the women walk. She observed their experimental changes of posture and body language. When she felt they'd internalized a bit of the feeling of walking through the world in a more self-assured way, she called them back into the circle.

"Roxanne, I'm going to walk. You come up to me too close. Invade my personal space."

As Roxanne closed in, Alex raised her hands and lowered her center of gravity. She made direct eye contact.

"Back off!"

Roxanne stumbled backward.

"That, ladies, is your first tool. Your voice," Alex said. "I just blew her back with a force of energy." She drew an invisible circle around herself. "This is *your* personal space and *you* decide who's allowed in it."

"But what if you get surprised?" Astrid asked. She had been following Alex's instructions with her usual Zen-like composure, her magnified blue eyes squinting from behind her thick glasses.

"Yeah, what if he comes up from behind and strangles you or knocks you down?" Maria added. "Or pulls your hair. Or grabs you by the throat and—"

"We'll get to that," Alex interrupted. "We're going to go in steps. By the end, we'll have covered a lot of different methods of attack, including surprise attacks. But I'll give you a hint. It's all about using your tools, your body parts, against the predator's weak spots, certain parts of his body." She grimaced. "I'm going to use the male pronoun for the predator, because statistics show that most attacks are by men. But I don't mean to imply that women sometimes can't be bullies or predators as well."

She glanced around the room. Most of them were with her, to varying degrees, with three exceptions. Ivy still looked defiant. Leslie wore her intensely bored expression. And Teresa stood slightly apart from the rest of the group, her body listless. Morbidly shy Teresa was a challenge. Alex knew not to push it.

"I wish we had more time. Maybe later. But for now, the purpose of this seminar is to teach you what you can do to facilitate escape."

For the first exercise, Alex had them practice adopting their stances and using their voices. As she expected, a few let out hearty howls, including Roxanne. The others looked flustered at the sound of their own voices.

"Louder," Alex ordered. "Blow them away with your power. You're creating a force field of energy. If you remember one thing from this class, remember you can win. It's like a switch. Don't switch into panic or immobility. Switch into power. Now, yell."

Ivy was beginning to find her voice of rage. Leslie, however, seemed bored. Alex wondered why Leslie had even bothered to show up. And poor Teresa was red-faced and shrinking. Alex made a mental note to keep a close eye on her, maybe talk to her after class if necessary.

"Okay, ladies," she announced. "Let's discuss the arms and hands and legs." She held out her arms. "We have fingers, palm, sides of palm, elbows, fist, fist with knuckles." As she spoke, she jabbed the air. "We punch, slap, grab, twist, chop and in general cause incapacitating damage to vulnerable areas with much less strength than you might imagine. Drive a palm into someone's nose and it doesn't matter how big he is." She kicked with her right leg. "We have both legs, including feet and knees to strike with. It takes very little to break a kneecap. A swift kick in the groin does not feel very good."

The class responded with nervous giggles.

"Can I have a volunteer?"

Maria ran up to Alex, practically into her arms. Alex detected the puppy-dog eyes of a girl with a crush. Something she was used to. It went with the territory.

She gestured to Maria's body, from head to toe. "There are many wonderful, vulnerable areas of the body that hurt when hit, no matter how big and strong the person you hit is." She started at the top again. "Just for example, right now, there's Maria's eyes." She made a poking gesture with her fingers at the eyes. "Nose." She drove a palm up, mock shoving the nose. "Ears." She banged both of her palms against the ears. "Adam's apple, side of neck, below ribs, groin, nerve on side of leg, and the wonderful kneecap, which is a ridiculous contraption, highly vulnerable to injury. Shin, tops of feet. What a shopping list!" She paused. Jean Heller had her hand raised. Her usually unanimated face was flushed with what appeared to be excitement. "Jean?"

"What about the side of the neck?" Jean made a karate-like chop at an imaginary neck.

"Yes, that would work. But like a few of the areas we've been discussing, that could be a very damaging, perhaps lethal, blow." She smiled cautiously. "But I like to see that you're using your imagination."

Jean smile a weird, twisted smile and was silent.

Alex had the group break up into pairs. For the next hour, she had them practice with the pads she'd borrowed from Sarge, doing a few simple, effective strikes and kicks. "Switch into rage!" she shouted.

Ivy Lightfoot was coming around, as Alex had expected. She made no comment but observed Ivy's increasingly enthusiastic kicks. Ivy was a tiger; Alex had known it all along.

Most of the rest of the women were doing just fine, including Jean, Astrid and Julie. Alex turned to the older ones. Marge looked a little disconcerted but was swinging her arms and legs with enthusiasm. Mrs. Juarez was a tough cookie, which wasn't a surprise.

Then there was Teresa. Poor Teresa. Her kicks were puny and she still refused to yell.

At the end, Alex had her charges get back into a circle.

"How did that feel?" she asked.

"Great!" Maria shouted.

Alex turned to Ivy, who fingered one of the many studs in her right ear and shrugged. "I was planning on leaving at noon."

"You coming back?" Maria asked.

Ivy's face contorted. "Maybe."

She'd be back. Alex had seen it before.

"Alex!"

Alex was headed down the path back to the lodge at the lunch break to check in with Jeffrey.

It was cold. A damp mist blew around them, the eerie kind that swirled in movie thrillers. Leslie stood before her, wringing her hands.

"Let's go inside," Alex said, shivering.

"No!" Leslie said.

Alex jumped. For once, Leslie had found her voice.

"Over here. It won't take long, I promise." Leslie went over to a wrought-iron bench. In a matter of seconds, she was crying.

Oh, no. She should have known. But she'd let her dislike of Leslie interfere with her intuition.

"I was raped in college," Leslie said. "A boyfriend's friend, after a party. I never told anyone. I was drunk and so was he. He begged me not to tell. I *hated* him for that." She lifted reddened eyes. "I know I'm not the warmest person in the world. After I was attacked, it got worse. I feel empty inside sometimes. I don't know how Chris stands me."

"You never talked to anyone about it after?" Alex asked. "A counselor? Your best friend?"

Alex, having grown up with a mother who gave advice for a living, had mixed feelings about the psychiatric world. But she understood that there were some situations that needed to be brought out, not left festering within.

"I never told *anyone.* And it's not like I'm living in a bubble. I read. I watch television. I know I'm not supposed to be ashamed. I know I'm not supposed to blame myself." Leslie shivered. "Marge told me you're bringing in a padded assailant for the afternoon session."

"I am. Maybe it might be a good thing to talk to someone first, let the seminar wait—"

"No!" Leslie said. "I want to take this class. You must get women like me all the time. They do it, don't they?"

Of course she'd had women like Leslie in her classes—women assaulted by men they knew or were dating. Usually not women so rich, stuck-up and pretty, though. Those women seemed not to gravitate to her classes. She felt suddenly guilty. She had to admit to a bit of reverse snobbery in her attitude toward Leslie. And, speaking of all that, hadn't she married Stacy in part to become a rich and stuck-up suburban type herself?

"I'd like to see you continue this afternoon, Leslie. Just do what you can. If you feel at all like this is going to make anything worse or bring up issues you can't handle, you must let me know. Okay? No need to make a big deal. Just do this—" Alex made a small gesture with her hand.

"Yes, I will. Thank you."

"Don't thank me yet," Alex said, using her tough, Sarge imitation. "I just want to hear you yell from now on."

Right after lunch, Alex brought in Uli.

A collective gasp filled the room. Uli was fully padded except for his head. He was carrying his head guard, a huge puffy helmet with eye and mouth holes.

"This is what we practiced in the morning for. Now you can use full force. Uli has been trained. Don't be afraid you'll hurt him. He's going to attack, he's going to use verbal insults. This is as close as we can get to a real attack." She paused. "I don't want anyone to stay who feels uncomfortable with this. Please. This isn't for everyone. If you want to leave, there's no shame at all." She glanced around the room. No one budged. "We're going to create mini-scenarios, building into higher levels of threat."

Leslie smiled weakly at her. Ivy grimaced. Alex looked at Teresa, who nodded almost imperceptibly.

For the rest of the afternoon, Alex demonstrated techniques. Then she let the women pummel, gouge, kick and chop at Uli.

As always, there were various levels of skill, levels of reaction. Some of the women were quick to react, drawing from some inner rage or strong self-protective urge. A few giggled nervously, had to be encouraged. Then it was Leslie's turn.

As Uli approached her, she went limp, then ran crying out the door of the Shed. The rest of the women stood stock-still, looking clearly uncomfortable. Alex went out to the patio.

"Leslie?"

Leslie was bent over, gagging. She straightened, looked Alex in the eye. "I want to do this."

"Leslie wants another turn," Alex announced to the group. "Let's give her a round of encouraging applause."

In the midst of the rhythmic clapping, Uli came at Leslie. When he went to grab her, Leslie managed a powerful palm strike to Uli's mask, where his nose would have been.

The group cheered wildly.

Leslie grabbed Uli's head with both hands. She thrust her knees into his face, a swift and vicious series of blows. To the group's shouts, she kicked his groin and smacked his ears with her palms. Uli fell to the floor, arms waving in a plea for mercy. Leslie stood over him, her nostrils flaring.

"Okay, okay," Alex called, joining in on the laughter. Sarge's theory was that women were actually the more aggressive of the species. They were wired to protect themselves and their young. At some of these classes, Alex had seen substantial proof of that postulation.

Teresa was the worst, as Alex had expected. Still, she delivered a serviceable kick to the knee and a tiny little yell.

The most surprising was Jean. It was late in the day and they were practicing more advanced scenarios.

Uli approached Jean quickly from behind, growling, "I'm going to get you, baby." He grabbed her tight around the waist.

Jean went ballistic, thrusting her hips back and back-fisting him in the groin, forcing him to let go and bend over. She spun around and twisted his neck, sending him sprawling to the ground. The rest of the women watched, half of them amused and half of them aghast. Jean stomped on his chest with her heel, then grabbed his throat.

Alex decided to speak up. Jean's rage was palpable. "Good, Jean," she said. "I think that's enough."

Jean stood, wild-eyed for a moment. Then her body wilted and she shuffled, puppet-like as before, back to the group.

At the end of the session, after Uli had left, Alex addressed the group, seated in a circle around her. "How did that feel?"

Surprisingly, it was Maria who expressed the first reservation. "I don't know," she said. "It made me feel angry the way he taunted me. Bastard. Now I'm feeling weird. I'm feeling like I did something bad, hurting him."

"Screw him!" It was a loud, resounding cry. All heads turned. To Leslie. "No one should ever be able to do that to you," she added, her voice quivering.

All right, Leslie. Alex silently cheered.

"I feel drained and sore," Marge said.

"That's normal," Alex said. "Are you sorry you came?"

"No," Marge said. "I know the difference now. What it feels like to turn fear into rage. I'll never forget the feeling of fighting back."

Nearly everyone nodded. Including Ivy.

"Any more questions?" Alex asked.

Jean raised her hand.

"Jean?"

"Can you tell us about the laws of self-defense? What if a man verbally abuses me on the street and I, for example, kill him?" Jean asked in her odd, toneless voice.

There were a few titters among the group.

"I've imagined it with some construction workers," Roxanne said.

"I understand," Alex said, trying not to grin. "But it's a valid question. I can't go into the details of the law here, but the general principle is the same everywhere in this country. Basically, the laws say you have the legal and moral right to defend yourself. If you are attacked physically, you can defend yourself using whatever force is necessary and reasonable to keep from getting injured. This is also true if you haven't been physically attacked yet, but you believe you will be."

Alex took a breath and looked around. They were staring at her with intent faces.

"Okay, first there has to be a threat, physical, verbal or both. Then, you must believe the perpetrator is going to attack you and has the ability to do so. Last, he must have the opportunity. That means if he's running away, his back to you, he doesn't have the opportunity. Of course, as in all things, it can be more complicated, but the bottom line is this: If you are being attacked or about to be attacked, you have all the right in the world to defend yourself. Does all that make sense?"

Everyone nodded.

"All right, then," Alex said. "Let me hear your voices!"

A gratifying collective shout filled the Shed.

Alex went to a box by the west wall. She came back with Sarge's videos, which she handed out to all attendees. "See yourself winning," she said. "Draw on the beast-woman inside you. You have it wired in you from prehistoric days. Remember most of all that this isn't about fancy techniques. It's about knowing you can fight back and believing in yourself."

Stacy had never liked Sarge or her philosophies. He said Sarge's beast-woman analogies sounded like bad cartoon material. Nevertheless, Alex had never abandoned them, just as she could never stop teaching during the marriage. She just hadn't referred to them when he was around.

Alex felt a twinge of guilt. This was the kind of thing she knew she'd have to deal with if she started teaching again. She pushed the thoughts away for the time being. There'd be time to examine her relationship with Stacy as it really was. But not now. Not yet.

As everyone was leaving, Alex approached Teresa, who shrank back, her face red. "I'm so sorry," she stuttered. "I'm terrible, I know it."

Alex smiled gently. "No, you're fine. You need to practice feeling strong, that's all." She hesitated, then spoke. "If there's anything—"

Teresa shrank back more.

"Hey, she's always been like that," Maria said, coming up to them. "She's afraid of her own shadow, man. She's been like that since she was little."

Teresa's eyes fluttered, the look of a trapped bird.

"It's okay," Alex said. Maria was about to go on again about her sister, but Alex held up a warning hand. "You did fine today."

Teresa stared at her, doubtful.

"You did." Alex smiled at her. "Go at your own pace. You know what? I know it was a big thing just for you to come. You're brave, girlfriend."

Teresa beamed at her, then scurried to the exit.

Alex felt as drained as her students. She glanced at the sky, then headed back to her little cozy granny unit, so nicely tucked behind the Campbell residence. She was feeling comforted by the place, her own small space. It was going to rain soon. From the look of the clouds, hard. The local pundits were forecasting a bad winter.

NINE

Two nights later, the rains came. Alex was startled awake by branches slapping against her windows and the relentless pounding of the torrential deluge. She tossed and turned until nearly dawn, when the storm quieted to a steady but relentless downpour. She was sound asleep when the cell phone on the nightstand rang.

"Alex, did I wake you?"

Alex's heart sank. "No," she lied. "How are you, Hunter?" Stacy's father sounded as patriarchal as ever. His tone had the silky assurance of a man accustomed to reverence. His question was rhetorical. He couldn't care less if he woke her.

A silence ensued. Long enough for her to think the connection had broken. Hunter finally broke the quiet. "I've left messages."

"I meant to—"

"Don't explain," he interrupted. He cleared his throat. "As to the holidays, I assume your lack of response indicates you don't want to spend them with us."

"I'd love to spend the holidays with you." *A lie.* "I was going to call." *A partial lie.* "I've obligated myself to work up here. They really need me." *Mostly true.*

There was a pause. Then she heard a deep sigh on Hunter's part. "Well, the truth is, I don't think any of us feel like there's much to celebrate."

Alex felt herself sinking into darkness at the unexpected throb in Hunter's voice. She was about to reach out as best she could, when Hunter reverted to his usual self.

"The lawsuit is proceeding much too slowly. After the New Year, things will get going. Rather, we'll *make* them get going. I would hope in the future that you'll be more timely in answering my calls. And that your plans will be flexible enough to accommodate the proceedings."

What a cold-hearted ass, she thought. It'd been a mystery to her why Stacy had been so fixated on pleasing him. But, then, it wasn't as though she wasn't familiar with fathers who were impossible to please.

"I'll return your calls." She paused. "I hope you and Bunny can find some time of solace during the holidays." Even to her own ears, her words sounded distant and perfunctory. She felt mildly ashamed at her lack of compassion but she was just as resolved not to be too hard on herself about it. She needed to nurture herself.

Good God. She was beginning to sound like Arlene's columnist persona. That was scary.

Jack was at her door thirty minutes later. She'd just dressed and was making coffee.

"We have some tree branches down in the far parking lot by the Shed. Thought you might help me clear 'em while there's a break in the rain." He held up a bag spotted with grease and pointed to her coffeepot. "Put that java in a thermos. I have doughnuts. Big ones with lots of sugar and bad fats." He winked at her. "Don't tell Marge."

Alex wanted to jump into Jack's arms, sink into his canvas coat and have him put his arms around her. She quickly suppressed the impulse and went to fetch the thermos.

They drove past the lodge, up the road past the cottages and into the last parking lot at the end of the road. They pulled saws and axes from the bed of the pickup and set out to clear the branches felled by the storm. It wasn't much of a mess and Jack probably hadn't really needed her help.

Alex knew what they were falling into, but so what? Maybe Jack needed a substitute daughter as much as she needed a substitute father right now. They chopped and sawed, hacked at the puny branches and dragged them to the pickup.

They took a break on a huge redwood stump, sipping steaming coffee and eating the doughnuts, which were so fabulously sweet and greasy she thought her taste buds would detonate.

Ring. Ring. Alex's cell phone broke into the calm. She let the ringing persist until the call was siphoned away into the message center.

"Might be important," Jack said.

"I'm avoiding the outside world," she said.

She didn't explain and Jack, bless him, didn't ask.

A few minutes later, Chris roared up, squealing to a stop and leaping from his Escalade. "Why didn't you answer your phone?" he said, red-faced with anger. "They caught the pervert who's been bothering us."

"What happened?" Jack asked.

"It was Teresa. He was in one of the cottages as she went in to clean."

"Oh, my God," Alex exclaimed.

"She's fine," Chris said. "I suppose thanks to you. She practically knocked him unconscious. He took off like a frightened sheep. They caught him down the road, trying to limp away."

"Right on," Jack said, clapping Alex on the back.

When they arrived back at the lodge, they were greeted by Deputy Szabo, the nice-looking officer who'd taken the original report a few weeks before. At Chris's insistence, they trooped to the back office, out of sight of the guests. Teresa was gone. She'd been taken, Deputy Szabo informed them, for a show-up.

"A show-up?" Alex asked.

"An identification in the field," he explained. "Our backup unit found the suspect not far from here, real disoriented." He looked like he was trying to suppress a grin. "The young lady roughed up the alleged assaulter pretty good. We've taken her down the road to identify him."

"Did anyone from the Overlook go with her?" she asked.

"No," Szabo said. "She's with two experienced deputies, one of 'em a female who's handled sex crimes."

Alex didn't like it. Teresa stuttered if a guest asked for extra soap. Someone from the Overlook should have gone with her. "What happened?"

"Well, according to the victim," Szabo began, "she came into the cottage and saw a man in a black overcoat and ski mask inside. She was blocking the doorway and he ran toward her and grabbed her around the middle." Here, he couldn't repress that grin. "The victim says she whacked his ears, then struck his nose. At this point he let go and bent over. She grabbed his head and delivered a knee strike to his chest, at which point he fell backward and she kicked him in the knee."

"Good for her," Jack said. He glanced at Alex. "Thanks to you."

The deputy seemed curious, but Alex didn't want to pursue that line of conversation just yet. "Then what?" she asked.

"The assailant got up and stumbled off before anyone else showed up. The victim's sister, Maria, was the first to arrive after that. The sister called down to the lodge and someone called nine-one-one." By the time he'd answered their questions, Teresa was back. As they brought her into the back office, Alex's heart sank. Teresa was trembling, despite the sheriff's coat thrown over her shoulders. Alex suspected she wasn't cold. Her expression was rigid with anxiety.

Teresa's face transformed when she spotted Alex. "I yelled this time," she said. "I didn't hesitate. Not for a second."

"Way to go, beast-girl," Alex said. "I am very proud of you." She could see Szabo gazing at her with intense curiosity.

One of the other deputies handed him a few sheets of paper, which he scanned. "The suspect is Shayne Elliot. He says he used to work here."

"Shayne Elliot," Chris repeated. "How do you like that?" He glanced at his father. "Another one of your rescue projects."

"I already told you," Jack said. "That was a mistake. I admitted that, didn't I?" He turned to Szabo. "I hired the boy because he's the son of

Hank Elliot, a buddy of mine and a good man. We knew the boy'd had a few brushes with the law, but we were told they were minor offenses."

A disturbed look passed over Szabo's face. "I know Hank. I know Shayne." He shook his head. "Why'd he get fired?"

"He was trouble from the beginning," Chris said. "He was only here a couple of weeks last summer. Rude, belligerent. We had him bellhopping, but that didn't work out, so we sent him to wash dishes and learn prep, which he thought was beneath him. The day he was fired, he apparently called our sous chef a bitch. Our chef threw him out on the spot."

"Bad egg," Jack said, shaking his head. "Well, at least he's taken care of now."

"We'll do our best," Szabo said.

"Open-and-shut case," Jack said.

Szabo shrugged. "No such thing, sir. Like I said, we'll do our best."

Shayne's arraignment was the next day. Alex attended by herself. It was going to be a wild, busy weekend at the lodge, deep into the holiday season. Everyone had to work. Still, it seemed right for someone to go and Alex volunteered.

She wanted to see the perpetrator in person. She wanted to see him go down. She wanted to be there despite having to go to a courtroom, despite having to wander among a sea of lawyers.

Shayne Elliot was six feet tall and skinny, with a wispy black goatee and stringy hair. He looked like most of the kids who hung out at Picasso's, the coffeehouse in Guerneville. The poetic, artistic crowd.

The family was at the arraignment, the mother crying. It was sad all around. Alex reminded herself that this was a kid with increasingly more serious offenses under his belt. Hank Elliot was in debt, it came out, and Shayne was appointed a public defender.

Alex sat up. She wanted a good look at the defense. It was a weary-looking woman who appeared earnest and sturdy, wearing an awful gray, dumpy pinstriped pantsuit. Alex thought back to Stacy's opinions about lawyer-lady wardrobes.

The public defender wasn't doing anything to dispel his disdainful comments. Alex recognized her type instantly. They were the prototypical bleeding-heart school counselors or social workers or public defenders. They drove used Hondas and believed in the ultimate good of all humanity. She felt a slight envy of these types. They didn't make fun of people and feel guilty later.

This particular woman, however, had a great face—slightly hooked nose and warm, brown, almond-shaped eyes, framed by dark blond hair cut just above the shoulders. The defender looked oddly familiar. Then she gave her name, Mary Szabo. Alex realized with a start that she looked like the female version of Pete Szabo, the Guerneville deputy.

Mary Szabo conferred for a few moments with Shayne Elliot, nodding intently, then entered a plea of not guilty. Alex knew enough about arraignments to know almost everyone pleaded not guilty. She was pleased, however, that the judge set a high bail, due to Shayne's past convictions. The preliminary hearing was set for January 2nd.

Shayne's mother wailed louder, the father scowled, looking angry and ashamed, and that was that. Alex prepared to head back to the lodge. She'd survived going to a courtroom. She felt okay. And now she could tell everyone that Shayne was due to get his punishment. Still, she felt uneasy.

She thought about the public defender, Mary Szabo. Poor woman, having to defend an obviously guilty loser. But that was their job, public defenders. Providing free counsel for the innocent and the guilty. For lousy pay.

On her way out of the courthouse, who should she run into but Deputy Pete Szabo.

"Deputy Szabo."

"Call me Pete," he said. He was trying not to do the guy thing, but the expression on his face was laughable, a suppressed *hey-baby*. That was okay, she thought, at least he was trying. Very professional.

"I just came from the Shayne Elliot arraignment. They appointed a public defender named Mary Szabo. I assume you're related?"

Pete Szabo grinned. "She's my sister. We're fraternal twins. Isn't that something? I arrest them and she sets them free."

"At least in this case she'll have a hard time."

"You don't know my sister." He didn't miss her grimace. "Don't worry. I think we've got him."

"Thanks, Deputy."

"Pete," he insisted.

"All right. Pete."

He grinned at her and flushed.

He was adorable, she had to admit. But not even remotely her type. She realized with a start that she was staring into space while Pete watched her with curiosity.

She turned to leave, waving a finger at him. "Tell your sister everyone knows that kid should be punished. Even you."

Poor Pete. He was just too easy. She walked away with the last word without hardly trying, while he struggled for an answer.

The Shayne Elliot arrest was a constant source of discussion all weekend as the entire staff of the Overlook rushed around making guests feel happy and comforted, despite recent events. Someone brought a copy of *The Press Democrat*, which featured the arraignment on the first page of the local news section. Alex could imagine the mother wailing at home. She wondered if Hank Elliot would be able to show his face at Stumps.

On Monday morning she was passing one of the cottages, jogging. The self-defense seminar had inspired her to get back in shape. She was starting out easy, a quick run around the property. She'd had to fight a nasty pang of guilt, pulling on her familiar Nikes. It made no sense, of course. She ought to be allowed to get in shape again, despite the fact that Stacy would never be beside her again, running the lovely trail that climbed the hill behind their house.

Teresa was coming out of the cottage, wheeling a cleaning cart. She signaled Alex over.

"What's up, Teresa?" Alex asked heartily. She didn't like the regressive shrinking act she was seeing.

"I'm so afraid," Teresa said.

"Don't worry. He won't be back." At least, Alex hoped not. He would, after all, be out on bail if his family could come up with enough money for the bail bondsman. She didn't mention this.

"No, it's not that," Teresa whispered.

"Teresa, he's guilty and he'll go to jail. He's confessed."

Teresa was trembling all over now.

"What is it?"

"The sheriffs, they pointed to him. He was on the side of the road. They made him walk toward me. I was in the back of the sheriff's car. He was limping. I thought it might be him. I knew it was someone. I remembered him from when he worked here. I told the deputies I wasn't sure. They said to look carefully. They kept asking."

"But you're sure it was him," Alex prompted.

"He wasn't wearing the ski mask or the overcoat anymore. I think it was him."

Alex felt a tweak of anxiety in her stomach. "The deputies didn't force you to identify him, did they?"

Teresa shrank into herself.

"You knew it was him, didn't you?"

She shrugged. "I recognized him from when he worked here. In the cottage, the person was wearing a mask and coat."

"Teresa, a lot of the case will be based on your testimony."

Teresa grew even more pallid. "In the court. In front of everyone."

Alex took a deep breath. "You know, my husband died not too long ago. In a terrible accident. We're suing. I have to testify in front of everyone. I don't want to go to court or take the stand or relive those horrible days."

Teresa stared at her wide-eyed.

"But," Alex continued, "I want justice done. So I'm going to go and testify." She paused, looking into the panicked face. "I'll be there when you testify."

Teresa was clearly struggling. "Promise?"

"Promise," Alex replied.

Well, hadn't she sounded righteous and brave? Oh well, she thought, no use getting into the intricacies of self-deception and denial. At least she'd reassured Teresa.

TEN

The Overlook Lodge was completely booked for Christmas. The place was frighteningly charming and festive, with lights and wreaths and ornamented trees in every single room including the restrooms. Alex wondered what a person would do if they had a holiday decorations phobia. There wasn't one spot in the place to escape from them.

Mark's holiday menus were masterpieces, no expense spared. But Mark was being a prime jerk, even for him. His moods were chaotic. One minute he was praising everyone, the next minute everyone was fired.

Alex wondered if she shouldn't talk to Jack about it. No, not Jack. Jack Campbell wasn't big on psychiatric explanations. Something she loved about him. He appealed to her ambivalent feelings about psychotherapy. One of the things she and Stacy used to make up were titles of pretend self-help books. *Yoga for Convicted Felons. Finding Your Inner Voice Through Karaoke. The Wishful Thinking Diet for Big Egos.*

Bottom line, there wasn't anyone she could go to. Deluded Jeffrey and deluded Astrid had Mark on a pedestal. Chris was crazy with making everything impossibly wonderful. Besides, it was the holidays. She needed the strength to stabilize her own borderline state of mind.

So, she went obsessive-compulsive and worked every shift she could. Let the whole thing be a haze of other people's celebrations, she thought. And she got through it okay, meaning numb.

After the Christmas Day dinner shift, she arrived back at her place to find a beautifully wrapped silver package with a blue bow sitting outside her door. She went inside and opened it to find a framed photo of Jack and Marge standing in front of the Overlook Lodge front entry sign, arms encircled. It was signed, "To Alex. With love, Jack and Marge." That sent her straight to the armchair for a good crying session. In the middle of the session, the phone rang. It was Arlene.

"Finally," her mother said. "I was getting tired of the phone tag. Did you get our card? We got yours."

Every year since she'd left home, she and her parents had exchanged nondenominational greetings, which included a donation to a children's charity. This year was the same. No, it wasn't the same. It was awful. She'd had to force herself to sign her name alone, leaving out Stacy's.

There was a silence, followed by Arlene clearing her throat. "We miss you. Honey, we really do."

The tears started streaming again at her mother's rare use of a commonplace endearment.

"Your father wants to say something."

No! She didn't say it, just let the protest echo inside her head.

"Alex?"

The gravelly voice of the famous man who etched his passion into blocks of stone sounded tentative, a tone Alex had heard in his voice so few times she could probably count them on one hand.

"We love you, my daughter."

Alex started gasping air in great, hiccupping gulps.

There was a silence during which Alex could envision the quick exchange of the phone.

"Alex, we'll call again, when it's a better time," Arlene said.

Better time? When would that be? "I'll call you. I promise. Right after the New Year," she choked out and hung up, feeling a palpable sense of relief that the conversation was over. She guessed there was a similar feeling in Annandale-on-Hudson three thousand miles away.

For the next few days, she dragged herself through her work, doing a bad job of seeming okay. Everyone, thank God, let her be. Finally, with Christmas over, that left only the New Year celebration.

New Year's Eve was the last gala event on the Overlook calendar before the annual weeklong break, when the lodge closed down for repairs. The place was booked solid for the stay/celebrate evening, including dining, dancing and flowing sparkling wine from Kendall-Jackson Vineyards.

To say it was a year she was glad to have over was not worthy of the word *understatement*. She was not looking forward to celebrating the coming of the New Year. She wasn't even close to feeling ready to act buoyant.

To complicate matters, Julie's difficult older sister, Bev, and her imperious husband—eminent surgeon, Dr. Glenn Bosch—were attending the festivities. Just before they were due, Wesley knocked a glass of red wine onto a customer's very expensive suede lap. All evening, Julie had been snapping at Jeffrey, the waiters, the bartenders and even Alex.

At 7:45, Alex grabbed Wesley and forced him into a corner. "What's with you two? You're acting like the President and his First Lady are coming."

Wesley stared at the ground, refusing to meet Alex's gaze.

"Can they be that bad?" she asked.

"You'll see," he said.

"Let me know what I can do to help." Alex sighed. She did understand having difficult relatives.

"Thanks." Wesley grinned. "If they get really obnoxious, maybe you can take them out." He did a karate chop in the air.

She grinned back. "Don't tempt me."

Sister and husband were late. At 8:20, Julie led the couple to the excellent table they'd held for them, screwing up reservations. Alex could see the tightness in Julie's posture and her frozen smile. She went into the kitchen to announce the arrival of the special pair.

As she pushed through the kitchen door, she came upon an ugly scene. At the pastry station, Jean clutched a propane torch against her breast. Mark was right up in her face, the veins in his neck popping out.

"Are you a complete idiot?" he screamed.

"I've never run out before," Jean replied.

"I could wring your neck," he yelled at the top of his lungs.

And now Jeffrey was beside Alex, a look of panic on his face. "What the hell's going on? I could hear Mark in the dining room."

"Jean made a mistake and he's going ballistic. Do you want me to go over and pop him one? Or tell her to? She knows how these days."

"That's not funny."

"I'm not sure it was meant to be."

Jeffrey sighed. "He swore on his mother's grave he'd reform." Fiddling with his tie, he marched over to the pastry station. "What's up?" he asked.

"This incompetent fool—I'm ashamed to say my own wife—has run out of propane. On New Year's Eve, our pastry chef has run out of propane, so she cannot torch her pumpkin crème caramels."

"Can't they be broiled?"

Mark's tone was cold and biting. "Oh, yes, my friend. *However,* as you may recall since you helped create the menu, we are broiling oysters for our appetizer. Wouldn't that be lovely, broiled oysters mingling with pumpkin crème caramel? *If* there was room to do such a thing, which there is not."

"Mark, Mark. Take a deep breath, chef." It was the Scandinavian college professor turned Zen sous chef. Astrid approached Mark, coming closer and closer, forcing him to back up. "We'll serve pumpkin pot de crème instead," she said with an air of finality.

Mark began to deflate. "Jeffrey, have your staff at their ass-kissing best when they explain the change to the public."

"The public will think it's all a charming adventure," Jeffrey said. "I think I'll add a lovely, free glass of port to the menu."

"Fine." Mark glanced around at his staring staff. "Get to work," he ordered. Quickly, everyone was back to bustling around. Except Jean.

As Alex turned to leave, she noticed Jean gripping her propane torch, staring into space and motionless. Her expressionless face hadn't changed throughout the blowup and it remained the same now.

Onward to the next crisis. Bev and Glenn Bosch.

Jeffrey, as he buzzed past Alex with a bottle of 1999 Saintsbury Pinot Noir, prepurchased for the Boschs by Julie, whispered, "They've been complaining since they got in the door."

Alex intercepted Julie, who was rushing over with the special New Year's Eve menu. "Let me do it," she said, trying to wrest the menus from Julie, who clung to them, looking deranged. "Am I going to have to take you down to get these menus?" she asked.

Julie let go of the menus. "You're going to have to listen to her inventory of allergies."

"I can handle it." When she arrived at the table, Wesley was already delivering an oak chair from the lobby.

"I can't sit on poorly designed chairs," Bev informed Alex. Bev lowered herself onto the hard, straight chair with the help of two canes. She took the menu, then placed it on the table without looking at it. Jeffrey was tableside, pouring the wine for Glenn to taste. Bev ignored him, focusing instead on Alex.

Uh-oh. Alex had a radar for these kinds of things. Bev was loaded. Painkillers, probably.

"I was in a car accident, four years ago. Broken back. It never healed properly," Bev confided, touching Alex's arm.

Jeffrey winced at her. He was waiting for Glenn to respond to the wine.

"Fine," Glenn said curtly. "Pour it."

Wesley had arrived and was standing like a puppy dog next to Alex. His face fell.

"It's good," Glenn said, at least astute enough to notice Wesley's crestfallen expression. But he still didn't sound thrilled.

"It won four gold medals," Wesley said.

Glenn picked up the menu without replying.

You mean bastard, Alex thought.

"I have severe allergies," Bev announced. "I can't eat anything from the menu. The chef is going to have to prepare me something I can eat.

I'll have the chicken breast broiled plain and steamed rice with no salt or anything else on it. A side of steamed vegetables—no white potatoes or corn or peppers of any kind. No wheat or anything with gluten."

Alex listened patiently to the litany of allergies and to the remarkable list of banned food, thinking about how she was going to deal with Mark when he was asked to make Bev's special meal containing almost nothing. Glenn apparently had neither allergies nor desire to be politically correct. He ordered the most expensive thing on the menu—the paillard di vitello con ruchetta, made with locally grown arugula and innocent little Sonoma County cattle babies.

She personally escorted each course out when it was ready. Mark, bless him, had arranged Bev's food into plates as beautiful as Impressionist paintings. With mind-boggling pampering, the Boschs grew more and more mellow as the evening progressed. Another bottle of expensive wine and two free glasses of Champagne didn't hurt the situation. Bev was apparently not allergic to alcohol.

Besides, Alex thought, it was hard to be morose, even for her. People were enjoying themselves too much. The food was fabulous, the spirits plentiful and the music embracing. While not exactly happy, she felt at least one notch past neutral toward the positive.

Just before midnight, Julie rushed over to her. "Thanks, you were great."

"It's easier when they're not yours," she replied.

"No kidding." Julie was trembling. "I'm totally freaked out. They're completely loaded. I've warned them about driving. He's a *trauma* surgeon. Bad enough I was arrested for drunk driving, but I'm the black sheep of the family. And I didn't have any passengers."

Alex detected alcohol on Julie's breath. At least she wasn't driving. She had poor Wesley for that.

At that moment, Wesley appeared. "It went okay," he gushed. "I think they liked it. They even thanked me."

"Oh, shut up," Julie said. "You sound like a worm."

"I don't care. Glenn gave me a fifty-buck tip."

Alex wanted to shake the poor kid. He needed to tell his aunt and uncle to go to hell. Probably his mother, too.

When midnight arrived, Alex was hiding in a stall in the women's restroom. She couldn't do the hugs and kisses routine and that was that. At least no one would ask her where she'd been when she returned to the confetti-strewn dining room. They knew better. Most of them were probably amazed she'd done so well this far into the evening. The event was due to conclude at 2:00 a.m. At 1:30 a.m., Mark rushed into the dining room, wild-eyed. The next thing Alex noticed was Mark and Julie in animated conversation at the end of the room. The last few guests looked up from their wineglasses, bleary-eyed but curious. Alex suspected a fight might be brewing. She couldn't believe either one of them could be that unprofessional, but she knew Julie was drunk and Mark was high on his own inflated ego and rushing male hormones.

Alex was about to race to the lobby to look for Jeffrey when Julie threw a glass of Champagne she'd picked up off a deserted table in Mark's face. "All I asked was for you to have Jean make my sister a special dessert," she said loudly, oblivious to the staring guests. "And yes, I did tell Astrid you're a conceited prick, but I was a little tense, if you can just imagine. How dare you come out here and scold me."

She turned to leave and tripped over a heel, falling to the ground. Mark stood over her, fists clenched. "Your sister can go to hell. Demanding bitch, just like you."

In an instant, it was chaos. Wesley flew out from nowhere and shoved Mark, who went stumbling back, crashing into the deserted table, sending dishes and glassware flying.

"You punk," Mark cried. "I should whip your ass." But he didn't move.

Typical. How many times had Alex watched bullies shrivel when confronted by someone tougher than themselves?

"Enough, enough." Jeffrey rushed up. "I don't have the words to express how unprofessional this scene is. I'm actually ashamed for you three and myself as your boss and coworker."

The rest of the evening would have to be spent picking up pieces, literally and figuratively. Alex felt tired to the bones. She begged to be excused and fled, ignoring the concerned looks.

ELEVEN

Someone was pounding at her door on New Year's Day at 7:00 a.m. Alex stumbled from bed and threw on a robe.

"Jack—" she began.

"Surprise!" Jeffrey cried. He held out a glazed lemon bundt cake. "Max baked it yesterday."

Alex glanced suspiciously at the cake. "Not for me and don't lie."

"Don't do this to me," Jeffrey wailed. "Would I be doing this if I didn't have a really, really good reason?" He thrust the cake at her. "Make coffee. I ran out of the house with this stupid cake and no coffee, before I had second thoughts."

He refused to tell her why he'd come until the coffee was made. They sat at the little table and cut large pieces from the cake.

"Mmmmm," Alex said, momentarily distracted.

"He's good, isn't he?" Jeffrey moaned. "He could be the pastry chef, I swear."

She swallowed a transcendent bite. "He's good, but he's not a professional." She paused. "You don't like Jean, do you?"

Jeffrey reddened. He licked his fork and pushed his plate away. "She's fine," he muttered.

"Jeffrey?"

"Well," he said, "she's a little odd, don't you think?"

Alex was thinking of Jean in the self-defense class, always asking precise questions in her dull voice, painstakingly practicing her moves. Even her loud cries were somehow affectless. As the class had bonded, Jean remained slightly removed. Her outer shell was in the group. Her interior, her soul, was elsewhere. But, Alex suspected, Jeffrey wasn't here to discuss Jean's eccentricities.

"Tell me," Alex said. "No use beating around the bush."

"Cliché," Jeffrey said plaintively.

They both smiled in temporary truce.

Jeffrey cut them each another piece of cake. "I'm getting high on the sugar, but I can't help myself." He feigned interest in breaking off a morsel of cake with his fork. With his gaze directed at the cake, he said, "We're firing Julie."

Alex, who had been in the process of swallowing, choked on her cake.

"Are you all right?" Jeffrey asked.

"You can't fire Julie," Alex sputtered after her throat was clear. "She's like family."

"Don't go getting Jack Campbell on me," Jeffrey said. "You saw her fighting with Mark last night. She's been fighting with everyone. Alex, do I have to mention she has a drug and alcohol problem that seems to be getting worse."

She knew it was true. But still, Julie did her job. And she was no crankier than a lot of people. Mark made her look like a saint. *Wait a minute.*

"It's Mark. He wants her fired, doesn't he?" She could tell Jeffrey about catching Mark and Julie in the janitor's closet but wasn't sure that particular indiscretion would really bolster Julie's case. Probably best left unsaid, she decided.

"It was a group decision," Jeffrey said.

"What group?"

"Chris, myself and Mark."

"What about Jack?"

Jeffrey sighed. "We didn't consult with him. We told him. It wasn't pretty. Chris had to remind Jack of his promise to start letting go of control."

"What about Wesley?"

"He's not fired. But he'll quit, of course."

She was already beginning to mourn Julie and Wesley's absence when something occurred to her. "Why come here and tell me?" She glared at him while he struggled for words.

"Chris is going to tell her," Jeffrey said. "I can't do it. I'm lousy at firing people, I admit it. If I can pass it off, I do. How's that for a confession? Only because you're my cousin and my confidante. You know more about me than anyone else, probably even more than Max."

"Jeffrey, tell me what you want."

"We were hoping you'd talk to Jack."

"Me?"

"You're the one who expects him at your door at odd hours."

"The point?"

"Come on, don't torture me. Obviously you two have gotten close. He'll listen to you."

She knew it was true. And, no matter what, Jack was going to have to accept change if the Overlook was going to survive.

She found him clearing brush at the far end of the meadow behind the cottages. Without her. He shouldn't have been out anyway. The thick drizzle was bone-chilling. The ground was too wet to be fooling around. Jack was muddy and moved with a desperate kind of energy.

He stopped hacking at a dead tree limb. "Julie always did her job. Now what's she going to do? And what about Wesley? Do my son and his partners think about things like that? They think about their own money, they think about their own survival, but they don't know what survival really is and I hope to God they never do. I know what survival is, believe me. I know what it is. I tried to protect him, but maybe I was wrong. I only wanted the best for him and for my wife."

His tirade verged on rambling, but she understood its compassionate intent. "Julie needs some time off so she can get help."

"Julie needs a job and a stable place to come to. She needs a support system." Jack came toward her, waving his hatchet. "Don't do this."

Alex instinctively adopted a subtle fighting posture. Jack just as quickly noted her guarded stance and dropped the hatchet. He was badly flushed.

"Are you all right, Jack?"

"Of course not!" he roared.

Alex jumped back.

"I'm sorry." He dropped his shoulders and his hands fell to his sides. The hatchet fell to the ground. For the first time in a long time, Alex wanted to take the initiative and embrace someone. So she did.

"I'm sorry, too," she said, breathing into his rough coat, which smelled like damp hide. He was squeezing her a little tightly, but she didn't mind.

"It's not your fault," he whispered. "It's not anybody's fault, except maybe mine. But I'll adapt, I promise you. You can tell them that, if it makes things better. I sure as hell won't. I can't speak to them right now."

"I'll talk to them," she said into his coat.

She didn't speak to anyone. She went back to her little place and got her car keys and wallet. She went down to her car and drove too fast down the lane, past the Campbell residence, then past the main lodge. Without saying a word to anyone, without leaving even a few words scrawled on a note, she fled.

She checked into an expensive corporate box of a hotel, off the freeway outside of San Rafael. Her room had two queen beds with brocaded gold bedspreads, burgundy carpeting, a burgundy-striped armchair and thickly lacquered mahogany furniture.

She had no luggage. She was still wearing her jeans and sweatshirt, with muddy running shoes. The desk clerk didn't bat an eye. She had a hairbrush from the car, bought a toothbrush and magazines in the gift shop and went up to her room. She put on the hotel-supplied bathrobe. She washed out her underwear in the bathroom sink. She read magazines on the bed, drinking a Chivas Regal from the minibar, until it was time for dinner.

Room service consisted of a turkey club sandwich, salad, fries and a piece of apple pie with whipped cream. She also had a carafe of wine, a red that was as boring as the hotel.

At around nine, she went down to the bar for a drink and was soon accosted by a decent-looking man in an Italian suit who seemed only mildly fazed by her trailer trash outfit. She brushed him off, finished off her drink and stumbled back to her room. She didn't dream. She was working on a state of semi-consciousness almost as deep as when she first found out about Stacy. When she'd been imagining him flying through the air, sailing freely, and then the phone had rung and she'd gotten a funny little tweak in her stomach. Nothing prepared a person for certain words spoken on the phone. Nothing.

In the morning, she bought a swimsuit from the gift shop and swam in the pool. In the early afternoon, she threw out the toothbrush, stuffed the swimsuit and hairbrush in a plastic bag and checked out.

When she got back to the Overlook, there was a note taped on her door from Marge. *COME SEE ME.* Alex had a piercing headache, probably one of the worst ones she'd ever had.

Marge answered the door. She studied Alex. "Are you all right?"

"Mostly okay," Alex said.

Marge motioned her in. "You're not okay." She led Alex to the ugly, comforting plaid couch. "Irma, Clyde, go lie down," she said to the leaping pugs. "Tea? Coffee?" she asked.

"Nothing. Thanks."

Marge sat silent, looking at her. "I-I-" She stopped, clearly unable to go on.

Suddenly Alex realized what was up. "Oh, my God. Shayne Elliot's preliminary hearing. It was this morning, wasn't it?"

Marge nodded.

"Did something go wrong?"

Marge nodded again, a pained expression crossing her face.

"Teresa blew her testimony."

"That was only part of it." Marge frowned, obviously reviewing the proceedings in her mind. "That public defender, Mary Szabo, she is sharp. First, she intimidated Teresa on the stand until the poor girl couldn't possibly seem credible. She admitted the deputies coerced her. Then Szabo made the deputies look incompetent. Worse than incompetent. She said they ignored the law."

Alex knew what was coming next.

"The judge threw out the case. I don't understand all the technicalities—"

Alex slammed her hand on the couch, causing Marge to jump. "What is wrong with lawyers?" she shouted. "I'd like to call that woman up and ask her how she feels getting dangerous monsters off the hook on *technicalities!*"

Poor Marge. Alex knew she was acting hysterical, and she hadn't meant to take out her feelings of guilt and frustration on Marge. Still, it wasn't right. She wouldn't really call the public defender, but if she ever ran into her, she didn't trust how she'd react.

Marge seemed to be reading her mind. "She was only doing her job," she said mildly. "The police, they should have been more careful."

But Alex wasn't in the mood for forgiveness and understanding. Just then, Jack spoke from the doorway.

"Lock him up and throw away the key, that's what's right."

Alex smiled gratefully at him, but she was aching inside. "I promised I'd be there," she admitted. "I gave Teresa my word."

Jack shrugged. "From what Marge tells me, it wouldn't have helped. Nothing would have helped. The police acted stupidly and that defender is a sharp one." He waved a finger at her. "Still, young lady, we were worried about you. *We* almost called the police, but Chris convinced us to wait until today and now here you are. Please don't do this again." He smiled at her. "You're too important to us now."

TWELVE

The traditional employee party was scheduled for Friday night, after which the restaurant and lodge would be closed for cleaning and repairs. It was, Jack informed Alex, the slowest and potentially rainiest time of the year. But they were lucky this year. The relentless rain of early January took a break on Wednesday, the day of the party.

It was, Alex felt, a blessing to have the place shut down for a week. Tempers were short.

Despite the latest difficulties, it seemed as though everyone was determined to have a good time. For her part, she avoided too many cocktails, hoping to curtail any tendencies toward maudlin behavior or sloppy conversation. Very few others seemed to be observing similar rules. By nine, most of the group was staggering drunkenly except for herself, Jean and Marge.

Alex milled around, making light conversation, rehashing the past couple of months since her arrival in a casual, almost flippant way, avoiding anything too heavy. She talked to Roxanne and Astrid and Ivy and Doug, the bartender. She talked to all of the Juarez clan, including Teresa, who still beamed at her with admiration despite Alex's failure to show up at the preliminary. Alex had already, in nineteen different ways, apologized and explained. Teresa had forgiven. She talked to Leslie, who also seemed to adore Alex now. She talked to Chris, who clearly did not adore her. She sought out and conversed with all the part-timers, including Maria, who practically crawled into Alex's lap. She outdid herself with small talk.

At nine thirty, Jeffrey sidled up to her, holding a glass of Chardonnay. "Having a good time?" he asked.

"Yes, I am, actually." Alex glanced around the room. "This place grows on you."

Jeffrey took a sip of his wine and grimaced. "Ugh. Oh, well, that's okay. Party wine. The red is worse."

"Where's Max?" Alex asked.

"In San Francisco, visiting friends. He's not into these work party things." Jeffrey took another sip of wine. "Yucky."

"Stop it. You're acting like you're drinking medicine."

He grinned. "Sorry, it's just a habit. Anyway, speaking of Max, he says he misses you. He specifically told me to tell you he's jealous that I see you all the time and he doesn't."

"That's sweet."

"I wouldn't describe Max as sweet."

"Sweet and sour, like a good margarita."

Jeffrey laughed. "He'll love that."

"Don't tell *him* I said that," Alex said.

"I tell him everything," Jeffrey said. A slight cast flickered over his face. "Well, almost." He took yet another sip of wine. "Yuck. Oops. I mean, yum." He set the wineglass on a table. "I'm switching to Perrier. I have to drive and I want to get going soon."

Suddenly, there was an odd cry from the other side of the room, a high-pitched bestial shriek that sent shivers up Alex's spine.

From their vantage point, she and Jeffrey could see Mark breaking apart one of Jean's party pastries and letting the pieces fall to the floor, where he was grinding them into sugary, pulverized powder under his shoes.

Jean was kneeling on the floor, grabbing Mark's foot and wailing. It was an extraordinary sound, both frightening and pathetic, causing everyone to freeze.

The freeze was broken by Marge. She hurdled from the pack of immobile observers and rushed over. She lifted Jean up with a surprising amount of strength, then turned to Mark. "Back off!" she shouted.

Alex felt a surge of pride. Marge's shout was deep and protective, right from her core, just as she'd been instructed.

The entire staff was staring, but now a tribal energy began to grow. As a group, they focused on Mark, who fell back a step, as though the group energy had physically shoved him.

"I was joking," he said feebly. "It was a joke."

He turned to Jean, who had stood up. "I'm sorry."

He had on that face. Alex had seen it before, on the faces of the husbands of the women in the shelters. Sweet, apologetic faces. Treacherous faces.

Jean looked around the room defiantly, then her body began to curl into itself until she was the usual Jean again, a big woman making herself little. "That's enough," she announced, her voice flat and toneless once again. "I don't want to dwell on this."

She kneeled down and began to brush uselessly at the pastry pieces. Quickly, Mark joined her, and for a moment they looked like children trying to clean up a hopeless mess they were terrified would get them into big trouble.

THIRTEEN

The phone rang at 11:00 a.m. Alex struggled in the tumble of blankets. She'd been lying awake in bed well past her usual rising time, replaying the Hellers' nasty clash in her head. The strange howling that had gushed out of Jean was the most disturbing part of the scene. Alex knew about psychic blackness. But the rawness of that primitive howling was disturbing even compared to her own recent downer perspective. She didn't want to talk to anyone and decided to let whoever was calling leave a message.

"Alex? Are you there?" the voice from the answering machine called into the room. It was Marge. "Mark is dead. Astrid found him in the *freezer*. Please, please, call as soon as you can. I'm at the main lodge."

Alex jumped up and grabbed the phone. Marge answered right away. She was too distraught to give many details. The sheriff's deputies had already arrived.

Immediately after, Jeffrey called from his car. He was ten minutes away and demanded that he pick her up so they could go over to the lodge together.

By the time Alex and Jeffrey arrived, the parking lot was a sea of sheriffs' cars, official-looking unmarked cars, an ambulance, press cars, and, most disturbing, two satellite-topped television news vans, one from the local Santa Rosa station and the other a Channel 5 Eyewitness News vehicle representing the Bay Area.

Alex moaned. Seeing the press, her first impulse was to flee. But where would she go? And even if she wanted to run away, she knew she couldn't. She was a part of the whole mess whether she liked it or not.

A young deputy strode up to the car and knocked on the driver's side window. Jeffrey rolled it down.

"I'm sorry," the deputy said in a not-sorry tone, "but we've got a problem here. The resort is closed."

"We work here. We knew the victim," Jeffrey said. "We have to go in there."

The baby-faced officer pondered this last statement with suspicious concern, clearly not wanting to relent any authority, especially to an effeminate man with a high-pitched voice. He glanced around the interior of the car, as though they were potential criminals.

"Is Deputy Szabo here?" Alex asked.

"He sure is," the deputy replied.

"Can you get him?"

The deputy hesitated.

"He knows us," Alex said.

Shrugging, the deputy said, "Don't move."

In no time, Pete Szabo strode over.

"What a hunk that guy is," Jeffrey commented as Pete approached with his athletic stride. "I love when men walk that way. So manly." He paused, adopting a look of shame. "How can I be noticing gorgeous men? It must be shock and denial. I don't really believe Mark is dead. It's too tragic."

That Mark's death was a shock, Alex had no doubt. But tragic? She wasn't feeling exactly shattered, she had to admit.

Pete leaned into the car, frowning. "Big trouble this time. Big, big trouble." His tone was concerned but calm.

"No kidding," Alex said. She felt reassured by Pete Szabo's presence. He seemed so simple and good, which she knew was condescending, but he did.

As soon as Alex and Jeffrey climbed from the car, the press predators started scurrying toward them, like invading insects from a bad sci-fi movie.

"Run." Alex grabbed Jeffrey's hand and pulled him toward the lodge. Pete did his best to fend off the worst aggressors as Alex and Jeffrey raced for the front steps.

Marge jumped up as they came into the lobby, but a deputy put his hand on her shoulder to prevent her from moving. Jack was hunched on the couch, his head in his hands.

They were led to another couch and asked to wait. Men and women rushed around carrying kits, pads of paper, cameras. It was surreal, like a movie-set crime scene.

Eventually, Pete came back. "Detectives Green and Harroway would like to talk to you," he said. "Alex first."

As he led her to her interview, Alex tried to get some details from Pete, but he was stubbornly reticent. She appreciated, at least, his rueful look. She had the feeling he'd like nothing better than to blab to her about the whole mess.

In the back office, the homicide detectives had set up a tape recorder on the large, scratched oak desk. They'd shoved the computer to one side and stacked the papers that usually cluttered the surface into a pile. They were only two regular-sized people but it felt like they'd taken over not only the desk but had swollen into the entire room, filling it with their investigative vibes.

Alex entered the room with her don't-mess-with-me attitude on high. She glanced at the tape recorder on the desk. She purposely took a chair on the other side of the room. She was having emotional flashbacks to the interviews after Stacy's death. She needed to stay calm.

"Could you come sit over here?" the woman deputy asked. She was probably in her early thirties, with pink cheeks and curly brown hair pulled into a partly successful bun. She looked friendly and untroubled, like a fresh-faced ranch girl. "I'm Detective Clarissa Harroway. You can call me Clarissa. This is Detective Rob Green."

The male detective nodded. He was older, maybe early fifties, with leathery tanned skin, a gray crew cut and a slight potbelly. He had cynical eyes, which he had directed at her as she trooped over to the chair near the desk. Interesting partnership, Alex thought.

The detectives had her describe her days at the Overlook from the beginning. She kept it as sketchy as possible. Clarissa asked most of the questions, in a slightly curious tone, as though she was making idle conversation. Alex wondered how Detective Green would play into this. She finally reached the last couple of hours she'd seen Mark alive, at the employee party.

Green straightened up from his slouch, squinting at her. "From your description, it sounds like a pretty mild event. Did you observe anything unusual?"

"Nothing unusual."

"No arguments?"

"Well, Mark and Jean had an argument. But that wasn't anything unusual."

"They fought a lot, Jean and Mark?" he asked.

"Mark fought with everyone," she replied.

"Did he fight with you?"

"He didn't have as much to fight about with me. Still, he even raised his voice to me a couple of times."

"But he had big fights with his wife?"

"Yes," Alex admitted.

"Who else? Who else did he have big fights with?"

She thought of Jeffrey, remembering Mark's humiliating tirades at her cousin. But those weren't fights, exactly. "No one else I can think of."

Clarissa and Green glanced at each other.

"I understand you teach self-defense," Clarissa said.

"Yes."

"That's great." Clarissa nodded. "You taught the women here, didn't you? What did you teach them?"

"Basics. Things most women could learn to do. I'm sure you know. A very simplified and introductory version of the things they taught you at the academy."

"From highly qualified instructors," Green threw in. "And you? I assume you have the qualifications to teach other people something potentially lethal?"

She'd seen this attitude before. Green wouldn't admit it, not in today's society, but he probably didn't approve of women taking things into their own hands.

Clarissa shrugged at her. "He's got this thing about proper qualifications."

Alex felt like she was being manipulated according to some unrevealed plan. But she couldn't resist taking the bait. "I have a black belt in karate. But more importantly, I trained with Naomi Goldstein at specifically teaching self-defense to women with no particular training. Women who need to learn to protect themselves and develop self-confidence." There. Now didn't she sound righteous?

"I know about Sarge," Clarissa said. "She does good work."

"I was a part-time instructor at her school," Alex explained. "After I married, I continued to do volunteer work."

Alex could see the respect in Clarissa's eyes. But not in Green's.

"Married?" Green asked. "You're up here alone. Is your husband still in the Bay Area?"

A sour panic rose in Alex's stomach. *See? That's what blabbing got you.* "My husband died eight months ago."

"I'm so sorry," Clarissa said. Green nodded sympathetically.

"If you don't mind," Alex said, "I don't want to talk about him. It has nothing to do with this case."

She watched Green pondering the statement. His lips moved when he was deep in thought, a little quirk that would drive her crazy if she had to work with him. She wondered if it bothered Clarissa.

"One of the women in your class fended off an attacker with your techniques in December," Green said. "There was a suspect, but the case was dismissed."

"He was the attacker," Alex said. "He got off, but I'm sure he was the one."

"Hmm," he said. "Jean was in your class."

"She was."

"And would you say she learned the skills pretty well?"

"Pretty well."

"She could use the skills if she had to?"

"Anyone could, if they had to. Why? How was Mark killed?"

Clarissa and Green glanced at each other once again, then Clarissa stood. "Thank you, Ms. Pope. That's all. We can't go into detail about the death right now. We'll be speaking to you again."

Alex left, thinking of Jean. Could Jean have killed Mark? She had to admit it was a possibility.

FOURTEEN

The rest of the cleaning and repairs were postponed indefinitely. Alex wondered if and when the resort would get back to anything resembling normal. Would she have to leave? It was an awful thought.

On Sunday, Jeffrey came over in the early afternoon. As soon as he arrived, he collapsed into her arms and burst into tears.

"You really did care for him, didn't you?" Alex said, holding him.

"No one understood him," Jeffrey mumbled into her shoulder.

It was a ridiculous statement. Mark was not hard to understand. She felt like Max, wanting to shake Jeffrey out of his delusions about Mark.

"I can't stop thinking about him. It was Jean who killed him, wasn't it?"

"Do you think so?" Alex asked.

"Isn't it obvious? You know how odd she is. Both Astrid and I tried to like her, to at least feel sorry for her. But she's a very peculiar person. A time bomb, honey. A real time bomb."

"What if he was threatening to really hurt her? He might have been."

"She didn't need to kill him," Jeffrey said.

"Only if she had reason to believe he was trying to hurt her badly or kill her. Reasonable force. But it could have been someone else."

"I don't know." Jeffrey sighed. "Anyway, if it wasn't her, who was it?" He smiled ironically at her. "You know, I don't have an alibi. Max was in the city, remember?"

"You didn't have a motive, either."

"No," Jeffrey said. "I didn't, did I?"

In a sign of the times, they learned most of the details of the homicide from television news. For the rest of the day and into the night, they watched every news show they could tune into, including CNN and MSNBC, both of which ran segments. It was a glamorous murder, worthy of national attention, at least for a few days.

So far, the actual details were sketchy. After the closing party, in the early morning, the first wave of scheduled weeklong deep cleaning began, with a professional janitorial crew tearing through the kitchen, attacking every surface, stomping around, effectively obliterating every possible clue in existence. A few crew members had even washed the outside windows, leaving irrelevant footprints all around the exterior, too.

In the late morning, Astrid had arrived. She and Mark had arranged to meet and take stock of the freezer and food pantries. When Mark didn't show up on time, Astrid decided to get started without him.

She went to the freezer. Pulled open the heavy door. Screamed, then screamed again. Lying on the floor, sprawled out on his back, was executive chef Mark Heller, ice-encrusted.

By the time they had watched many, many hours of reports, they were almost numbed, as though the whole thing was happening to other people. Jeffrey offered to sleep on the couch so she wouldn't be alone, but she packed him off. Alex wanted to be alone.

The next morning, she made coffee and read the San Francisco *Chronicle*, staring at the words but not absorbing anything. The murder was granted a small column at the bottom of the first page.

In the afternoon, she braved the most recent downpour in a yellow slicker, running to the Shed, getting pummeled by the rain. It was a hard, relentless storm, another in a series predicted for the next week. Already, there had been a couple of mudslides in Rio Nido. The river was rising. The Shed was dim and cold. Rain rattled against the skylights. Alex removed her socks and shoes and went to the center of the room. She began a series of karate forms. She let the time pass, absorbed. The body was amazing, she thought. It slowly remembered the complex combinations, clearing her mind of anything but the kicks, blocks and chops of the ritualized movements.

"Oh!"

Someone was standing in the shadows, near the small kitchen.

"You're very good," Jack said.

"I worked hard. I wasn't the star pupil. I'm not hugely athletic. I wasn't even middle of the pack, not at first. I thought too much. I overreacted to everything. I hated being tested. I hated the whole thing at times. Especially my teacher, a wise man who I thought was hounding me." Alex wiped her hand across her forehead. In spite of the chill in the room, she was sweating.

"But you kept it up."

"It gave me focus even when the focus was centered on hating how hard it was to focus. What I loved is that it had nothing to do with words. I grew up with too many words."

"Most people don't realize how imperative it is to focus. It can save your life." His face was ashen and a bead of sweat dribbled down his cheek from his right temple.

Alex studied him. He seemed not focused but dazed. But what else did she expect? He'd just had a dead body found at his resort.

"They think it's Jean," he said. "If it was, Mark attacked her and she'll get off on self-defense."

"They asked me about the self-defense course."

"I'm sure they did. Anyway, did you want to come to dinner tonight? Marge is making pork roast with homemade applesauce and potato pancakes."

It sounded wonderful, but she refused. She needed to burrow into her nest and hide, at least for a while.

But there wouldn't be any hiding. That afternoon, Hunter Carlyle called.

"Alex? I cannot believe you're at that resort where the chef was murdered. You can't stay there. You must go home."

Home. She shuddered. "I need to stay for the investigation."

He didn't bother to press her. "I have good news."

"Oh?"

"The defense lawyers are ready to depose you. Things are finally moving along. You're scheduled to meet with them a week from Tuesday, the fourteenth. You can come down anytime this week and meet with Bruce Phipps."

On Stacy's naming spree of everyone in his firm, Bruce Phipps had been christened Mister Rattles, a snake whose temperament was notably nasty even in the snake world.

"Bruce is the best at this kind of litigation in the state," Hunter said. "He's unstoppable."

"I've heard."

"He'll explain the purpose of the deposition—"

"I was married to your son, remember? I know what a deposition is. I understand suing for wrongful death and loss of consortium. What do you think we talked about over cocktails in front of the fire?"

Hunter groaned. "Not that."

She was quite positive Hunter never discussed law with his wife, Bunny. But that was them. Alex had been interested in what Stacy did. Or at least she'd tried to be. "Look, let's just take a little time before the deposition next week for a phone conference. I know how to act. But we can review it, if it makes you feel better."

"I'll have Bruce call you." Hunter sounded irritated but resigned. "Alex, it's different when it's you. You can hear all about it. It's not the same."

Alex spent the rest of Monday in her vegetative state. She watched the repetitive news reports. She dozed and drank tea. That night, she went to bed and slept as though in a coma.

The phone rang first thing Tuesday morning. It was Detective Clarissa Harroway.

"Ms. Pope?"

"You can call me Alex."

"Alex, we'd like to come and talk with you."

"Here?"

"We like to make it easy for you."

"What time?"

"Anytime after three would be best."

"Four."

"We'll be there."

"I take it you know where I live."

"Yes, we do."

Of course. They probably knew a lot about her. They'd been around interviewing everyone. The entire situation was probably a big web of evidence by now, trapping everyone into roles of suspects and tattletales.

At exactly four, the detectives knocked at her door. She'd decided she was going to have a better attitude. No use taking out her demons on them. She made coffee and set out a plate of assorted holiday cookies Marge had given her. The cookies had lasted amazingly well in their metal tin.

Green entered the room, sniffing. "Coffee," he said in a strangled tone.

"Organic Costa Rican. Roasted fresh at that nice place on Railroad Square in Santa Rosa," Alex said.

Green moaned shamelessly.

"I take it you'd like a cup," Alex said.

"He's addicted," Clarissa said.

"I'm not addicted," he protested. "Addiction is drugs or booze. Coffee is good. You heard the lady. It's organic, too."

"I take it you don't drink coffee," Alex said to Clarissa.

"No caffeine," Clarissa replied with the tone of a righteous nutritionist.

"There's not any good evidence it hurts anything," Green said.

"Not yet," Clarissa said, "but you'll see."

Alex had to smile. The two of them probably went through this every day.

"Some herbal tea?" Alex asked her.

"That would be great."

Alex had boiled some water in the kettle just in case. She put a mint teabag in a mug.

Pretty soon they were settled at the little table, eating the sublime cookies and sipping beverages of choice. A cozy party. Then Clarissa took the tape recorder from her black bag. A cozy interrogation.

No, not an interrogation. Interrogations were for suspects, Alex had to remind herself. This was an interview. She *was* going to be more cooperative. The sooner they caught the killer, the sooner the Overlook could begin to recuperate.

They asked her to describe every instance she'd observed Mark and Jean in conflict. They asked her to describe Jean in the self-defense class. They asked about the quirks of Jean's personality, to which they'd obviously already been alerted. Feeling like a traitor, Alex listed the various instances of Jean's odd behaviors.

In the meantime, the detectives ate all the cookies. Green drank a pot of coffee. Clarissa had three cups of tea, with heaping gobs of honey. Alex felt like she was feeding starving orphans.

"I'm sorry," Clarissa apologized, finishing off the last cookie. "We didn't have time for a real lunch."

"Can I make you a sandwich?" Alex offered.

Green looked tempted.

"No, thanks," Clarissa said quickly. "We're almost done for today. A couple of last issues."

"Yes?"

"First, the autopsy on Mark Heller. We were waiting for the report before we talked to you again. According to the coroner, Mark was subjected to two blows. One stunned him, the other killed him. The first was to the temple. The second was to the neck, the carotid artery. The nature of the blows indicates a blunt, relatively soft instrument—for example, a hand making a karate chop. You are familiar with those kind of blows."

"Of course. To be used in self-defense."

"We're not getting into motive here yet. My point is that any of the women in your class could have used these blows, including Jean Heller."

"I have no doubt Jean could and would defend herself if attacked. But it would have been self-defense, as I was explaining."

In unison, Green and Clarissa rose.

"Thank you for the nice refreshments," Green said. "We'll be contacting you. Next time, we'll try and eat ahead of time."

Alex was developing a weird fondness for these two. It went to show what unusual circumstances bred in people. The next time she heard from them was a call late Wednesday afternoon, one day after her interview.

"I thought you might like to be informed before you hear it on the news," Clarissa said.

Alex knew what was coming.

"Jean has been arrested."

FIFTEEN

The "Celebrity Chef Murder," as they christened it, was a gold mine for the press. Prominent California chef, abused wife. The ethics of self-defense. Larry King and Paula Zahn and Geraldo Rivera blathered about the case on their nationally televised programs. Reports started to filter in concerning Mark's reputation in San Francisco.

On Thursday, KRON Channel 4 revealed that Joy Kronenberg, the chef and owner of hot spot Circle Two, told investigators she fired Mark after he'd been arrested for domestic violence. Jean had refused to press charges, however, and the case fell apart.

Alex was screening all her calls, both regular and cell phone. It was only a matter of time before they dug up her story, she was sure of it. She was fighting panic.

Jean's preliminary hearing was scheduled for 8:30 a.m. on Friday. Jeffrey had already told Alex that the lavish-spending Hellers were in constant debt. Mark had also been paying heavily to the IRS on back taxes. There was no way Jean was going to get an expensive private attorney.

The courtroom was full. Alex and Jeffrey had to skirt reporters to get into Courtroom 3, presided over by Judge Eileen Morse, in charge of in-custody felony cases. Judge Morse was a well-preserved sixtyish woman with a short, stylish haircut. The courtroom was brightly lit and chilly. Maybe to keep everyone awake when the lawyers droned on.

Jean was fourth on the docket. A stir went through the crowd as the bailiff opened the door to the holding chamber. Judge Morse called for silence.

Alex sat up with a sharp intake of breath. Never a sharp dresser, the blue prison garb didn't change Jean all that much. The disturbing thing was her look. She walked into the courtroom with her deadpan face and herky-jerky gait as though she was coming in to make croissants.

When Judge Morse asked her if she could afford a private attorney, her negative response was affectless. She proceeded to answer the short list of questions with abrupt nonchalance, causing even the judge to glance at her curiously.

In the meantime, Alex was staring at Mary Szabo. She was thinking of Mary's brother, Pete. Really, they could have been identical twins except for the gender differences. She was wearing an appalling brown suit that resembled a paper bag. She appeared puzzled and concerned as she conferred with Jean, her gaze intense.

The whole thing was over in short order. Jean pleaded not guilty and that was that. It was a weird aspect of law. *In and out, one of the list. Now, go to jail. We'll discuss bail next week.*

"She looked guilty," Jeffrey said.

They were in her car, traveling down Guerneville Road, intent on doing something normal, which in this case was stopping at a favorite produce stand in Sebastopol before heading back to Guerneville. Jeffrey wanted to bring Max some mangoes.

"Jeffrey, she looked exactly the same."

"That's what I mean. She always looked guilty to me."

"You're reading that into her face. She has the kind of face that's so absent, you can put your own meaning into it. You might be projecting your own demons onto Jean."

Jeffrey sighed. "I see the world around me, no matter what you or Max say. My point is, look at the facts of the case."

There was no point in endless speculation. Alex changed the subject. "That's the same public defender who handled the Shayne Elliot case, Pete Szabo's sister. I hope she uses her skills as well this time."

"That woman needs a makeover," Jeffrey commented. "She's very pretty, but she seems to be bent on hiding it. That outfit. There should be a law against that color of brown for fabric. And who doesn't wear at least a little makeup when they're appearing in public? But the brother is a ten in my book. He's gorgeous."

"He just has the advantage of wearing a uniform," Alex replied.

"You're not kidding," Jeffrey said. "Straight as an arrow, though. I can tell, the way he looks at you."

"I didn't notice."

"Liar."

She didn't bother to protest. Besides, they were just arriving at the wonderful produce stand called Mandy's. Alex was thinking about mangoes herself right now. She was thinking about bananas, pineapples and papayas. She was thinking about an entire tropical fruit salad.

Alex ended up making enough tropical fruit salad to feed a troop of Nicaraguan soldiers. By late Saturday afternoon, she was consuming yet another bowl of it when the phone rang. By now, she never answered. She only screened.

"Ms. Pope, this is Mary Szabo, Jean's attorney. I need to talk to you as soon as possible—"

Alex dropped her spoon, sending a grape rolling across the table. She grabbed up the phone. "Hello?"

"Is this Ms. Pope?"

"Call me Alex."

"All right, then you can call me Mary. Did you hear what I was saying?"

"Yes, about talking to me. What about?"

A pause. Alex could almost imagine the grimace on the lawyer's earnest face. It was definitely a troubled pause.

"I've had a chance to meet with Jean this morning."

"You saw a client on the weekend?" Alex asked, surprised.

"From behind glass. Only non-contact visits on weekends. It isn't very private and I would have preferred to wait until Monday when I was more familiar with the case, but Jean insisted."

That meant Mary intended to study up on the case on Sunday. Alex had to give it to the woman. She was a hard worker.

"What does this have to do with me?" Alex asked.

"It's complicated," Mary replied.

Mary Szabo had had the case for a day and a half and already the complications were mounting. Alex felt sorry for her. She shouldn't have, though. It was about to become clear that she, Alex, was among the complications.

"Jean wants your help," Mary said. "I can't possibly explain all of this on the phone. I'd really appreciate it if you would block some time on Monday for a meeting."

"Can't you fill in a *few* details?" Alex asked.

Mary sighed. "Jean insists on seeing you. Please, that's all I can say for now."

Alex was thinking about Jean. Not a pleasant woman. But she understood the pain of accusation and, worse, self-accusation. In a way, she owed this to Jean. "What time on Monday?"

"Are you all right?" Marge asked.

It was Sunday morning. Alex was at the Campbells' door, holding a Tupperware container of tropical fruit salad.

"Not really," Alex admitted.

Marge led her to the kitchen. The pugs licked her ankles on the way through the living room. She sat at the kitchen table and let Marge mix up buttermilk waffles to go with the fruit salad, informing Marge of Jean's request.

Marge stared into the bowl of egg whites she was whipping as they formed into stiffened peaks. "Don't anticipate what might happen. Try not to worry."

Alex's throat tightened. Her eyes started to blur.

"That isn't all, is it?"

Alex intended to lie. Instead, she blurted out, "I have to go to a deposition Tuesday concerning a lawsuit about my husband's death."

"You'll do fine," Marge said. "You speak well and—"

"Screw them!" Alex interrupted, surprising both Marge and herself. Marge almost dropped her waffle spatula. "I never wanted this lawsuit. My in-laws need me to make the case. I'm not sure how I'll be. I'm very, very concerned about how I'll be." She grimaced, feeling the words pull themselves from her gut. "There are some things I don't want to discuss. Not now. Maybe never."

Marge went over to the cupboard by the sink. She removed a prescription bottle and brought it over to Alex. "I can give you a few of these," she said.

Alex took the container. It was Xanax.

"Jack hasn't been sleeping well, what with everything. That keeps me awake. These help. He won't take them, but I don't mind taking them when I need to."

Alex opened the container and shook out three pills. "That should be enough," she said. "Thanks, Marge."

SIXTEEN

The Sonoma County Hall of Justice was an oddly shaped structure, four rectangular segments with a courtyard in the middle. The public defender's office was located on the first floor of a segment, one of the middle doors along the long hallway lined with doors.

Alex checked in with the receptionist. A few moments later, Mary Szabo appeared through a side door. She led Alex to a small office and pointed to a brown vinyl chair in front of the neat but crowded desk. Amazingly, the vinyl chair was the same mud-brown color as Mary's suit.

"I see you found us okay," Mary said once she'd sat down behind her desk. "People tend to get lost the first time around in this peculiar building."

The public defender was wearing almost no makeup except for a little blush that didn't match her coloring and a touch of mascara that was a shade too light to make a noticeable difference in her appearance. On the other hand, Alex had noticed on their walk to the office that Mary moved gracefully, like her brother. Underneath the dumpy dowager outfit was a pretty nice body. And her face was attractive enough to withstand the insulting makeup assault.

Alex glanced at the desk. On it were several framed photos, the type people littered their work areas with. Two of them pictured Mary with another woman. One photo appeared to have been taken at Yosemite, both women wearing heavy backpacks. In the other, the women were seated on a couch with two cats on their laps. In the camping photo, both women looked vigorous. In the second, Mary's friend was haggard and bald, probably a good twenty pounds thinner.

"That's my partner, Kim," Mary said.

"She looks nice," Alex said, trying to keep the curiosity regarding Kim's condition from her tone, but apparently she was unsuccessful. Mary studied Alex's face.

"She had chemo, but it's over now. She's in remission," Mary said, in a light, controlled way.

"That's hard," Alex replied. "I'm sorry."

"It would have been harder if she hadn't gone into remission," Mary replied on cue. That, Alex realized, must be her stock, relatively upbeat answer.

Mary was staring at her. Alex shifted in her chair. The defender had a way of scrutinizing her that was a bit unsettling.

"It's all just a part of life, isn't it?" Mary said. "The pictures on my desk are a good reminder that pain is part of life." She smiled. "As if I need reminders in this job."

Alex wondered if Mary left the photos out all the time. What did some of her more conservative clients think?

"Are you wondering if I leave them on my desk for all the world to see?" Mary asked. She smiled at Alex's startled look. "Yes, I can read minds. Not really. But I'm good at figuring out what's in people's minds, whatever you want to call that. It's handy for being a lawyer." She pointed to the photos. "I sometimes take them off my desk. If I think it might interfere with my relationship with the client. I don't like it, but it's the real world, isn't it?"

"Yes, it is."

"In your case, I didn't think you'd mind. Kim and I have been together a long time, twelve years."

Of course she couldn't care less if Mary Szabo was a lesbian, but they might as well get the whole sexual preference thing out of the way. She knew people made mistakes about her, Alex, sometimes, even lesbians who prided themselves on their gay-detection radar.

"I'm not gay," she said. "Not even a lipstick lesbian."

She smiled at Mary's raised eyebrows, but the public defender quickly erased the expression from her face.

"Just setting the record straight, so to speak."

Mary grimaced at the bad pun. "All right then, I think we have enough of the personal squared away." She gestured at a stack of papers. "I've had time to study the police reports, the autopsy findings, the interviews, the results of the search of the Heller residence. The prosecution has a solid case. I've gone over this with Jean. Now, here's the problem. She insists she's innocent. Let me ask you this. How many of my clients do you think tell me they're innocent?"

Alex knew the answer. Lawyer lore. "All of them?"

Mary laughed. "No, but almost."

She had a nice laugh. Deep, guttural. However, from the strain on the lawyer's face, Alex had a feeling that Mary wasn't laughing much these days.

Alex couldn't help her next words. The feelings behind them had been lurking ever since December. "What about Shayne Elliot? Did he say he was innocent? Did it matter to you at all?"

"Shayne Elliot." Mary thought for a moment. "Of course. The boy charged with attempted assault at the Overlook." No laugh this time. "I can appreciate it if you're angry at my defense of Mr. Elliot. It was a terrible, bungled case and I did everything I could to show that to the judge. That's my job."

"To get criminals back on the street?" Alex truly believed he was guilty and she suspected that Mary felt the same way.

"My job is to see that all of our citizens have an equal opportunity for justice and a fair trial," Mary said stiffly. "I'd rather see a few guilty go free than see horrendous bungling and poor tactics in our police and judicial system. That's my choice. Otherwise, I would have hired on at the district attorney's office and prosecuted bad guys." She picked up the thick volume of papers lying in front of her. She tapped them into a neat pile. "I'm sure you want me to do the same for Jean Heller."

"Of course I do."

"To put it briefly, Jean not only insists she's innocent, but she wants to plead not guilty. I've explained that the evidence is exceptionally strong against her and will only get stronger as the prosecution builds its case. I've explained the battered-woman syndrome and the laws of self-defense and the reality of our current justice system. I believe with a fair degree of certainty that I can plea bargain for a very light sentence."

"Do you think she did it?" It was a ridiculous question, but she had to ask, even knowing what the answer would be. The lawyer answer.

"That would matter in a world where the truth is always absolute and completely accessible. That isn't the world we live in. Her innocence or guilt is not the point here. The point is that the prosecution has a very strong case, leading to probable conviction. Technically, the burden of proof is on the prosecution. But in reality, I am saddled with showing reasonable doubt as to her guilt, and what truth is involved here is the truth that I don't think I can do that." Mary had to lean back in her chair and take a breath. Then she leaned forward, staring intently at Alex, who was struck once again with the startlingly blue color of Mary's eyes, which, like her brother's, grew darker when the siblings were feeling intense emotions. "She's going to ask you to help her find the 'real killer.' What I'd like you to do instead is convince her of the reality of her situation."

It was Alex's turn to gasp for air. "Me? Find the killer? Why me?"

"She apparently thinks you're Wonder Woman," Mary said, breaking into what looked like a reluctant smile.

Jean thought that? Alex couldn't imagine Jean thinking that about her, much less saying it to anyone.

"Alex, I don't know how to say this but other than straight out. She's going to plead with you. I've seen versions of this before. All I can ask, and I don't want you to take this personally, is that you not let your ego or sympathy or any other feelings take over your rationality. Jean needs to take a defensive stance involving self-defense. If she pleads innocent and insists she didn't do it, she'll wind up in jail on murder one. That's the bottom line."

The Adult Main Detention Center was conveniently located in the building next door. Alex and Mary checked in at the bulletproofed reception area. They were buzzed into a back hallway and whisked up an elevator. A deputy let them into one of the interview rooms.

Dreary would have been a euphemism to describe the pale green room. It was so ugly one could imagine people confessing just to get out of it. It smelled of nasty disinfectant reminiscent of crushed bugs. Everything felt sticky to the touch.

A few minutes later, Jean shuffled in. The deputy uncuffed her. Mary motioned her into a metal chair with mustard yellow padding. When the deputy left, Jean wasted no time.

"I didn't do it, Alex," she stated flatly.

Mary spoke up. "Since we last talked over the weekend, I've thoroughly reviewed what we have of the prosecution's case. Now I can say with more certainty than ever that the case against you is very strong and, to make matters worse, there isn't a shred of evidence pointing to anyone else. Jean, please, I'm not disputing your claim. I'm telling you the reality of your situation."

"What about the person in the overcoat?" Jean asked with a persistence that bordered on affect.

"Person in an overcoat?" This was the first time Alex had heard of this.

"I told the police, I told this woman, but no one will listen. I saw a tall person in an overcoat." Jean spoke with what appeared to be a growing sense of urgency.

"It's not relevant," Mary said.

"It *is* relevant," Jean insisted. She leaned toward Alex. "Mark went back to the kitchen after the party to do some work. He was a night owl; everybody knew he was there a lot of the time by himself. I came back there after he did, because I'm stupid. I wanted to make up with him, like always. We argued and he grabbed me." She frowned. "I pulled away and ran out to the car. That's when I saw a figure in the headlights. A tall person in a dark overcoat."

Mary held up a police report. "In the search of the Heller residence, a bloody sweater was found in the bathroom hamper."

"I told them the blood on the sweater was Mark's and why it was there," Jean said. "I scratched him accidentally when I pulled away. If I'd killed him, would I have kept the sweater?"

It was an interesting point, Alex thought. She glanced at Mary, who was looking pained.

"Tell her what happened next," Mary said.

"I sped away, was doing at least seventy down River Road, and a deputy stopped me. I told him I wasn't drunk, just had had a terrible fight with my husband and was headed home. He let me go with a warning." Jean waved her hand at Alex. "Why would I admit to having a terrible fight with my husband if I had just killed him?"

Another interesting point, Alex thought.

"There are two ways to look at everything." Mary stood and began to pace back and forth in the squalid room, which had grown quite warm and stuffy. She had to make short, careful turns to avoid bumping against the furniture. "Look at how the detectives and prosecution are assessing this material. Jean was there. She had motive, she had the means—her newly learned self-defense training—and physical evidence links her not only to the scene but to a struggle at the scene."

"But it's all so obvious and stupid. Why would I do something so ridiculous?" Jean was clearly baffled.

Mary sighed. "I'm going to be frank with you. People—even smart people—commit crimes that are not well-conceived."

"I didn't do it," Jean said, with more emotion than Alex had ever heard in Jean's words, except for the odd wailing the night of the murder—and that wasn't technically speech. "Alex, help me. It's the truth, I swear it. I did not kill Mark. I will not plead guilty. If you don't help me, I won't change my mind. I'll go to jail for the rest of my life if I have to. I'll work in food service and become a model prisoner. God knows, it might be a better life than I had before."

Alex took a deep breath. "I don't think I can. I wouldn't know how to begin."

"I didn't kill my husband," Jean shot back, staring right at her.

Alex shook head. "I can't. Besides, your lawyer is probably right. You can make a good plea bargain."

"I didn't kill my husband," Jean repeated quietly, forcefully. "Just like you didn't kill yours. But they're both dead and you're free and I'm locked up. Can you really ignore me and just go on with your life? Will you sleep at night?"

Alex's mouth fell open. "I have to go." She jumped from her sticky chair.

"I know about you," Jean called as Alex stumbled to the door.

"It's true, I don't really like her. She's manipulative and just plain weird," Alex said. "Honestly, do you like her?"

Mary was walking her to her car in the parking lot near the main sheriff's office. Mary looked up at the thick black clouds covering the sky. "Rain coming again. I'm getting so tired of the rain."

"Answer me," Alex insisted.

"I don't think in those terms. Jean is my client and a human being. She deserves my best defense and any personal feelings I might have is not only pointless but in violation of my principles and goals. I knew what I was getting into with this job. And I believe without any hesitation that every single person in our society is entitled to a fair trial with adequate representation."

"Wow," Alex said. "I've never met anyone who can go on that long without taking a breath."

"I'm not sure what to make of that observation."

"I think it's a sign of your conviction."

They had reached Alex's car. A few heavy drops of rain were already beginning to fall.

"Uh-oh," Mary said. "I should've brought the umbrella. I'd better run. Anyway, I hope you feel good about making a reasonable decision to not take this mess on."

The drops grew larger and fell with loud plunking sounds on the hoods of the cars surrounding them.

"I don't actually know if I've decided." Alex smiled at Mary's blush. "You're cute when you're blushing."

Mary's cheeks turned redder. "I'm not blushing. It's the cold rain. And you're flirting. I thought you said you weren't a lesbian." Mary adopted her all-business look. "I'm sorry. That was unprofessional."

Alex grinned at the defender. "If we're going to get through this, I think we're both going to have to try and lighten up, at least a little. Agreed?" She held her hand out.

Mary put her hands behind her back. "I'm not shaking unless you reassure me that you're not going to go off and do something foolish, like mess around with Jean's case."

Alex shrugged and withdrew her hand. "Just go along with me for a day or two." She paused and frowned. "I have to think over what just happened in there. And I have to go down to the city tonight. I have something important to deal with tomorrow." She threw her arms in front of her face in mock defense. "Don't read my mind or whatever it is you're doing. I don't want to talk about it, especially to a lawyer."

SEVENTEEN

That evening Alex drove to San Francisco and checked into the elegant Omni Hotel. She had her favorite, Chivas Regal, from the minibar in her suite, then had tuna and barbequed eel and salmon nori rolls for dinner at the sushi bar of a nearby Japanese restaurant decorated with too many aquariums stocked with too many psychedelic fish swimming brazenly like proud hostages in their confines. She drank too much warm sake, then staggered back to the hotel late in the evening along the mostly deserted streets, unafraid. Let anyone try and mess with her. She was not in the best of moods.

At the requested time of 8:00 a.m., Alex was awakened by the front desk call service. Then she promptly fell back to sleep and woke up in a panic at nine.

She showered and dressed, trying not to think much. Just before leaving the room, she remembered Marge's Xanax. She went back to the bathroom and swallowed all three pills.

By the time the taxi dropped her off at the Gold Mine coffee shop on Battery Street, she wasn't feeling anxious. She wasn't feeling much of anything, except a bit woozy. Waiting in a booth in the steamy café were Hunter and Bunny Carlyle. Next to them was Bruce Phipps. Mister Rattles.

All three of them watched her approach. She felt very light on her feet. She slid in next to Bunny and picked up the menu. "I'm really not hungry, but I'd love some coffee. Why don't you go ahead and order?"

"We already have," Hunter said.

Alex glanced down at the half-eaten plates of food in front of the threesome. "Sorry I'm late." She glanced at the three stern faces. Even Bunny, who usually just looked preoccupied, was frowning at her.

The coffee shop was bustling with white-collar workers speaking quite loudly to Alex's suddenly sensitive ears. The overheated place smelled of greasy bacon and waffles, which was making her suddenly sensitive stomach feel queasy.

Alex accepted coffee from the harried waitress. She stirred in two teaspoons of sugar and sipped at the hot liquid. Then she looked from face to face.

"I know what to say," she insisted. "I'm prepared. I really am."

The pills were definitely starting to affect her mind. For some reason, she was remembering when she and Stacy had announced their marriage plans to the Carlyles. They were at the country club, in the elegant dining room—eating mediocre expensive food. She'd had dry, stringy chicken breast smothered in a gloppy dill sauce.

Besides the food, she remembered the hideous hypocrisy of the whole thing. Hunter and Bunny had clearly hoped Alex was a passing fancy of Stacy's. The marriage plans were greeted by one of the most gruesome and phony displays of best wishes that Alex could ever remember witnessing.

But they'd learned to tolerate one another, she and the Carlyle in-laws. Even at the funeral, she'd felt their pain, she'd embraced them with genuine empathy and they'd returned the embrace with similar sincerity.

It wasn't until the Carlyles had brought up the lawsuit that it had gotten ugly. Alex understood she should have wanted to sue. My God, everyone sued. She understood that she had a necessary part to play, if there was going to be a lawsuit. She understood about the money and her future. But the whole thing made *her* want to die.

Now, looking into these faces, she understood something deeply unsettling. No matter what the lawsuit resulted in—and they had a good case—she knew she blamed herself for the accident. And, she now realized—despite or maybe because of her drugged state—that the Carlyles blamed her too.

"Alex, are you all right?" Mister Rattles asked.

"I'm fine," she stammered. She took a big sip of coffee. She had to get back on earth. Right away. She had almost called Bruce Phipps *Mister Rattles* to his face.

"Alex, listen to me," Bruce Phipps said, speaking slowly, frowning. "I know you think being a lawyer's wife has prepared you for what's coming up this morning. But I tell every client the same thing, even the ones that *are* lawyers. It's different when it's you."

Alex sighed. "Okay, okay. Tell me."

"The most important thing—I can't stress it enough—is to answer only the questions asked. Be cooperative but reticent. Don't volunteer anything, and above all don't elaborate. Understood?"

"Understood." She grimaced, looking at the three skeptical faces. "I mean it. I understand."

By the time she and Rattles had sent the Carlyles packing and climbed into a cab to go six blocks to the defense lawyer's office, she was most definitely in an altered state of mind.

In the cab, she studied Bruce Phipps's nose. He had started removing his nose hairs. Without them, he wasn't a bad-looking man, something one would notice if one wasn't staring at the nose hairs. Of course snakes didn't have hair, she thought with wonder. Not a speck of hair.

Bruce glared at her. "Are you all right?"

"Never better," she slurred.

The conference room of Warwick, Pippins & Raber was, if possible, more ostentatious than the one at Hunter Carlyle's firm. There must have been a small forest's worth of mahogany used to construct the massive table, chairs and miscellaneous furnishings. The artwork was conservative and original, involving ridiculously pompous landscapes and activities suggesting wealth and privilege.

When Alex and Phipps arrived, they were introduced to the already seated parties, including the defense lawyers and the court reporter. Alex knew she should be paying more attention to who was who. She just didn't care. Let them ask the questions and that was that. She just wanted the whole thing over with, particularly with Bruce Phipps eyeing her like she was some kind of mental case about to lose it.

"Alex?" It was Bruce Phipps, nagging at her. "Answer the question."

"Would you repeat that, please?" she asked.

The head defense lawyer, an overweight man with black hair that appeared to be a wig, scrutinized her, then repeated, "Are you under the influence of anything that would impair your ability to understand or respond truthfully to the questions I'm going to ask you?"

His name was . . . Raber. That was it, Raber. He looked like a fat, quivering cartoon character wearing a black wig. *Elmer Fudd*. That's what she'd name him. Not that clever, but she was under stress.

"Are you under the influence of anything that would impair your ability to understand or respond truthfully to the questions I'm going to ask you?" Elmer Fudd repeated for the third time.

It was a standard question. She answered in the standard way. "No, I'm not."

They asked her all the usual questions about who she was and how she was related to the deceased. They asked her about the state of their marriage prior to the accident. Loss of consortium, blah, blah.

Raber was a smart man. She could see that. He needed to get to the gym more often and find a better wig shop, but he was sharp. Alex would listen to Bruce Phipps's advice. She'd be terse with her answers. She reminded herself of this, because her internal voices were becoming lively.

"Ms. Pope, do I need to repeat the question?" Raber said, breaking into her reverie.

"No, I heard you." She took a deep breath.

"I bought the parachuting adventure for my husband's birthday." *No more words. Keep quiet.*

"Did you understand what the adventure consisted of?"

"Yes."

"Can you tell us what your understanding was?"

"A tandem jump. Stacy had never jumped before. This was supposed to be extremely safe. He went up with an instructor, jumped with the instructor."

"His first jump? Was he excited?"

Alex hesitated. "Yes."

"Was he nervous?"

Again, she hesitated. "I guess so."

"Yes or no? Was he nervous?"

"Yes." She breathed out. She waited. *Don't ask me how nervous he was,* she thought. Thank God, Raber chose to move on.

"Your husband signed a waiver, didn't he?"

"Yes."

"Did you and he discuss it?"

"Yes, we did." She smiled. "He was a lawyer. He read every word. Then he made jokes about the loopholes if anything happened to him and I had to sue."

Bruce Phipps's mouth fell open. He shook his head vigorously at her.

"I see," Raber said. He glanced at the other lawyers. Alex swore she could see his body quivering cartoonishly with barely concealed glee. He asked a few more boring questions about the waiver, then paused. "I'm sorry, but I have to ask a few questions about the event." He cleared his throat. "On the day of the jump, were you present at the airport?"

"No. I was home making a birthday dinner."

"How did you learn about the, um, accident?"

Tears welled up in her eyes. Everyone waited while she dabbed at them with a tissue handed to her by Bruce Phipps.

"A phone call. He was on his way to the hospital, but he died on the way. They told me the instructor died on the spot. Why did they have to say that right then?" She choked down a lump in her throat. Bruce Phipps was still shaking his head at her. "It was a woman. I never met her, but she was named Carly. She was the friend of someone in one of my classes. That's how I picked that parachuting company."

In this of all places, she was finally talking about it. Bruce Phipps's face was growing purple, but she didn't care.

"Of course you were upset," Raber crooned. "Devastated."

"Devastated." She sounded out the word. It wasn't good enough, but she couldn't think of any word that would be. "Yes, I was devastated."

"Here you had bought what you thought was a marvelous gift and then this tragedy. Of course you were devastated. Worse, you must have felt almost . . ." Raber paused, then almost whispered, "Guilty."

"Yes," Alex choked out.

"And you sought help for these feelings?"

"You mean did I go to therapy?"

"Yes, some kind of grief counseling," he prompted.

Even in her current state of mind, she knew what he was getting at. The bastard. Her internal voices were screaming self-accusations and at the same time she could have strangled the lawyer. "Elmer Fudd," she said. They all looked at her like she was on drugs, which, of course, she was.

"Excuse me?" Raber said.

"Never mind," she said. "I didn't get any counseling. I went into my home and hid for months." She laughed then, causing the defense lawyer's eyes to brighten. Screw him. "I like to take action. I like to keep things moving ahead. If I believe in a psychology, it's the kind where you use an attitude of moving ahead. But I wasn't even doing that, after Stacy died. I was just hiding."

She waited. She knew how smart Raber was. There was an inevitability here; she almost looked forward to it. Poor Bruce Phipps. She hoped he didn't have a stroke.

"Let me ask you this," Raber said, his voice calm and curious, as though voicing an afterthought. "Why did you buy him a parachuting adventure, of all things?"

Alex felt as though she were awash in a cleansing light. "He was terrified of heights," she said. She didn't wait for the questions. She just plowed ahead. "I know what you're going to ask. Why the parachuting then? Because Stacy hated being afraid of anything. It's what I loved about him. Afraid of heights? Conquer it. How? Not *therapy*. Parachuting, of course. But he was too afraid to buy it for himself. So I bought it for him."

She looked around the room. They were all staring at her. She didn't care. She was in some heightened state, both traumatized and peaceful, both muddled and precise.

"So," she concluded, "you can ask me anything you want. You can fight among yourselves. In the end, whatever happens, you know what? It was my fault. And the last thing I wanted was some counselor to convince me otherwise."

EIGHTEEN

The next morning, Alex woke up with no idea where she was. It took several seconds for her to identify the hotel suite. There was spilled red wine on the carpet. An empty bottle and glass sat on the table nearby. She took a moment to be grateful she hadn't overdosed, then groaned.

Before she could ponder her predicament too thoroughly, she hobbled to the shower and ran hot water over her cottony head and numb body. She dressed, checked out and stopped for a huge Starbucks mocha with whipped cream to go. She drove down Lombard to the bridge. She didn't think about anything until she was in Marin County.

She had to pull off at the Mill Valley exit. She drove into a Chevron station and parked behind the car wash and rested her head on the steering wheel.

She was an idiot. Worse than an idiot. An embarrassment to the human race. She was beyond humiliated. The deposition played before her closed eyes like a very bad video.

What had been the worst? The moment where she'd confessed she bought Stacy the parachuting adventure because he hated being terrified of heights, with Bruce Phipps trying to shut her up. No, how about the temper tantrum, where she'd shouted she'd been forced into the lawsuit? *Oh, my God.*

When she'd stopped trembling enough to drive, she sped up the freeway with the imaginary deposition video replaying endlessly in her head.

Still, there was some shadowy part of her standing back, amused. She could sense a hidden trickster having a field day. Even more ironically, she had the strange feeling that Stacy, if he were still alive, would have appreciated this latest development.

Alex decided she would tell Mary in person. It was only fair. When she called the next morning, Mary informed her that Jean was having her bail hearing later that morning.

"It's a homicide case. She'll either get no bail or such a high bail that she won't be going anywhere but back to the pokey."

"Do people still say 'pokey'?"

"I have an old-fashioned vocabulary."

"Were you raised by old people?" Alex asked.

There was a pause on the other end of the line.

"Well, yes," Mary replied finally. "Pete and I were raised in part by our grandparents."

"I've found that kids pick up old-fashioned phrases if they were raised by elderly people," Alex said. She was wondering why the Szabo twins were raised by the grandparents, but it was probably way over the limit to ask. She changed the subject. "I need to talk to you about Jean."

Silence. Then, "Oh?"

"I'd like it to be in person," Alex said.

"I see," Mary said carefully.

They arranged a meeting for later in the afternoon, after the bail hearing.

Alex was tired. Very tired. She'd had bad dreams all night. The worst one just seemed unfair; she felt betrayed by her unconscious. In the nightmare, she and Jean were parachuting in tandem. They'd plummeted, struggling with apparatus neither of them knew how to use. Alex woke up sweating as they were about to smash into the ground.

Mary greeted Alex in the waiting area. This time, the defender was wearing an attractive outfit—a plain blue oxford shirt and khaki slacks with a black leather belt. Black leather boots. A little butch, but not nearly all the way to motorcycle dyke.

"You look nice," Alex commented when they'd settled into their chairs in the office. She was surprised to see a deep red flush rise from Mary's neck, all the way up to her cheeks.

"Thanks," Mary stammered. She cleared her throat and frowned, adopting her business persona. "Jean's bail was set at half a million dollars. I don't think anyone will be coming forward to pay. She has little contact with her parents and no siblings. She has few close friends, I take it."

"Not many that I know of," Alex said.

"Now," Mary said, "what's up?"

"I've decided to help Jean."

What did she expect? Alex's declaration was greeted first with a look of shock, then dismay, from Mary.

"This is a waste of time, mine and yours," Mary said in an icy tone.

Alex knew she herself was tired and looked it. But she didn't look as tired as Mary. She hardly needed Alex messing up her plans on top of whatever else was exhausting her.

"What if Jean isn't lying?" Alex said. "How would you feel if she went to jail even if it was only for a short time? Don't you think she deserves just one chance to show she's not lying? I'm that chance."

Alex wasn't prepared for Mary's response.

"Oh, God." Mary moaned and covered her face with her hands. "Oh, God," she repeated, mumbling into her hands. When she took her hands away, her eyes were bloodshot.

"I understand wanting to be a savior. Believe me, I understand better than you can imagine. But this decision of yours is not going to help anyone."

"The person in the overcoat," Alex said. "What if he or she really was there?"

"Alex, this isn't television."

"Listen to me," Alex said. "I've thought a lot about this. Mark fired Shayne Elliot. Then Shayne started haunting the place, exposing himself, damaging property. It got worse. He almost assaulted someone. He might have if she hadn't learned how to fend him off. What if he's an escalating case of violence? It's not impossible, you have to admit. What if he was there? What if he went in after Jean left and killed Mark? It's possible."

"Anything is possible," Mary said. "But there's absolutely no evidence to suspect Shayne or anyone else but Jean."

"Mark not only fired him, he humiliated him in front of the entire kitchen crew. And the kid has a history of weird behavior."

"From what I've heard, Mark had a tendency to alienate people. If we open that can of worms, an awful lot of people would be suspects. But there is *no* evidence. Alex, I want to say this tactfully. I sense you may not be able to be objective in this case."

"Are *you* being objective?" Alex snapped. "You're tired and overworked and you don't like Jean."

Mary's eyes fluttered. The public defender closed them and took several deep breaths. Alex waited until Mary opened her eyes.

"I won't tell you no, because I know it's useless and I can't anyway," Mary said. "What I will tell you is this. Jean's preliminary hearing is scheduled for January twenty-seventh. I didn't ask for a continuance because I didn't think I needed to. I'm not an unreasonable person. If you provide me with good, solid evidence in order for us to ask for some time, I'll do it. So, go for it. But better get going. You're going to have to perform a miracle."

"Wow, another major tirade without a breath. You're amazing," Alex said.

"I don't know if I'm in the mood for levity," Mary replied, but there was a tiny hint of a smile on her face. She picked up the thick folder on her desk and waved it at Alex. "With Jean's permission, which of course she'll grant, I can give you access to whatever reports I've received. You may not believe me, but I'd be thrilled if you got at the truth. I'm not against truth. I just have to prioritize. I'll help you if I can, but it won't be much, I'm afraid."

"You won't regret this," Alex said.

"Okay, Nancy Drew." Mary sighed, rising. "Let me go make copies." Alex waited in Mary's office while the defender made copies. When Mary returned, Alex stood. "I had a crush on Nancy Drew."

"I was the type who worshipped horses," Mary said. "I had a crush on Elizabeth Taylor in *Black Beauty*."

"I had that, too. I'm surprised sometimes that I'm not gay. But who knows how these things work?"

Mary was grinning now. Alex thought Mary needed to grin more. She had a great face, too appealing to be so strained.

"Isn't that the truth?" Mary said. "By the way, you look nice, too."

An awkward silence ensued. Mary led Alex out to the reception area.

"I'll be in touch," Alex said.

"I'm sure you will," Mary replied, holding open the reception door.

Alex wasn't sure if the defender sounded pleased or upset at the prospect.

NINETEEN

Alex sat at her little table, drinking coffee and reading reports. Everything pointed to Jean. She picked up the autopsy report and shivered. Mark's name was typed neatly in a box at the top of the form, followed by a detailed analysis of his dissected body and his organs. Not to mention the gruesome effect of freezing. Particularly on his brain whose "architecture was disrupted by freezing fluids." Poor Mark. He was a bully and an abuser. But to have his brain turned to Swiss cheese . . .

Next she considered one of the most damning pieces of evidence: an interview with a neighbor who'd seen Jean's car speed up the road to the Overlook after the closing party and come tearing down again.

Then there was the matter of Jean's being stopped on River Road for speeding, during which time she'd admitted to the deputy that she'd gone back to the Overlook to argue with Mark.

The damning evidence went on. There was the San Francisco restaurant owner's revelation of firing Mark because of alleged spousal abuse. There was the bloody sweater found in a hamper in the Heller residence.

When she was arrested, Jean had trotted off to the sheriff's substation in Guerneville and blathered self-incriminations without a lawyer. But why not? She knew she hadn't killed Mark. Why not be honest?

The phone rang. Alex didn't answer. But when she heard Sarge's voice on the message machine, she picked up.

"Alex Pope, do you know I'm getting hounded by reporters for my expert opinions on self-defense and murder? I'm getting hounded to talk to you and get you to talk to the press."

"No! No interviews. Please, please don't tell them anything about me."

"Don't worry, I'll handle my end. I just wanted to warn you. I have a friend at Fox News. God, woman, I'm sorry. My friend tells me you should watch the ten o'clock news tonight."

Alex's stomach churned. "I knew it was only a matter of time. Thanks for the warning."

"Do you want to come down here?" Sarge asked. "Watch with me, Uli and the Furies?"

"No, thanks, but I appreciate the offer."

"Anytime, open invitation."

Jeffrey called next. "I had a psychic moment that you needed me."

"Maybe so," she admitted.

"You need me *and* I need you," Jeffrey said. "Jesus, if we didn't know it was Jean, I'd suspect Max. He's almost happy Mark's dead. Listen, I think we both need to talk. Come out to dinner with me. I heard about a secret treasure not far from here."

"Can we be back by ten? I need you to watch Fox News with me."

"Alex, maybe you shouldn't be following every moment of this case."

"This is different."

"We'll be back by ten. Promise."

When they hugged, Alex smelled alcohol on Jeffrey's breath. "Have you been drinking?"

"Just a glass of Ravenswood Zinfandel before I left the house."

"A glass?"

"All right, two. I was going to ask you to drive tonight anyway. I want to drown my sorrows in sake at the restaurant and I'm feeling wretched enough to make you listen to me snivel and stay relatively sober to boot. Could I be more self-serving?"

"Probably not. Don't worry about it."

"You're a doll."

"Shut up. I won't do it if you use dated fag lingo."

Jeffrey put his arm around her. "What can you expect from a dated fag? Let's get going."

Kiro's was located in an dreadful strip mall off Redwood Drive in Rohnert Park, a planned community of tract homes and apartment complexes in southern Sonoma County. The restaurant, however, was charming, run by a gracious extended Japanese family.

Jeffrey ordered a large carafe of warm sake as soon as they were seated. He sighed deeply, swallowed his first pour from the tiny cup in a single gulp.

They ordered miso soup to start, with a seaweed salad to share, then a vast selection of sushi. When the waitress left, Jeffrey refilled his sake cup and downed it again.

The waitress returned quickly with their soup and seaweed salad.

"Put something in your stomach," Alex advised. "Then start talking, because I can't stand watching your miserable face without an explanation."

Jeffrey sipped from a bowl of miso soup. "Mmmm. If this is a sign of things to come, at least our stomachs will be happy." He lifted a bit of luminescent greenish salad with his chopsticks and dropped it into his mouth. "Yes. Yes."

By now, Alex had tried her soup. It was very good.

"I wish Max liked Japanese food. He seems like the type that should," Jeffrey said. "But I probably don't need to worry about that for long since he's probably about to dump me."

"You guys have gone through all sorts of things and survived as a couple."

He shrugged. "Things are *very* tense."

"Of course things are *very* tense. Someone we know was just murdered and dumped in a freezer."

They hadn't noticed the waitress arriving with the first round of sushi. She twitched at Alex's words but maintained a neutral expression and calmly set down the tray arranged with a pristine selection of raw fish and rice.

Jeffrey popped a piece of octopus nigiri into his mouth and moaned. "I feel pain, I feel pleasure, simultaneously. I'm having a cosmic moment."

"You're having a sake moment."

"Whatever." He held the carafe up to the nearby waitress and signaled for more. She nodded. "You know I loved him."

She knew her cousin pretty well. She knew he didn't mean Max. "I gathered that."

"No, I mean I *really* loved him. I love Max, too. But with Mark, it was an obsessive passion. Max knew. He ignored it, pretty much, except if we were arguing."

She picked up a piece of maguro sashimi and dropped it into her mouth. "Marvelous."

"See? Try the eel." He poked at the pickled ginger with his chopsticks. "Brace yourself. Take a drink."

The sake slid sensuously down her throat and warmed her gut. "I'm ready."

"Two years ago, there was a fancy foods convention in Las Vegas. Mark and I went together. You know Las Vegas. It's all a big fantasy." He paused, looking pained.

"You slept together," she filled in for him.

Jeffrey set down his chopsticks. "Why am I not surprised you guessed?"

"Mark used sex as one of his tools. You know, he was screwing Julie. I caught them."

"I sort of knew. Why else would he want her fired? Here's the sickest thing. I didn't care who else he screwed. I was upset he didn't want to screw me after that one trip to fantasyland. I'm sorry if I'm being too gross. It's the truth."

"Oh, Jeffrey, I wish the human race was less predictable. He screwed you on a trip, then he started rejecting and berating you after that, right?"

"Why am I trying to confess? You can confess for me and I'll just nod in agreement."

"It depends what you're confessing to."

Jeffrey's eyes widened. "I didn't kill him."

"I didn't say you did."

"Obviously, it was Jean."

"I don't think it was Jean."

"You think it was me?" His hands shook as he reached for his sake and drained the cup one more time.

"As a matter of fact, I don't."

He poked at a piece of glistening pink salmon but didn't pick it up. "What about Astrid?"

"Astrid? I think she had a bigger crush on him than you did. More obsessive, really, because it wasn't about sex. She was dependent on him, or so she thought, for his talent."

"Exactly. And she has no alibi, from what I hear."

"But she didn't have any reason to kill him."

"On the face of it. But let me tell you a little piece of information. Something was going on between Mark and Astrid."

"Fine, so Mark was sleeping with nearly everyone. Maybe there was sex."

"Call it faggy intuition, but I think it was something else." He dropped a piece of tamago nigiri into his mouth and chewed. "There," he said, when he'd swallowed. "Nice bit of business, huh?"

"The whole thing," Alex agreed. "Any more confessions or ratting on anyone?"

"That's it for now," Jeffrey said.

At ten, they were slumped on her couch. She and Jeffrey watched a recapitulation of the case until, in the last segment, Alex's picture flashed onto an inset at the top of the screen.

The stiff-haired newsdroid rattled on about Alex's self-defense class and Jean's participation. But that was old news.

The breaking news was the revelation that, in an odd coincidence, Alex herself had lost her husband, Stacy Carlyle, only recently in a freak tragedy where Alex's husband and his parachuting instructor, jumping tandem, had fallen to their deaths. Worse, the instructor had been found to have a previous history of depression. There was speculation that she may not have pulled the reserve chute, essentially committing suicide and murder.

Although not enough evidence was found to bring criminal charges, the newsdroid mentioned a lawsuit being brought to court by Alex and the parents of the dead man, Hunter and Bunny Carlyle.

"I can't believe this," Jeffrey exclaimed. "What the hell relevance does this have, except filling the airwaves with people's pain and anguish so the voyeurs can get their thrills?"

"No big deal," Alex said. Tears rolled down her face.

"Screw them!" Jeffrey cried. "I'm so sorry, honey."

"I mean it, it's no big deal." She wiped her face. With a jolt, she realized she meant it. She had watched a hundred reports, at least. Maybe two hundred. They couldn't make her feel any worse, not anymore.

Tears started rolling down Jeffrey's face too. He was back on his Jeffrey track. "I promise I won't bring this up anymore. But I miss Mark so much." He sniffed.

Alex felt annoyed, then guilty. How could she be so cold? She knew what grief was. Why couldn't she let Jeffrey have his version?

"Now it's my turn to confess," she said.

"*You* killed him."

"No, but I am going to prove that Jean didn't."

"But she did."

"She didn't."

"Honey, we've known each other forever. All this rehashing of the business with Stacy. I know how you feel about the accident. Don't let your guilt cause you to do something you might regret when—"

"Don't analyze me," she interrupted. "I'm not going to change my mind."

TWENTY

During her vegetative period in the mansion after Stacy's death, Alex had watched crime shows on the Court TV channel—*Forensic Files; I, Detective; The System.* She was fixated on death anyway, so why not watch the cases that finished neatly, all the loose ends tied up?

She developed a fascination with a former F.B.I. agent named Marlene Denton who solved cases by coming up with detailed psychological profiles. Marlene Denton had a show called *Solving the Impossible: Tales of a Profiler.* She learned on Marlene's show that no stone should be left unturned and that the smallest of details unearthed the truth.

After sending Jeffrey home, Alex watched a few repeats of *Solving the Impossible.* At 3:00 a.m., she crawled into bed, her mind spinning. She dozed, woke again, then dozed. At 8:00 a.m., she woke one more time, her mind still searching for possibilities. She asked herself what Marlene Denton would do. Inspect the crime scene personally, for one thing. Then she would have to do the same.

The sheriff had only recently removed the yellow police tape. Alex tromped over to the main building. It was drizzling and foggy, a cold, wet January day in a month that had seen almost no sunshine. The ground was spongy, the tree branches drooped and it seemed the entire world sagged with moisture.

Leslie's car was parked out front. Alex banged on the front doors. After an interminable wait, Alex could see Leslie coming across the lobby. As Leslie got closer, Alex noted the welcoming but guarded look on her face.

Leslie opened the door. "It's good to see you. I feel like everyone is in hiding."

They walked across the deserted lobby, which smelled like mushrooms.

"The furnace was set too low," Leslie said. "I'm praying we didn't start any mold problems. Mold is this generation's asbestos. God forbid it creeps in here. As it is, Guerneville is probably one of the mold centers of California. Let's go into the office. It smells better in there."

"Actually, I wanted to look around the kitchen," Alex said.

"Why?"

"I know this is going to sound crazy, but I'm trying to help Jean. She swears she didn't kill Mark. I promised I'd see if I could help."

Leslie looked like she might start to cry. "Jean did it, didn't she?"

"I don't think so."

"What makes you think that?"

Alex grimaced. "I don't know yet. I just feel like she didn't."

Leslie hesitated. "I don't know how to put this. You know, with the counseling I've had recently, I've had to look at past issues and how they've driven me to do things in my current life. I saw the news about your husband. You know you recently had to deal—"

"Don't psychoanalyze me."

Leslie appeared to crumble. Tears welled up in her eyes.

"I'm sorry," Alex said. "I didn't mean to snap at you. I'm just tired of people making assumptions about my motives. I need to see the kitchen. Please."

"I just wish we could get the whole thing over with." Leslie waved her hand around the lobby. "I was finally feeling like Chris and I could make a life here. Then this."

"How's Chris holding up?"

"If you want to know the truth, he's been a bit odd. No matter how much he denies it, he's strongly affected by Jack. He always has been. Now Jack is in a funk and Chris is running in circles." Leslie placed a hand lightly on Alex's shoulder. "It would be best to have it over, don't you think? I know how you feel about Jack and Marge."

"I won't drag it out too long." She stepped back to get away from Leslie's touch.

Alone in the kitchen, Alex turned on all the lights, but that didn't erase her willies. The place had been scoured by the janitorial crew but had a creepy feeling.

Putting herself in the profiler mode, she tried to view the scene objectively as an unusually clean restaurant kitchen. Jean had told detectives she and Mark argued just outside Mark's office cubby. He grabbed her, she scratched him, and then she exited from the rear kitchen door, the same one she'd come in.

The second person, the killer, could have entered through the same unlocked rear door after Jean fled. Of course, there'd be no physical proof of a second person. The janitors had trampled inside and out, creating tons of fingerprints and footprints, car tire marks and God only knew what other false evidence.

Alex steeled herself, then walked to the hallway. The freezer was the first door on the right. She pulled open the heavy door. A blast of cold air and a mechanical humming greeted her. She propped the door open with a chair. In the middle of the floor, an outline of a body, Mark-size, was chalked on the floor.

Mark had been a sturdy man. Still, Alex had to admit, Jean was a bruiser. She could have dragged Mark into the freezer. Alex shook her head. She had to clear her mind. Even she was thinking about Jean as the perpetrator.

"What are you doing?"

Alex spun around.

It was Jack. He looked irritated.

"I was looking at the crime scene."

"Leslie told me you're looking for a phantom killer."

Alex's heart sank. Jack had never used an irritated tone with her. "It can't hurt to look into things. A few days and I'll stop, I promise."

Jack stepped into the freezer and stared at the chalk lines. "Come up with anything?"

"Not here. The neighbor down the road who saw Jean's car also saw a person in an overcoat coming up the road. But he claims people come up the road all the time."

Jack seemed to be considering this latest bit of information. "It's not much to go on."

"I know. But it's something."

He fumbled with a button on his coat, avoiding eye contact. "It's cold. Are you done in here?"

Alex glanced around. She wasn't feeling very profiler-like, now that she'd been interrupted. "I guess so."

They went into the kitchen. Jack stood with his arms hanging at his sides, looking chagrined. "Sorry I snapped at you. Want coffee?"

"Yes." She was surprised at how much Jack's brief hostility had affected her. She couldn't help thinking of Chris. She suddenly realized how much wanting Jack's approval could affect his son.

"Chris says the publicity will have people coming in once we open again," Jack told her, "but I don't know. And even if they come, who will cook for them?"

They were sitting in the dining room at an empty table, cradling coffee cups.

"Astrid. She's good, really good."

Jack shook his head despairingly. "She's not a leader." He stopped speaking and stared across the room, his gaze unfocused.

"Jack, are you okay?"

"Not feeling that great these days." He cleared his throat. "You know how fond Marge and I have become of you. We saw the report on the news about your husband."

Alex stirred more sugar into her coffee. "Know anything about parachuting?"

She thought a strange look passed over Jack's face. He was silent for a moment. Then he said, "A little. Enough to know those beginner tandem jumps are usually safe."

Hesitantly, she said, "There's some question as to whether the instructor was suicidal. At least that's the case my husband's father and the other lawyers are making. They've insisted on this lawsuit and I need to be a part of it. It's called loss of consortium, what I've suffered. I *hate* that term. I only blame one person. Me. I instigated the whole damn thing."

Jack's face crumpled. "No," he mumbled. He stood abruptly. "Don't blame yourself, you didn't have control over any of it. Look at what's happening here. I could blame myself, letting my son take over, letting him hire that chef."

"Of course you're not to blame for Mark's murder," she said. "You made choices based on reasonable assumptions, then—" She stopped. "My case is different."

"Our own situations always are." Jack's tone was reasonably calm but his hands trembled and his right eye had developed a slight twitch. "I only wish we could all do the right thing and never make terrible mistakes. But we do bad things. Then we have to live with the consequences." He put his hand on her shoulder. "You are a fine person. I'd be proud to have you as a daughter. I hope your parents are helping you out with this. You never talk about them. But I'm here. I'm always here for you, Alex." Before she could reply, he held up his hand. "Bad headache. Have to go."

With that, he marched out of the dining room with the watchful gait of a man being chased.

As she was walking through the parking lot, headed back to her place, Chris's car pulled up. He motioned her into the passenger seat.

"We have to talk out here. I don't want to disturb Leslie. She's fragile right now," he explained when she'd climbed in.

Alex thought he was looking just as fragile as Leslie, perhaps more so.

"What are you doing?" Chris said, his voice pained. "I can't believe you. You come here and you're sticking your nose into everything from day one. But this thing with Jean takes the cake. I know you don't care if you mess me up, but what about my father? He's suffering already. Do you want to send him over the edge?"

"I talked to him. He knows what I'm doing. He's okay," Alex said. The windows of the car had fogged from the warmth of their bodies. She felt claustrophobic in the tight, confined space with Chris glowering at her.

"How dare you make judgments about my father's condition. I've lived with him my whole life. He's in bad shape and your meddling will make it worse."

A pang of guilt seared her middle. She knew there was truth in Chris's accusations. She'd seen Jack's edginess. She just hadn't wanted to face it.

"Leave it alone," Chris said. "For everyone's sake. I want to reopen the lodge in a couple of weeks. Don't mess it up. I know enough about law to be pretty sure they'll plea-bargain with Jean and it'll be over in less than a month, if we're lucky."

She knew he was right. She knew she should stop. To Chris, she nodded neutrally. "I understand everything you're saying."

"Good. I knew you'd listen to reason."

And she would stop. But first, she had to conduct one interview.

TWENTY-ONE

From behind the screen door, Gus Pearlstone peered at Alex. Behind him, his wife, Esther, peered at her, too.

"Mr. and Mrs. Pearlstone?"

"More police?" Gus asked.

"She looks like she's selling something," Esther said out of the side of her mouth.

The Pearlstones lived on Dearborne Road, below the entrance to the Overlook, second house on the right after turning from River Road. It was an old yellow cottage set close to the road. The small patch of front lawn was inhabited by a battalion of statuary: plastic, stone, cement and wood. Emissaries from an eclectic band of mythologies, there were elves and lions, Snow White and her seven dwarfs, Buddha, St. Francis and Rudolph the Reindeer, among others.

Alex was standing on the front porch, an equally busy area filled with flowerpots, assorted patio furniture, old shoes, raincoats and a few garden tools.

"I'm not from the police and I'm not selling anything," Alex said. "I'm working with the defense team for Jean Heller."

"The woman who killed her husband?" Esther asked.

"The woman who's accused of killing her husband," Alex clarified.

"She did it," Gus said.

"She killed him," Esther agreed. "Aren't you the one with the husband who fell out of the airplane? We saw it on the news. Very tragic. You teach women how to fight."

"That's her," Gus said.

"Gus says women shouldn't fight," Esther informed her. "He's a chauvinist."

"I thought if I could just come in for a few moments, just a couple of questions."

Esther poked Gus on the shoulder. He shrugged. "All right, Miss Bruce Lee," he said. "Come in."

Every surface of the living room was occupied with figurines and more statuary, tinier than outside but just as eclectic. The Pearlstones themselves were not much bigger than some of their larger statuary, measuring in, Alex guessed, at somewhere around five feet tall, somewhere in the elf category. They both stood up straight, however, and moved briskly for their age.

"We're collectors," Esther said proudly.

"I can see that," Alex replied.

"Coffee? It's already made."

"That'd be nice."

Esther marched to the kitchen, leaving Gus to get Alex settled in a pumpkin-colored vintage fifties armchair, while he settled onto a matching pumpkin-colored sofa. Esther came back from the kitchen with a steaming cup shaped like a pinecone. "Don't break it," she admonished Alex. "Those are hard to find." Esther joined her husband on the couch and they both stared at her expectantly.

"You told the police you saw a car speeding up the road at about midnight on the night of the homicide? A white Mercedes?"

"It was fifteen minutes past midnight," Gus said. "It was a late-model pearl-white Mercedes coupe. It was going maybe fifty-five miles an hour, very fast for this road."

"He's very observant," Esther said.

"I can see that," Alex said. "How did you happen to be able to be making such astute observations at that hour?"

"This should all be in the sheriff's interview," Gus said.

"I'd like to hear it from you."

"The detectives asked me if I'd seen anything unusual that night. I told them about the Mercedes."

"And you said you saw the same car come down again."

Gus tapped his watch. "At twelve-forty. Driving even faster and wilder, like a crazy person, coming down the hill."

"He has insomnia," Esther said.

"I can't sleep," Gus concurred.

"So he takes naps in the afternoon and sits on the porch half the night," Esther added.

"Was that the only unusual thing you saw that night?"

"Yes," Gus said. "That's what I told the detectives."

Alex took a sip of surprisingly good coffee, which she'd been neglecting due to the disturbing shape and color of the pinecone mug.

"It wasn't all he saw," Esther said.

"What?"

"It wasn't all I saw," Gus said.

"But that's what you told the detectives."

"They asked what I saw that was unusual. I told them about the Mercedes and they weren't interested in anything more, from what I could tell. So I didn't tell them what else I saw."

"What else did you see?"

"A person in an overcoat going up the road. Same person coming back down the road twenty minutes after the Mercedes came down."

Alex sat bolt upright.

"When?"

"Went up just after the Mercedes, so it was maybe twelve-seventeen. Back down, walking fast, twenty minutes after the Mercedes came down the hill."

"You didn't tell the detectives?"

"I told you they didn't seem interested. Besides, it wasn't unusual. We have drug dealers with a small driveway up four houses from here, close to the entrance to the Overlook. They have all sorts of bums parking on River Road and walking up to their house. The neighbors call the sheriff if any of those characters park on private property, and they can't park on the road, no curb. I see people walking up and down the road all hours of the day and night. Didn't think anything of it."

"Was it male or female?"

"It was tall," Gus said. "The road isn't well lit. A car, I could see. A person, not so good."

"Should we tell the detectives?" Esther asked.

"What good would it do?" Gus said. "They caught the murderer, as far as they're concerned. They're not interested."

"No, they probably aren't. But I appreciate your cooperation." Alex drained the last drops of coffee from the pinecone mug.

"Take it," Esther said, gesturing at the mug.

"I can't."

"Take it," Gus insisted. They both smiled at her with empathy. "You've been through a lot."

"Thank you very much," she said and she really meant it. She cradled the mug in both hands and hurried from the cottage. She couldn't wait to call Mary Szabo.

"I'm sorry, Alex. It doesn't mean anything."

"How can you say that?" Alex removed the phone from her ear and held it out in front of her like it was an offensive weapon.

It was evening. She'd left a message on Mary's voice mail at work as soon as she'd returned from the Pearlstones. Then she'd tried not to wait for the return call. By seven, she'd almost given up and was unreasonably pissed off at Mary, a feeling she tried to quell when Mary finally returned the call.

"Did you hear what I just said?" Mary said.

"No, I was too horrified to listen," Alex said. "I had the receiver away from me."

"Please, listen. The Pearlstones were right. They see people coming up and down the road all the time in black clothes. I know the house the

Pearlstones are referring to. I've defended some of the kids who live there. The sheriff has been around to that house many times. They just haven't been able to stop all the illegal activity completely."

"But doesn't it at least open a possibility? That a person in an overcoat was headed up to the Overlook?"

"Of course it opens the possibility. But think of my position. Is this a strong enough piece of new evidence to change Jean's situation one iota? Let me answer my own question. No."

Mary was probably right. The police were probably right. Was there anyone in the entire world who knew Jean was innocent? There was one. The real killer.

"Are you finished now?" Mary asked.

"I still have ten days, don't I?"

"In reality, you have fewer. I need to get a continuance, remember?"

"I'll be in touch." Alex hung up. She was convinced the killer was the person in the overcoat. That person, she just knew, was Shayne Elliot.

TWENTY-TWO

Astrid's house was on a side street in Guerneville, a tiny gray clapboard with white trim, tucked into a private drive lined with four other cottages.

Like everyone else, she looked drained. Her place, on the other hand, was bright and cheery in a spare, Scandinavian way. The tiny living room had glistening hardwood floors. A glass and chrome coffee table sat on a woven multicolored cotton rug in front of a love seat and armchair. A blue-tiled counter separated the small kitchen area from the living area.

"Sit. I made tea. Do you like Earl Grey?"

"That's fine."

Astrid went out to the kitchen and returned with a pretty white tea set. When she poured the tea into the porcelain cups, her hands shook.

"I'm so sorry about Mark," Alex said.

"I can't believe that woman. I never liked her or trusted her." Astrid shot Alex a challenging look. "Oh, I know in America you're supposed to take the woman's side, especially when they're oppressed. In this country, where you see everything in black and white, good and evil. But I can't help myself. I find myself blaming her."

Alex took a sip of tea. This wasn't going to be easy. "Jean says she didn't do it," she said. "I told her I'd help her."

Astrid's eyes grew wide. "You agreed to help that woman?"

"You just mentioned black-and-white thinking. Everybody is assuming she did it. No one is willing to think out of the box."

"Out of the box? This isn't an advertising campaign. It's people's lives." Astrid frowned. "What do you want from me? Do you think I killed him to get his job?"

"No."

"I don't want his job, I never did. I'm not talented enough. I will never again find such a good mentor."

"He was very important to you." Alex tried to maintain an encouraging tone.

Astrid took a breath. "I started professional cooking later in life, after a boring career teaching economics, with a dull husband, also in teaching. I went to the California Culinary Institute. Mark taught a seminar. Once I tasted his food, saw his genius, I persisted until he hired me. I had already heard rumors about his problems. I didn't care, and I never regretted my alliance with him. I could handle him." She smiled grimly. "Mark was not dull."

Alex saw something behind the anger and dismay in Astrid's face. Was she hiding something? She sure looked like she might be, just as Jeffrey had suggested.

In any case, Alex wanted to get to the point of the visit. She explained her Shayne Elliot theory, complete with current evidence.

"It sounds far-fetched," Astrid said.

"I know, but just hang in there with me for a little while and I promise I'll stop bothering you," Alex said.

Astrid grimaced. "All right. I feel like I owe you that. All of us do, who took your class. I walk down the street with more confidence. I think more about how I walk through the world, what my body is saying. The other women say the same thing." Her expression changed slightly, an ironic grin. "I don't know. Maybe Jean was justified, at least in defending herself. But she didn't have to kill him."

"Except I don't think she did," Alex persisted.

"I know that." Astrid sighed. "What did you want to ask me?"

"Tell me about Shayne Elliot. He was fired because of you, wasn't he?"

"He was fired for a number of reasons, among them insulting me, yes, and not taking direction from me because I was a woman."

"He said that?"

"He didn't have to. It was obvious. He was belligerent and egotistical. Shayne was a big mistake. Everyone noticed."

"Who noticed?"

"Mark noticed. Even Jack noticed. I think this was the only time they completely agreed that Shayne Elliot was no good."

"Tell me what happened. What did Shayne do to get fired?"

"He didn't think peeling potatoes was good enough for him. But, as you may know, arrogance won't necessarily get you fired in a restaurant kitchen, if you're talented. Shayne was not. He had delusions of grandeur, but he was inept. On the day he was fired, I had to have him redo an entire crate of very expensive Sharlyn melons, which he cut wrong."

"That was when he called you a bitch?" Alex asked.

"Have you heard this story already?"

"Not in its entirety."

"Yes, he blew up at me," Astrid continued. "Mark came over and tried to get him to apologize. He told Mark to go screw himself. One thing led to another, but Mark had years of experience over Shayne and he got in the last word in front of the entire crew. Then Shayne actually picked up a knife."

"You're kidding!" Alex was shocked.

Astrid shrugged. "It wasn't real. It was a gesture. Dramatic. Mark fired Shayne then and there. Mark knew he wasn't going to be stabbed in front of a crew of people."

"How did Shayne react?"

"Furious. But, to be frank, a bit like Mark. Both just full of hot air—is that the right expression? Just glared and slinked off."

"Did you see Shayne at any time after he was fired? Did you hear of any threats?"

Astrid hesitated. "No. But I wasn't surprised when they arrested him for the assaults."

"Did Shayne ever talk at work about killing, anything odd you can remember?"

"I work with teenage boys all the time. They talk about killing and armies and revenge and space wars all the time. It's in their hormones. I never pay attention. The only boy I know who didn't was Wesley. He was a boy you could have a conversation with."

Alex made a few skimpy notes on the pad she'd brought, while Astrid watched with interest.

"First a teacher of self-defense, now a sleuth," Astrid commented.

Alex closed the pad. "Not a very good one."

"Don't underestimate yourself. You're persistent."

Astrid hesitated. "About Jeffrey."

"Jeffrey?"

"Is he holding up?"

"Fine, at least under the circumstances," Alex said.

"I only mention this because you're related." Astrid turned her gaze from Alex to a framed poster on the wall. It was a large replica of Edvard Munch's *The Day After*. It made, Alex thought, a grim statement in the otherwise upbeat room. "He was very fond of Mark," Astrid continued. "Maybe too fond. Mark found this disturbing."

"How do you know?"

"Mark told me. Jeffrey might be grieving more than anyone suspects."

It was odd, Astrid not meeting her gaze.

"Is there something else you want to tell me?"

"No!" Astrid said too quickly.

"Are you sure?"

Astrid met her gaze now. But her look was veiled. "Nothing else."

TWENTY-THREE

What did she have to go on so far? Not much. But the more she heard about Shayne Elliot, the guiltier he seemed.

Now what, though? she wondered. Obviously, she needed more evidence. She was driving down Main Street, just passing Armstrong Woods Road. She slipped into a parking spot.

Before she climbed from the car, she took a few deep breaths and tried to envision the orange cone of protective light surrounding her. But for a moment, nothing. No light, no protection.

She shuddered, surprised, remembering the only other time her visualization had failed her in a public place—at Stacy's funeral, as she'd climbed from the black limousine at the cemetery. The rest of that awful afternoon, she'd had to suffer a hideous rawness like someone whose skin had been scraped away.

She waited, knowing not to get out of the car in that state of mind. It took a few minutes and a vigorous internal pep talk, but finally she was able to put up a weak protective barrier, a pale orange cone of light that would have to do.

Alex headed into Picasso's, the local coffeehouse. It was crowded for a late Monday afternoon, mostly with local kids, failed writers, old hippies and moms with strollers. The place smelled wonderfully of strong coffee. The baristas—all wearing sleeveless black muscle shirts emblazoned CAFFEINE POWER—were two gay boys with tight biceps and a dyke with even bigger arms.

All three of them, smiling lecherously, rushed up to help her. Alex ordered a cappuccino. To be diplomatic, she gave the gay boys a fag-hag smile and then winked at the cute dyke, expressing a not-gay-but-sincere gesture of appreciation. She took an isolated stool along the exposed brick wall opposite the service counter.

Shayne Elliot was standing among a boisterous crowd of Goth kids. They were packed at a couple of tables pushed together at the back of the room. He was wearing a black overcoat that fit Gus Pearlstone's description of the one worn by the person going up and down the road to the Overlook. Alex glanced around the room, counting at least twelve other young people in similar dark overcoats.

Shayne was raving about something, judging from his body language. She noticed a few rolled eyes among his audience. All of this, she admitted to herself, was pretty typical. She'd grown up in a rural area, too, albeit a rarefied collegiate one. There often seemed to be a kid tolerated despite his or her obvious problems. It took a lot to be completely ostracized in a small town, especially among the already alienated kids.

She sipped her cappuccino, thinking she should have ordered decaf. She was getting shaky, after three cups of Astrid's dark tea and now this. She thought of Detective Green's caffeine addiction. Maybe it was a hazard of the job, which seemed to consist of searching for clues fueled by caffeinated beverages.

She was about to leave, feeling either frustration or caffeine-induced derangement, when Wesley walked in. He passed by quickly, not glancing in her direction.

He headed to the crowded table in the back and was greeted with a high-five and an elaborate handshake from Shayne. He went to the counter, ordered a coffee in a huge to-go cup and took it back to the table. Someone pulled up a chair from another table and Wesley sat. Shayne directed an arm-waving tirade in Wesley's direction. Wesley nodded and gave him a thumbs-up.

Wesley looked gaunt. His usually pink-cheeked complexion had faded into a pallor. She was still studying him when he turned. She shrunk back, but he fixed his eyes on her. He got up and headed in her direction, carrying his plus-sized cup of coffee.

"What're you doing here?"

"Drinking coffee. I didn't know you hung out with Shayne Elliot."

Wesley shrugged. "Everybody hangs out with everybody here in nowhere land."

"After what he did?"

"He wasn't convicted."

"Does that matter? He's got serious problems."

Wesley glared at her. "Who doesn't?" He took a big gulp of his coffee. "Maybe I'm more sympathetic to Shayne nowadays."

"Wesley, I'm so sorry about what happened."

"It wasn't your fault."

"How's Julie?"

A dark look passed over Wesley's face. "Fine," he said. He took another sip of coffee. "He got what was coming to him."

"Mark?"

"Who else? If I was his wife—not really, you know what I mean—I'd have done the same thing. It was self-defense and at least she'll get off."

"Maybe, maybe not." Alex hesitated. She had to take this carefully. "What if she didn't do it, though? I think it was someone else and she swears it was."

"Oh, shit!" Wesley had been bringing his cup up to his mouth. At her last words, he'd missed his lips altogether, spilling coffee all over his white T-shirt.

"Let me get some napkins," Alex said.

"No!" He backed away, looking agitated. "I gotta go."

"I just have a few questions."

"I don't know anything." He continued to back away. Alex glanced to the rear of the room. Shayne Elliot was watching them.

"It'd be better if you told me what you know."

"Forget it, you're not the police," Wesley stuttered. With that, he turned and fled.

Alex left right after. As she was headed toward the door, she glanced back. Shayne Elliot was staring at her.

Despite the caffeine, she was bone-tired. She'd also not eaten recently. The lack of blood sugar, that was bad. She had to get some real food in her stomach; her head was beginning to spin. Instead of going back to her car, she turned the corner onto Main Street and headed to Stumps.

Alex spotted a seat at the counter, next to the realtor, Fred Gurkey, who was just finishing. She noticed a few stares as she sat. Hazel was over swiftly, handing Fred his check, then getting set to pour coffee for Alex.

"No. No coffee. Just water."

Meanwhile, Fred Gurkey was pulling out a credit card. "Gotta go," he said. "Late for an appointment." He watched as Hazel disappeared with his credit card. "Think I'll go up to the register." He hesitated. "Sorry about that bad business over by you."

He looked odd, like he was hiding something. Alex was getting used to this. Maybe it was a form of dementia developed by fledgling investigators. All of a sudden, everyone looked like they were hiding something.

Fred fidgeted, crushed a real-estate flyer he'd been holding in his fist. He nodded toward Hazel, who was at the register. "Gotta go." He stared at her, his lips working with unspoken revelations. Or so she was imagining. She was so hungry that she hardly cared.

As soon as Fred was gone, she took up the menu. She was definitely in need of nourishment. Maybe then the delusions of hidden secrets among the populace would fade and she could concentrate on nailing Shayne. Unless the whole town was in on a conspiracy with him, she had to focus on Shayne.

She had just ordered a bowl of split pea soup, an English muffin and a salad with blue cheese dressing, when Bill Hanson plunked down on the stool vacated by Fred Gurkey.

"Remember me? Wesley's coach at the junior college? We met the first time you came in here with Jack."

"I remember you."

"What a mess up there. How's Jack holding up?"

"Not great."

He picked up the menu and inspected it. "Didn't plan on this, did you, coming to stay up here?"

He seemed straightforward and concerned, not a meddler. She thought about his question.

"I feel more bad than sorry. Like I dragged my bad karma along with me." As soon as she said it, she felt a surge of embarrassment. Not just for referring to karma, but for the personal disclosure to a near stranger.

Bill lifted his eyes from the menu and gazed at her. "Tell you what," he said. "I believe in karma. I think a person pays on some level when they don't do right. Who says we don't come back over and over until we get it right? Maybe next time—if I don't treat my players right—I'll come back as a greyhound chasing a fake rabbit around a track."

Hazel was standing over them. "And I'll come back as a stiff who asks for everything special-order and never leaves a tip." She placed a tureen-sized bowl of soup in front of Alex and took Bill's order. After inspecting Alex's soup, he ordered the same, with sourdough toast and a side of fries.

"I was using karma more like an expression," Alex said. She sniffed at her soup, thick with ham chunks and diced carrots and potatoes. Her stomach growled.

"Eat," Bill encouraged her. "I know how you were using the term. I was a religion and philosophy major before I changed to physical education." He watched while she spooned several bites of soup into her mouth. "They make the best pea soup here—I can't tell my wife, she has a family recipe she got from her grandmother. It sucks, to tell you the truth."

"Delicious," Alex replied.

Bill drummed his fingers on the Formica. "Seen Wesley lately?"

"Just today, as a matter of fact, at Picasso's."

"I'm worried about him."

She thought back to Wesley's haggard look and nervous disposition. There was reason to be concerned.

"That chef of yours, he was a bad man," Bill said. "I hate to think what he'll come back as. Wesley and his mother needed their jobs. The Campbells and the Overlook were a source of stability for them. Getting

Julie fired, that was the bad act of a bad man."

"You know what happened with Julie and Mark?"

Bill shrugged. "It's a small town. Everyone knows Julie. It's not hard to put two and two together. And the worst part is that Wesley got the worst punishment, having to be a knight in shining armor."

Hazel arrived with Bill's food. He accepted the soup, fries and toast gratefully. He blew on a spoonful of soup and held it tentatively to his mouth. "Good."

Alex had been eating her soup forever but seemed to be making little headway. It was the largest bowl of soup she'd ever seen. She stopped and took a breath. She needed a soup intermission.

Bill grinned at her. "Wimp."

"Just wait," Alex replied. "I'm resting."

Bill whistled appreciatively, then frowned. "Julie got her license back this week, from what I heard. Maybe she'll get to living her own life now and Wesley can come back to school."

"I hope so."

True to her word, Alex finished her soup. To prove herself not a wimp, she felt compelled to order dessert. She could only handle cherry Jell-O with Cool Whip, the lightest thing on the menu. Alex had hardly ever encountered Jell-O growing up, much less Cool Whip. They fascinated her. She especially liked the kind with fruit suspended in it. It was quite sculptural.

When he was finished with his soup, Bill got the apple pie with a scoop of vanilla ice cream. He patted his stomach bulge. "Gotta start hitting the gym more."

After they'd finished their respective desserts, Hazel arrived with the checks. "Where's Jack been?" she growled. "Tell him to get his butt in here. If anyone so much as looks at him sideways, I'll kick 'em out."

"I'll tell him," Alex said, standing. She was full, but it felt good. She glanced down at Bill, about to say good-bye.

Oh, no. The delusions of widespread public confessions were returning. Bill's lips twitched; his eyes regarded her imploringly. She would ignore the delusions. Maybe they'd go away.

"See you around, Bill," she said, turning to go.

"Wait," he said urgently. "Sit down for a minute."

When she'd sat, he glanced around, then leaned toward her. "You know Pete Szabo?"

Alex blinked. "Yes, as a matter of fact, I do."

"Good boy. One of the best. Was one of my best wrestlers, although not as good as Wesley. Could have gone away on scholarship, but he always wanted to be a cop, like his father."

"Weren't Mary and Pete raised by their grandparents?"

Bill looked pained. "When the Szabo twins were nine, the parents were killed in a car crash on River Road. Head on. Hit by a drunk driver. The dad was a fine cop with the Santa Rosa department before that. The grandfather was a firefighter. Runs in the family, this public service thing." He shook his head. "Anyway, Pete and I are still close." He glanced around again.

She nodded, waiting for him to go on.

"Seems like Pete stopped Wesley a few nights ago for a busted taillight. It was around midnight. The kid had a bag on the seat next to him. He was acting so suspicious that Pete asked him what was in the bag. Wesley said it was prescription drugs that his Aunt Bev accidentally left in the car. They drove to his house, where Julie confirmed the story. They even called the aunt, woke her up. She confirmed the story. So Pete just let the whole thing go. But he doesn't like it. And I don't like it." He stared at her. "I don't like Wesley hanging around with Shayne Elliot. I think he might be getting Wesley mixed up in trouble. I'm trying to help Wesley, not hurt him. Maybe you can use this information to get to Shayne."

"Yes," Alex said. "Thank you."

She left Stumps with a surge of confidence. There were secrets out there and people willing to reveal them. She'd get Shayne, if she persisted. She was sure of that now.

TWENTY-FOUR

That evening, she left a message on Julie and Wesley's answering machine. When Wesley didn't return her call, she tried again the next morning. And again a few hours later.

Finally, she called Jeffrey and asked for Wesley's address.

"You're still meddling in police business, I see."

"From a certain point of view. Don't nag. It won't accomplish anything. Just give me the address." She wrote down the street and house number and was about to demand directions but Jeffrey volunteered the information, apparently resigned to her meddling.

The Summerfields lived between Guerneville and Rio Nido, about two miles south of the turnoff for the Overlook. Alex nearly missed the turn for Blackbird Lane. The road sign was nearly completely obscured by hanging branches from the nearby cypress trees.

About a half-mile up the winding lane, she pulled in front of a cheaply built beige duplex whose exterior was beginning to mold. The front yard had patchy clumps of grass scattered among large expanses of mud. Toy guns, dirty nude baby dolls and Hot Wheels sat grimy and abandoned for the winter on the neighbor's side of the yard.

Wesley flung the door open after Alex's persistent pounding. After a moment spent staring at her, he shut the door in her face. She took up another round of relentless pounding.

The next-door neighbor, a henna-haired young woman with a child clinging to her skintight jeans, opened her door and peered out. Alex kept banging.

"Something wrong?" the neighbor asked.

Before Alex could answer, Wesley opened his door again.

"Is everything okay, Wesley?" the neighbor asked.

Wesley motioned Alex in. "Fine," he said to the neighbor.

The living room of the duplex was furnished cheaply but with taste, a mixture of Target and Cost Plus with a few splurged items from Macy's thrown in. The walls were filled with framed art reproductions. The selections were well-chosen museum copies, not the generic impressionists and landscapes found in shopping mall outlets.

Wesley watched her take in the room. "My mom wanted to be an art historian, but she had me instead."

It was a sad bit of self-blame and probably a lame excuse on Julie's part, but on this particular visit Alex wasn't about to get into any dysfunctional family folklore. Wesley looked worse than he had at Picasso's. His hands were trembling and he smelled like nervous sweat.

"What do you want?" he blurted out.

"Don't be rude, Wesley."

Julie had appeared from the hallway that led to the back rooms. If possible, she looked worse than Wesley. She was rail-thin and so pallid that her skin had a greenish hue. She was wearing a faded blue terrycloth bathrobe over a pair of pink pajamas with red trim.

She shuffled into the room, pushing back her unwashed hair. "Can I get you some coffee?" she asked. "We have coffee, don't we?"

"She won't be staying long, Mom," he said.

"I want coffee," Julie whined.

"I made some," Wesley admitted. "It's in the thermal carafe."

He took off for the kitchen, leaving Alex alone with Julie, who ran her fingers through her greasy hair. "I know I look like shit."

Alex nodded noncommittally.

"Wesley told me you think Jean didn't kill Mark." Julie let out a harsh laugh. "I could have killed him. I thought about it."

"Mom! Are you crazy?" Wesley came in with a tray holding three steaming cups of coffee in lovely pale yellow mugs. He'd poured cream into a small matching pitcher and put sugar cubes into a bowl with small silver tongs. "I brought you some anyway," he said to Alex, then turned to his mother. "She's looking for the killer. You don't make statements like that."

"I can if I want," Julie said petulantly. "Besides, we have alibis." She picked up the cream container and poured half its contents into her cup, added four sugar cubes, then stirred vigorously. "We were here all night together. Since we *weren't* invited to the closing party. Not that we expected to be."

"Actually, I didn't come here to ask about where you were," Alex said. "I came to ask about Shayne Elliot. Do you know where *he* was that night? Or anything else that might link him to the murder?"

"You see!" Julie almost spilled her coffee into her lap. "I told you that little shit is no good. I told you not to hang out with him."

Wesley stared at his untouched cup, gripped in two hands. He looked up, his eyes wide. "You think *Shayne* did it?"

"He's an evil punk. I warned you not to get involved with him." Julie was trembling all over by now.

"You're warning me not to get involved with losers?" Wesley replied with quiet mockery.

Alex suddenly recalled her childhood trips to stay with Jeffrey and his parents. In the middle of a visit, a comment would trigger a confrontation between her uncle and aunt, which they would leap into as though no one else was in the room, sucked up in their own private drama.

With her aunt and uncle, she had felt powerless to intercede. Now, she purposely held back. She knew from personal experience that people playing out their demons were apt to reveal more than they intended.

"I'm an adult," Wesley said with studied calm. "I can pick my own friends."

"Sex criminals? Murderers?"

"I won't get into anything with you about sex criminals. You want to start discussing some of your old boyfriends?"

"I'm your mother!"

"I have to take care of you. I have to drive you around and do your errands for you. That gives me the right to have an opinion."

"I've got my license back, don't I? I don't need you anymore."

"Sure you don't. We'll see," Wesley said.

"Yeah. We'll see, big boy. We'll see who needs who."

As though they were simultaneously waking up from a dream, Wesley and Julie noticed Alex, who was sitting and sipping her coffee. Wesley jumped up. "You have to go. I don't know anything about Shayne."

"Do you know anyone who does?" Alex persisted.

He shrugged.

"Come on, Wesley," Alex urged. "Does he have a best friend? A girlfriend?"

"He has a girlfriend." Julie piped up.

"Mom!"

"Don't protect him. He's a creep."

"I'm not protecting him."

"Then what are you doing? Just give her the name."

"No."

"*Give her the name*," Julie said authoritatively.

Wesley looked like he might cry. "Patty Westaway. She lives in Guerneville, on West Elm. She works at the stationery place."

"I'm sorry, Wesley. You have to understand, I just want to find out the truth."

A mix of emotions crossed his face. "The truth. We all know how important the truth is."

A bit of adolescent nihilism better left alone, she thought. She headed for the door with both Summerfields eyeing her. As she stepped down from the porch, she glanced over to the neighbor's. The henna-haired mother was watching her, too, peeking from behind a tattered curtain.

TWENTY-FIVE

Alex went straight to Guerneville and parked on Main Street. The stationery store, Witherspoon's, was three doors down from Stumps. In addition to paper and office supplies, it sold a smattering of tourist memorabilia, including T-shirts, paperweights, caps, shot glasses, mugs, posters and tiny statues worthy of the Pearlstones' collection.

Having been in with Jack for paper clips or staples or the like, Alex had met the owner, a woman of seventy or so named Mrs. Witherspoon, who had inherited the store from her father.

Because of the recent influx of office-supply superstores in nearby Santa Rosa, Witherspoon's was surviving on sales of the tacky tourist stuff and the generosity of the local loyalists who were willing to pay nearly double for their pens and push pins and yellow notepads. Jack, of course, was among them.

Mrs. Witherspoon recognized Alex. She was a small, agile woman dressed in black slacks and a flowered retail smock that hung loosely over her wiry torso.

"Where's Jack?" she asked.

"He's back at the lodge," Alex said.

"Is he all right? What a terrible thing."

"As good as can be expected."

Mrs. Witherspoon shook her head. "I'd like to blame the newcomers, but there's always been a wild element to this place. You know, the first homicide in Guerneville was in eighteen-seventy. It was a hot summer night and a man was shot in the heart outside a bar right here on Main Street." She tapped Alex's arm. "Well, that chef of yours deserved it, from what I hear. I don't blame the wife and I don't blame her learning how to defend herself. I say more power to women getting strong."

Alex smiled. "If I ever teach a self-defense class again, you're welcome."

"I hope you mean that, young lady. I won't be condescended to." Mrs. Witherspoon smiled back. "I was getting bored with tai chi. I might just take you up on that. Anyway, what can I get for you?"

"I came to talk to Patty."

Alex realized she'd seen Patty in the store before, just never talked to her. Patty was a short pretty blonde with quite large breasts.

Mrs. Witherspoon leaned in and whispered, "The deputies came around asking about that Shayne last month. I keep telling her he's no good, but she won't listen. Is he in trouble again? You're helping the deputies, I see."

Alex said a silent prayer, thanking the universe for allowing Mrs. Witherspoon to invent her own explanation, which, if you pondered it, did have some element of truth.

"Yes," she said.

Mrs. Witherspoon squinted at her. "Why would you be helping them? Why would they need you?"

Alex waited. She had the feeling that Mrs. Witherspoon was going to supply all her own questions and answers.

"Like an undercover," Mrs. Witherspoon whispered. "Not suspicious." She nodded wisely. "I won't say more. I don't want to ruin your cover." She waved over at Patty. "Come here. Do you know Alex? She works at the Overlook and she's a very nice woman. She has a few questions to ask you. You can go in my office. Don't worry, I'll take care of business for a few minutes."

Patty glanced at Alex, then at Mrs. Witherspoon. "Is this about Shayne? I already told the sheriffs everything I know. Okay, he has a few problems. Why can't everyone leave him alone? He got off—he's free."

Mrs. Witherspoon grimaced. "What a nasty business."

"He's seeing a counselor," Patty said in a tired voice. "I don't want to go into the back office and I don't want to talk to her. I know what she's up to." She turned to Mrs. Witherspoon. "She's been following Shayne around. She's been bugging people about him and she isn't with the police."

With that, Patty stalked off, intercepting a rare winter tourist family with three whining children who had wandered in. The children were fingering breakable items on a glass shelf near the entrance.

"You're not helping the police?" Mrs. Witherspoon asked.

"I *am* helping them," Alex said. "They just don't know it yet."

Mrs. Witherspoon stared at her as if making an evaluation of her character. "Don't explain. I don't like Shayne, either. I'm sorry Patty won't help, but if you're not with the police, I can't make her do anything."

"I understand."

"Well, good luck, whatever you're up to. And tell Jack I want to see him in here. I miss that man."

On her way out, Alex endured a hostile stare from Patty. She didn't blame the girl. It wasn't her smartest move, coming over to the store like that. But what the hell? It wasn't like she was an expert in all this. At this point in time, she'd just have to pray that she more or less bumbled into the truth.

She was almost to her car when her cell phone rang.

"Hello?"

"Why are you doing this to me?"

She didn't recognize the voice. "Who is this?"

"The person you're stalking."

"Shayne?"

"I repeat, why are you doing this to me? I got off on the charges fair and square."

"How did you get my number?"

"How did you get my girlfriend's name?"

"I'm not afraid of you, Shayne."

"I'll bet you're not. I know you could knock the shit out of me." Shayne's voice turned nasty. "I can see you, you know. Walking down the street."

"Where are you?"

"I'm in my car, just around the corner. The red Toyota."

Alex saw him. He was in a battered Corolla, clutching a phone.

"I want to talk to you," Shayne said.

It was the middle of the day. A quiet winter day, but still there were a few street occupants, window-shopping or running errands. She walked down Main Street and turned the corner, approaching the funky Toyota.

Shayne rolled down his window. "Get in."

Alex peered into the car. It was a mess of fast-food wrappers, crumpled newspapers and empty soda cans. The seats were torn. There were no visible weapons, but there wouldn't be anything obvious.

"Do you think I'd attack you in the middle of town?" Shayne said. "And if I tried to drive, *you'd* probably kill *me*. Get in."

Alex glanced around, taking in her environment and avenues of escape and proximity to the nearest pedestrians. She opened the passenger door and pushed away a pile of crumpled candy wrappers, then slid in.

Shayne put both hands up. "See? No weapons. It's not a trap. Can you take away knives or guns?"

Alex shrugged. In fact, she could. But she wasn't going to tell him that. She sniffed. The car smelled like body odor. She glanced at Shayne more closely. He had beads of moisture at his temple. His lips were trembling. She really hoped he didn't try anything. Cars were awkward. She didn't want to hurt him badly, whatever he'd done.

"I'm not going to go through any bullshit," he burst out, his voice shaking. "You think I killed that chef, don't you?" He laughed. "I wish I did. What an asshole. But I didn't. What's the matter? Don't you think the wife did it? You taught her how."

"I have reason to believe otherwise," she said neutrally.

"Yeah? Well, just because I messed up doesn't mean I killed anyone. Okay, I have a few problems. But I'm not a murderer. I'm, like, doing anger management and"—his face reddened—"sexual counseling."

Alex waited, watching him. For some disturbing reason, she felt he was telling the truth. She felt frustrated and annoyed with herself. Maybe that was another beginning—"investigator delusion." One developed irrational sympathies for suspects if they whined with enough conviction. She needed to get a grip. Find a way to break his cover.

Shayne wiped at his temple with a sweaty palm. Then he sat up, grinning wickedly at her. "You think you're smart, but you're not. You know why?"

"No, I don't."

"Because," Shayne said in a triumphant tone, "I wasn't even in town that night, the night that jerk got murdered. How do you like that, girlfriend? Did you bother to check that out? I was visiting my grandparents in Ukiah for their anniversary and about a hundred people, including my parents, can vouch for that. You're pretty stupid, you know that? I don't care if you beat me to a pulp, I can't help saying it. Like, isn't that the first thing you check, the alibi?"

Alex's heart sank. "Why didn't the detectives ask you? I never saw a report about you."

"They never got around to interviewing me. They had his wife arrested and they didn't care anymore about anybody else, including me."

That was it. Shayne was right. She'd blown it. She was stupid and deluded and a lousy detective. Good-bye, efforts on Jean's behalf.

But Shayne wasn't done. "But maybe you're right. Maybe the wife didn't do it. Maybe somebody else did it, came in after her and all. It's possible. Very possible. In fact I know it is." He shot that wicked grin at her again.

"What do you mean?" she asked.

"Do you really want to know?"

"Of course I do."

"I don't think you do."

"Don't fuck around with me," Alex growled. She was descending into her worst street language. Nice. But the situation called for it.

"I don't think you do because it's easy to blame the sicko who everyone hates. But what if you have to blame one of your friends? That's all you have left if I didn't do it, one of your nice friends up there at the Overlook who you love. Very sweet."

"Shayne, do you know something?"

"I just suspect. A little evidence, but enough to suspect."

"What is it?"

Now Shayne laughed. "I'm not going to tell you. I don't want to get involved. The last thing I'm doing is going to court, for any reason. Screw that. I'll never go into that Hall of Justice again." He bent down and picked up a crumpled grocery receipt. He smoothed it out and picked up a pen, then scribbled something and handed it to her. "Talk to this dude. He's Wesley's best friend. I wrote down where he lives."

Alex took the scrap of paper and twisted to get out of the car. As she turned her back to Shayne, he reached out and gripped her shoulder. In an instant, she had the hand pinned. She rotated it so that his arm was incapacitated. She reached her other arm up, ready to tear out his windpipe if she had to.

A feeling of repulsion washed over her. Shayne had a leering expression of pleasure on his face. "I love it," he purred. "Hurt me."

Alex dropped his hand and jumped from the car.

"Keep up that counseling," she said, slamming the car door.

TWENTY-SIX

Unless Shayne's grandparents, parents and ninety-six other people were lying, Shayne couldn't be the killer. She didn't like it, but there was nothing she could do, was there? That left Jean or probably someone else from the Overlook.

Alex went back to her Lexus on Main Street, but she didn't go anywhere. She wondered if it might be time to drop the whole thing. Jean was likely the guilty party. Yet, Alex thought about her encounter with Shayne. He might have been trying to mess with her, but was he implying that Wesley was the real suspect?

Wesley's alibi was his mother. Alex knew from watching her crime shows that the weakest alibis were provided by people close to the suspect, especially relatives.

Shayne was absolutely right about one thing. The whole detective thing had suddenly become less compelling, now that she was possibly about to investigate those she was fond of. Her reverie was interrupted by a yuppie woman in a monstrous black Cadillac Escalade honking at her, demanding her parking space. Alex pulled out and flashed a peace sign at the angry-faced woman.

When she got home, she tried the phone number Shayne had given her. It was disconnected. He'd also scribbled an address. She could go back to town and check out the address, but she was feeling lethargic.

She slumped down on her couch and felt the old anxiety and dread coming back. Why couldn't it have been Shayne, if it was anybody? She really should drop it. But she couldn't get the image of Jean out of her mind, pleading with her to find the real killer.

What if she stopped? Jean would be convicted. The real killer, if there was one, would be free. But stopping was more than that. A twinge of anxiety fluttered in her stomach. If she stopped, where would she be? *Face it*. She'd pried open a Pandora's box of emotions and hidden motivations. That was the thing with those boxes. Once opened, they refused to be closed.

She'd try to find Wesley's friend. But it would have to wait until tomorrow. She picked up the television section of the newspaper and was relieved to find many crime shows due to play over the next few hours. She had a bottle of excellent Cabernet Franc that Jeffrey had bestowed upon her. And a frozen pepperoni pizza. Those things available, the rest of her day and evening was planned.

That morning, already Wednesday and time running short, she was well aware, as she drove to Rio Nido and turned onto a small lane and pulled in the driveway of a moldy former resort whose cottages had been converted into cheap housing for students and various others with low incomes.

"Are you Matthew?"

A boy in his late teens, dressed in a pair of torn jeans, answered the door at the address Shayne had given her. Despite the chill, he was bare-chested and barefoot. He was just short of six feet and muscular, with curly brown hair and a gold hoop earring in his right ear. "That's me."

"Can I talk to you for a couple minutes?"

"Depends. What're you selling?" His tone was mildly curious and friendly.

"Nothing. It's about Wesley," Alex replied.

"Wesley?" His tone turned guarded. "What about him?"

"I was told he's your best friend."

"Who told you that?"

"I'm afraid I can't say."

"Who are you, lady?"

She didn't have much to lose, so she said, "Shayne Elliot told me." She wanted to see his reaction to the mention of Shayne's name.

A snort of disgust arose from the boy. "Wesley and I *used* to be best friends. Lately, it's been tough. I mean, I still love the guy—we've known each other since we were in, like, kindergarten, but there's only so much a person can take, you know what I mean? He hanging around with Elliot now? That's a drag, man. Elliot's a sick loser."

"Can I come in for just a few minutes?" Alex persisted.

He eyed her warily. "Are you a social worker?"

Alex was realizing the downside of sleuthing. It seemed to necessitate quite a bit of deception. "Something like that," she said.

"Are you trying to help Wesley?" His tone lightened. Like Wesley, the boy had an open, friendly face. He inspected her. "They're making social workers a lot more user-friendly these days." He backed up and gestured for her to come in. "I got into a little trouble when I was thirteen. My social worker was real scary-looking. Anyway, she sort of saved me. Now I like social workers. Sorry, I don't mean to be sexist about her looks."

"No problem."

"Want anything? All we have is Mountain Dew right now. Or milk, but it's probably sour."

"No, thanks." Alex removed a worn purple Frisbee from a green plaid chair and sat.

Matthew cleared debris from the couch until he'd made enough of a spot to sit. "So, what's up with Wesley?"

"I was hoping you could tell me."

"I work part-time at the Safeway. Last time I saw him, he was shopping, probably because his load of a mother was too drunk or stoned to do it."

Alex was surprised at the anger in the boy's voice. "When was that?"

"A few days ago. Yeah, like Sunday. I only work weekends, I'm taking a full load at the JC. Premed."

"Premed? That's impressive."

"Pretty good for a guy with a burnout meth addict for a father and a mother who died of an overdose."

Alex suddenly understood Matthew's willingness to express his disgust with Wesley's mother.

"My family is total white trash," Matthew continued. "They don't know any better. Wesley's mom, she's from this rich family. I have no respect for her or for her sister. Now Wesley's getting fucked up, too. But you're trying to help him?"

Alex's heart hurt. "Yes," she lied.

Matthew sat, hunched over, rubbing his fists together. Then he straightened up. "I wouldn't say anything, unless I thought it would help him."

"I understand," she said.

Matthew picked up the purple Frisbee Alex had tossed onto the dirty carpet and tossed it through the doorway into the kitchen. It hit a glass jar on a counter near the sink, sending the jar crashing onto the linoleum floor. "He begged her not to drive when she was high, but she would anyway. Then she got busted and he dropped out of school to take care of her. That's when I kind of gave up on him. Not completely, because I'm not like that. But, you know, I have to stay concentrated on myself and my studies so I don't wind up like my old man or my mom. I have to visualize success, know what I mean?"

"Yes, I do."

He looked at his watch. "Gotta go. I'll be late for anatomy." He reached for a pair of worn Nike basketball shoes and shoved his large feet into them. "Did you know the foot has twenty-six bones? That's a lot of bones."

"Please," Alex said. "Finish what you were saying about Wesley."

He frowned at her. "Think about it. How is his mother going to get her stuff if she can't drive?"

"Her stuff?"

"Don't be lame. Her *stuff*, like her drugs. What kind of social worker are you?"

"Wesley was picking up drugs for her?" A buzzer went off in her head. She remembered Bill Hanson's story of Wesley getting stopped by Pete Szabo late one evening.

"It's the sister, Bev, isn't it?" she asked. "She's giving Julie drugs. When Julie couldn't drive, she was sending Wesley to his aunt's house to pick up prescription drugs for her."

"Pretty twisted, huh? Late-night runs so the husband doesn't find out. The two sisters in this little drug gang together." Matthew jumped up. "I really gotta go."

Alex stood. "Thanks, Matthew."

"Forget it. You just find a way to help him, okay?"

"I will."

Matthew grabbed a Raiders sweatshirt from the floor and a backpack and ran out the door. "Shut the door after you," he called.

So Wesley was making drug runs for his mother. Did that make him a killer? Not necessarily. But it did have him driving around late at night with ugly motives. And he was certainly a tall person whom she'd seen wearing the popular teenage dark overcoat. As to motive, he had every reason to hate Mark. She was excited and yet miserable. Almost torn in half.

But wasn't that the nature of personal growth according to someone like Carl Jung? The ability to hold conflicting thoughts and emotions simultaneously without going crazy? Something like that. Anyway, she didn't have time for any more philosophizing.

TWENTY-SEVEN

Just before noon, she called the Guerneville substation of the Sonoma County Sheriff's Department and was told that Pete Szabo was out sick for the day. The receptionist refused to give her Pete's home address, so—being the brilliant detective that she was—she looked it up in the Sonoma County phone book.

After a quick lunch, she hopped in her car and drove down to Graton, a small village between Sebastopol and Forestville. Pete lived down a long gravel driveway off Mill Station Road.

When she arrived at the end of the drive, she found him chopping wood in his front yard, wearing a blue plaid shirt and a pair of worn carpenter's pants. The whole situation was very scenic, she thought. Good-looking man swinging axe outside rustic cabin with smoke rising from its chimney. A yellow Lab barked at her car.

Pete glanced up. She had to smile at his look of surprise. He dropped the axe and wiped his hands on his pants, then headed down the patchy lawn toward her car.

He didn't look exactly put off. In fact, she thought he almost looked pleased to see her. Good. She hated manipulating with female wiles, but she could wing it if she had to. She climbed from the car. The yellow Lab lumbered over and tried to sniff her crotch.

"Feather! Cut it out." Pete shook his head. "Don't worry, he won't hurt you. He's a great dog. That's his worst habit."

"Feather?"

"One of my friends' kids begged to name him that," Pete explained. "I didn't have the heart to say no."

Alex bent down to pet the slobbering Lab. "I never had a dog. I had a cat. Her name was Harriet, a little tabby stray who wasn't afraid of anything and had a terrible temper. I found her when I was ten years old on the side of the road and I begged to keep her. She wasn't supposed to come into the house—my parents didn't like the idea of house pets. But I used to sneak her into my room at night and put her back outside early in the morning. She came to live with me here in California after I left college. She adored being an inside cat and lived to be twenty-one years old, just died two years ago." Alex felt a lump in her throat. "A little more than a year before my husband died."

To her surprise, Pete's eyes filled with tears. "I'm so sorry," he said with deep feeling.

Had she dropped into some parallel universe of nice men today? Between Matthew and Pete, she was beginning to think so. Might as well enjoy it while she could. God only knew, there were enough not-so-nice males out there.

"I need to talk to you," she said.

"I didn't think you tracked me down to talk about your cat." Pete frowned at her. It was an almost obligatory-looking frown. "Mary told me what you're up to. Listen, Alex, you know I can't tell you anything that's confidential. I can tell you what's already public information, but then why would you need to ask me?"

"I just wanted your opinion as an expert," she said.

Pete hesitated. "I have opinions. I don't know how expert they are." He gestured to his cabin—a pleasant log structure with bright blue trim. "Okay, at least we can get out of the chill for a few minutes."

She followed him in.

"Coffee?" he asked once they'd entered the pine-paneled living area. The room was heated by a glowing wood stove in a corner. She noted the worn leather furniture and intricately patterned Navajo throw rugs.

Alex laughed.

"What?" Pete asked, glancing around.

"No, it's the coffee offer. I was thinking of Detective Green. I'll bet he never refuses a cup."

"Oh, you mean Mr. Caffeine? The guy's a nut case by the end of his shifts." He made a cup shape with his hand. "Anyway?"

"I'd love some."

While his master was gone, Feather slunk over, eyeing her crotch with intense doggie fascination. She glared at him and he wagged his tail guiltily.

Pete came back with two enormous mugs. There was already a set of cream and sugar containers on the table in front of the couch.

"I mostly eat and drink in here when I'm alone." He made an exaggerated macho face. "Not that I'm alone much."

"I'm sure you're not," she said, smiling flirtatiously. *Oh, brother.* So easy getting men on a certain track, she thought. *But we're all biological creatures, aren't we?*

Pete dropped his gaze and reached for a spoon. He dumped four heaping loads of sugar into his mug. He struggled not to look pleased.

Alex sipped her coffee. "Good."

"You know it's against the law to make bad coffee in Northern California," he said. "Except for the poor and elderly. And my sister. She can't cook and she can't make coffee."

"I'll bet your sister doesn't appreciate comments like that," she said. "She seems so serious."

"Mary? She comes off uptight at first. But she's got her other sides, believe me."

"I'd love to see them. I like her."

"Really? She thinks you hate her."

Alex blinked. "Not at all. Next time I talk to her, I'll—"

"Don't *tell* her I told you," Pete said sternly. "Me and my big mouth."

"I won't say a word," she said quickly. The last thing she wanted was to discourage Pete's big mouth. She was desperate enough to bat her eyelashes at him. She was embarrassed for herself. "It's about Wesley, the night you stopped him and found the drugs."

Pete froze, coffee mug in midair. "Who told you that?"

Alex considered. She hadn't made any promises about confidentiality to Bill Hanson. So she told Pete about her discussion with Wesley's former coach at Stumps. Pete listened, nodding.

"Bad business for a good kid," he said when she'd finished.

"Do you believe the explanation?"

"That the sister left them in the car?" Pete sighed. "Okay, this is just an opinion."

"I understand."

"I think the sister is giving some of her meds to Wesley's mother. Look, she's the wife of a doctor, she's got chronic pain, you add it all up, and she's got access to a lot of good stuff. Pretty picture, huh? Wesley going to Santa Rosa to pick up for his mother."

Alex nodded. "It probably wasn't the first time, was it?"

"Almost definitely not. Julie was on DUI suspension for six months, wasn't she?"

"Something like that."

"You know what I predict?" Pete asked.

"What's that?"

"She's got her license back. I give it a couple weeks at best before she gets herself in trouble again. We make bets about her type at the station. How soon until we have to arrest them or scrape them off the road again."

A loud cracking sound, like a gunshot, rang out suddenly, causing them both to leap up and adopt defensive postures. Feather let out a few obligatory defensive barks. It was only a log bursting into deep flame in the wood stove. Alex took a deep breath to settle her rapid heartbeat and sat back down. She spoke up quickly, before the interruption caused Pete to think twice about his loose tongue. "Let me ask you this . . ." She paused. "Just opinion, okay?"

"Okay." Pete sat down, looking guarded.

"The sisters backed him up. So, essentially they lied for him."

"Right."

"Let's say he'd gone out one night on a run like this and something happened that night. If he said he was home the whole time, his mother would probably lie for him, wouldn't she?"

"Where are you going with this?" Pete asked. "If you know something that you should be telling us, meaning the authorities, I can't answer more questions."

"But—"

He stood, looking enormously conflicted. "I'm sorry, I can't."

Poor Pete. He looked as forlorn as Feather being reprimanded for crotch-sniffing. "I have a lot of wood to split."

As Alex drove down the twisting driveway, she caught a glance through her rearview mirror of Pete and Feather standing on the porch. Pete was waving and Feather was wagging his tail. Honest to God, in a contest for too damned cute, they'd both have to win.

She felt surrounded by nice men and friendly dogs all of a sudden, including both Jack and Pete. That was great, as far as friends went. But, to be honest, Alex was more fascinated by cats and men like Stacy. Creatures with an edge.

TWENTY-EIGHT

When Alex returned home, Jack was headed up the driveway to her place. She honked at him. He came up to her window, looking dour.

"Busy?" he asked.

"No." She could barely suppress a smile. "Come up and have coffee."

"Something funny?" Jack asked.

"It's a coffee joke. I'll explain another time."

Jack was quiet the entire time she made the coffee. He sat at her little table, staring out the window.

When she sat next to him, he said, "Marge and I are retiring."

"What?"

"Nice community in Arizona. Better than the Florida one Chris wanted to send us to. Fred Gurkey found it for us." Jack sniffed and his Adam's apple wobbled. "This is one of the hardest choices I've ever made."

"I'll miss you," she said. "Very much."

"I'll miss you, too," he said.

Alex slipped her hand into his. "Don't be hard on yourself. You told *me* that, remember?"

Jack squeezed her hand. "It's not the same. I can't explain, but it's not." He jumped up, letting go of her hand. "Talk to you later," he croaked, rushing out the door and slamming it after him.

She couldn't blame him and Marge for jumping ship given the enormous effort it was going to take getting the Overlook on track again. Still, it seemed odd. Why suddenly let the recent obstacles defeat them? They'd weathered all the other ones.

She decided to let her questions rest. She knew what Jeffrey would say—that she was letting some weird Freudian sense of abandonment influence her judgment.

Not ten minutes after Jack left, the phone rang. It was Jeffrey.

"Want to go to a movie with me and Max? We're going to The Hut tomorrow night."

"What's playing?"

"It doesn't matter! Some foreign nonsense. But won't it be good to go out? We can eat popcorn and try to feel normal. I use the term loosely, of course."

She awoke the next morning intending to continue her sleuthing, but could hardly get out of bed. It was Thursday; time was really running short now. She realized with a jolt how profoundly tired she felt. So she went back to bed and spent almost the entire day reading several older copies of the *New Yorker* that she'd collected from the lodge in the weeks before the Mark Heller incident. By the time she drove over to Jeffrey's place, she was feeling more rested and calm than she'd felt in a while— and at least marginally prepared to try and feel "normal."

"I'm in despair!" Jeffrey wailed. "I feel like an intellectual failure. I didn't understand a minute of that film."

"Jeffrey, it was only a movie," Alex said.

She, Jeffrey and Max were traveling down River Road, crawling along in a nasty storm. The windshield wipers on Max's ten-year-old Plymouth Caravan struggled to keep up with the deluge, feebly swiping at the rain thundering against the glass.

They were returning to Guerneville from the little town north on the river, Monte Rio, having experienced a "normal" evening out, at the local art movie house, a large converted Quonset hut that served organic popcorn and politically correct espresso.

"I don't know how you can feel anything, including despair," Max objected, his hands gripping the steering wheel tightly, his eyes focused on what he could see of the road. "I didn't have a clue what was happening. I don't think anything was."

"You're the one who paints purple sheep. You should be able to comprehend abstract film," Jeffrey argued. "Isn't one supposed to react subliminally or something? I mean, I feel guilty. I feel like I missed the deep meaning."

"Ever heard of the tale of the emperor's new clothes?" Max threw out. "That flick was a regally bare-assed imposter."

"Maybe that was the point. To confuse us," Jeffrey retorted.

"I'm confused," Alex said.

In fact, she was more distracted than confused, trying to ignore the possibility that they were going to coast off the road and plunge into the river. The rain was slapping the van, sending it shuddering from side to side.

"Max, don't go too heavy into the analogies. Look at how you're having to drive. Do you want these to be your last words?" Jeffrey said.

"You brought it up," Max said.

"I brought up my emotions," Jeffrey countered.

"I was just alluding to the fact that some art is empty," Max said. "Like the nude emperor. So the audience reads its own state of mind into some nonsense and thinks it's profound."

"And what if the filmmakers did that on purpose?"

"Boys, boys." Alex stopped them. "Look at my knuckles. I'm gripping the seat for my life. Can't this wait until we get back? If we get back."

"Isn't this fun?" Jeffrey cried. "Babble and perish in the dark and stormy night!"

Strangely, it was. Alex was feeling nicely distracted and safe, at least emotionally, with Max and Jeffrey's couple-bickering. The physical perils were another story, but even those were forcing her to be in the moment.

They managed to reach Parker Hill Road in one piece, then climbed the winding road to the cottage. They made a run for the porch, aiming for the blurry porch light, getting lashed with rain while the wind shook the branches of the surrounding trees.

Soon, Max had a nice fire going in the fireplace. Jeffrey was in the kitchen making hot toddies.

"Will there be floods?" she asked Max.

"A few more of these heavy rains too close together and there might be trouble, from what the old-timers say."

Jeffrey came into the living room with three brandy snifters, each with a healthy amount of warmed amber liquid. "Rémy Martin."

Max accepted a glass, raised it to his nose and sniffed. "Delightful."

"Nothing but the best for my closest people," Jeffrey said, holding up his snifter. "Here's to better times."

They drank to their toast, then sat silently for a moment, letting the alcohol warm their stomachs and infiltrate their bloodstreams.

"Jeffrey told me you're playing detective," Max said.

"I told Jean I'd help her," Alex said, although Jeffrey was making faces at her to shut up.

"You really think she didn't do it?" Max asked. He rubbed his finger around the rim of his glass.

"I'm almost positive she didn't."

"Who did then?"

"I don't know. I suspect."

"Interesting," Max murmured. He turned to Jeffrey. "If Alex's trail led to me, would you stand by my side?"

"Max!" Jeffrey exploded. "I can't believe you. This is not the time for mind games. Alex really is looking for the real killer."

Max downed the rest of his large toddy and stood. "Anyone besides me ready for another?"

It was obvious that Alex and Jeffrey had barely gotten started on their drinks, so Max headed to the kitchen without waiting for an answer.

"I hope you're not taking him seriously," Jeffrey said.

"He knew about your fling with Mark," Alex said.

"Alex! He didn't kill Mark."

"How do you know I didn't?" Max said, returning with another large toddy.

"You wouldn't be playing around like this."

"I might," Max responded. "Ask Alex. Might be trying to outsmart her. Or just acting stupid. Most criminal acts are stupid, committed by people acting stupidly."

"Max, enough," Alex said firmly. "I know what you're doing. Punishing Jeffrey. You hate when men abuse him. Now you're doing it. I won't tolerate that. I'll leave and take Jeffrey with me if I have to."

"You're right, Alex." Max sank onto the couch and took Jeffrey's hand. I'm sorry, honey."

Jeffrey sighed. "Back to couple's counseling?"

"I'm not that sorry," Max said, grinning. He turned to Alex. "I didn't kill him. But I could have. So could a lot of people, as I'm sure you're discovering. I don't envy you. I don't know why you're driven to do this, although I can speculate, but I'm pretty sure that when you find the killer, you'll find you won't feel any better."

"Don't listen to him," Jeffrey interjected. "He's such a skeptic."

"I'm nothing of the sort," Max replied.

"Enough!" Alex raised her hands to her ears, covering them. "I have to go. No more babble for tonight."

The bedside phone rang at two a.m. She hadn't gotten home until midnight.

"Hello?" she said drowsily.

"It's Wesley. You have to come back to my house."

"Is everything all right?"

"If it was, would I be calling you?"

"I meant . . . are you hurt . . . is anyone—"

The phone went dead.

As soon as she pulled in front of the Summerfields' duplex on Blackbird Lane, the door opened. He waved her into the living room.

A chair lay toppled on its side, a glass broken on the wooden floor, shards lying in a pool of reddish-brown liquid.

"Where's Julie?" Alex asked.

"Strangled in the bedroom."

Alex blanched.

"I'm kidding." Wesley shrugged. "It's what you were thinking." He went over to the toppled chair and righted it. "I'm going to get something to pick up that glass."

Alex glanced down the hall that led to the bedrooms. Where *was* Julie?

Wesley returned with a broom and dustpan. He cleaned up the broken glass, then looked up. "Want coffee?" He grinned feebly at her, his look an oddly touching mix of despair and irony. "I have a new dark blend from Sumatra."

"Wesley," Alex said, frustrated, "what's going on?"

"You're so smart, you tell me." Wesley went over to the couch and slumped back, stretching his long legs out onto the coffee table.

"This is no time for guessing games."

Wesley glanced at his watch. "It is time for a game. It's called The Waiting Game." He stood up. "I make the first bet. I'll bet we have time for coffee. You don't want to miss this Sumatra blend, believe me."

A few minutes later, he returned with the coffee and went back to the couch.

"Have much do you have on me already?" he asked.

Alex's mouth dropped open.

"Enough to go to the sheriff? Probably not." He sipped at his coffee. "Try it," he urged. "It's got nearly zero bitterness."

"Where's Julie?" Alex asked. "Does she need help?"

Wesley shrugged. "That's the game, Alex."

"I don't understand."

"Naturally. I haven't explained. I'm not going to either unless you try my Sumatra blend and rate it among all the coffees you've been drinking while you've chased everywhere trying to track down Mark's killer."

She was wondering if Wesley had gone over the edge. She was inspecting the room for anything she could grab to use as a weapon if she needed it. In the meantime, she took a sip of coffee. "Very smooth," she said. "The best one yet."

"Thanks."

"Now—"

"All right. All right." Wesley sat up. "The name of the game is Waiting for Julie." He pointed to his watch. "At one a.m., Julie, who got her license back, drove away. Now Julie can run her own errands again. Isn't that nice?"

"Where'd she go?"

"You tell me."

"She went to her sister's to pick up drugs."

He waved his arm around the room. "And?"

"You had a fight. You didn't want her to go."

"And?"

"I don't know."

"Come on, think."

Alex thought. "Was she high already?"

"Naturally," Wesley said. "The roads?"

"Terrible," Alex said. "Wet and slippery. Poor visibility."

"Now put it together."

Alex's stomach sank. "Why didn't you call the sheriff?"

"That wouldn't stop it. We have to play the game to the end. She's going to crash the car. What we don't know is how badly she'll be hurt." The control in Wesley's face began to crumble. Tears slid down his cheeks. "I can't protect her anymore," he said between gulps of air. "I've done too much and it only makes it worse. It's like quicksand."

"Mark?" Alex asked. "Did you do something to him, trying to help Julie?"

Wesley took a deep, wet breath. Before he could speak, the phone rang. He jumped up and managed to spill what remained of his coffee onto his white T-shirt. Wesley ran over to the phone, dabbing at his chest. He listened and jotted something down on a piece of paper.

"Okay, I'll be there," he said and hung up. He turned to her, his arms hanging at his sides. His entire chest was stained with a large brown blotch of Sumatra blend.

"Where is she?" Alex asked.

"Memorial Emergency. Just a few scratches and bruises, but the car is pretty bad. I better get going." He picked up a wrinkled napkin from the counter and dabbed at his chest with it. "I went there to talk to him about giving my mother her job back. I had to go to Bev's anyway. I couldn't get the Overlook out of my mind. So I decided to go up there, knew he might be there working late. Jean was just leaving. Mark was already pissed. He said some really bad things about my mother. *Really* bad things, Alex. I hit him. A karate chop to the temple. I saw it on the video you gave my mother."

"Wesley, he was hit twice. He was dragged to the freezer."

"I know. I watched the news like everyone else. I didn't do that."

"Why didn't you go to the sheriff?" Alex asked.

"I had to protect *her*. So no one would find out about the drugs, about her and her sister." Wesley sighed. "Look, I gotta go."

"You think someone came in after you."

"I told you. I didn't kill him, so someone definitely came in after me." He paused. "Look, I don't want to go pointing any fingers, but Mark and Astrid, they were always huddling in corners, whispering about stuff."

Alex thought back to Jeffrey's allusions to funny business between Mark and Astrid. "What stuff? Did you overhear anything?"

"No. But I don't think it was about sex." He smiled grimly. "I hoped it was. Maybe then he'd stop trying to screw my mother. But I know when I see two people doing the sex vibe thing and they weren't."

"You think Astrid killed Mark?"

"I don't know who killed Mark, except it wasn't me and it wasn't Jean. I'm just telling you something weird I saw. Look, I really gotta go."

"Let me drive you," Alex said.

Wesley grabbed a rain slicker from the coat stand. "No."

"Wesley?" Alex asked.

"Yeah?"

"Can I ask you a favor?"

"What?"

"Don't tell anyone what you did just yet."

"Okay, whatever."

"Are you sure I can't drive you?"

"No," Wesley said. "You better go get some sleep. Sounds like you're going to be busy chasing murderers tomorrow."

TWENTY-NINE

As soon as she got back to her place, Alex called Mary Szabo. It was 5:00 a.m.

"Hello?" said a groggy voice.

"Mary?"

"No, Kim. Who's this?"

"It's Alex Pope. It's important. I know it's late. Or early. I'm sorry."

There was a brief silence, then another groggy voice came on the line. "Alex?"

"Can you get a continuation? I know it's last-minute, but it's critical."

"A continuance? The prelim is on Monday morning. It's Friday. There are procedures I have to follow for a ten-fifty, which I don't have time for."

"But is it impossible for you to ask for one?"

"No, but it's unlikely that it'll work. And, to even consider trying, I need to have a damned good reason. Do you have one for me?"

"Yes, but I can't tell you what it is yet."

"Alex, do you hear yourself? I have rules I have to follow."

"I was married to a lawyer," Alex said. "I know about working rules to your advantage."

"That's done with good ammunition, which I don't have." Mary moaned. "You have to give me something to work with. Please."

"What if I could provide you with someone who could testify that Jean was telling the truth?"

A silence ensued. Alex suspected that Mary was startled into wordlessness.

"Would that be good enough?" Alex prompted.

"Who is it?" Mary asked.

"I can't say."

"Alex!"

"Tell them you have some new evidence, but you need a little more time to substantiate it. Get me a little more time," she pleaded.

"It's not that simple. Normally a request to continue needs to be served to appropriate parties, in this case the district attorney, two days before the hearing. It's Friday, as we've established."

"That's the normal rule," Alex persisted. "How do you bend it? My husband always said the legal system was invented to be bent. At least in this case it's being bent to save an innocent person."

There was another silence. Alex could imagine Mary in her pajamas— or whatever she did or didn't sleep in—mulling over the situation. The silence lasted perhaps thirty seconds but seemed like forever.

"The D.A. owes me a big favor," Mary said at last. "If I can get him to agree to approach the judge with me today during the judge's calendar, we might be able to work something out."

"She didn't do it, Mary. I can prove it and find the killer to boot. I just need a little more time."

"You know, even if we went ahead with the preliminary, we could work on this in the discovery phase—"

"Just give me the weekend. We can end this now."

"All right. All right."

"Thanks. Thanks so much."

At exactly eight, which seemed a decent time, Alex called Astrid. It was not a pleasant conversation. Astrid was just short of rude. With a great deal of persuading, however, she agreed to see Alex that morning.

It had finally stopped raining. On the radio during Alex's drive to Astrid's place, the announcer listed flooded areas, along with a few mudslides in Rio Nido. The river was two feet short of the Guerneville Bridge.

When she drove through town, Alex spotted flood-watchers crowded on the bridge, watching the water rise to potential disaster level. She was tempted to stop, drawn like the rest to see Nature threatening despite all attempts at human control. But she was too busy pursuing the threats of human nature despite all attempts at control, so she had driven on.

Astrid was tight-mouthed and polite, drawing Alex into the cheery living room filled with sunshine. Through the windows, Alex could see the sun's rays refracting brightly on the dampness. The entire world seemed bathed in crystal light. It felt like a good omen. She needed a good omen.

"I have a few more questions," Alex began.

"I told you everything I know about Shayne Elliot."

"I'm afraid it isn't possible for Shayne to have killed Mark."

Astrid's eyes widened. "And you still think it wasn't Jean?"

"I know it wasn't Jean."

"Why haven't you gone to the police? I'm not sure I should be answering your questions." Astrid stood up, wringing her hands. "Is it Jeffrey? Is that why you're taking this on and not going to the authorities? I told you what I know about Mark and Jeffrey. I told you everything."

"Astrid," Alex said, "I know you're hiding something."

Astrid dropped her face into her hands and began to sob. Alex waited, infused with a sense of triumph mixed with remorse. She *was* getting good. Tearing down people she knew, using their weaknesses to get them to the sobbing point. Nice.

"I feel like such a traitor," Astrid said, her words barely intelligible through her clutched hands. She looked up, her face pale and tear-stained. "It's so absurd for you to think I would kill him. You can't imagine how absurd."

Alex thought it was time for a little well-placed honesty. "I don't know if you killed him. I do know you're hiding something."

Astrid smiled wanly. "It hardly matters anymore if I am, does it?" She went over to a pretty pine hutch. From a drawer, she removed a rolled piece of paper. She removed the rubber band and handed the paper to Alex, who unfurled it.

"It's a drawing of a restaurant," Alex said. "A little bistro, it looks like."

"My restaurant," Astrid said. "Mine and Mark's."

Alex looked up at her. "You and Mark were leaving the Overlook to start your own place."

"Mark hated the Overlook. He barely tolerated Chris, who he thought was a greedy incompetent fool, and he couldn't stand the father, who he thought was a deluded, incompetent fool. But he knew he could establish a reputation up here at the Overlook quickly, then he and I could move on. We could become wine country celebrities. Mark didn't want Jeffrey to be a part of the new place."

"How soon were you leaving?" Alex asked.

"We already had a realtor in Santa Rosa who we'd sworn to secrecy. He was lining up a place for us in Healdsburg."

"Healdsburg? Wouldn't the rent have been very expensive?"

Astrid shrugged. "We were using my money and the money of some wealthy friends of mine. I have a lot more money and rich friends than I have talent. Mark and I made good partners."

She seemed to read the aversion on Alex's face, which Alex had been trying very hard to suppress.

"I understand how you probably feel about Mark. He was a manipulator and a bully. I'm not an idiot. I saw his bad points. But I thought I could provide him with some balance." Astrid sighed. "So, you see, I lost everything when he was killed." Tears rolled down her cheeks. "I miss him. My life feels incomplete without him. You lost a husband— you know how hollow a person can feel. Hollow. Yet hurting, how is it possible? A shell of a person who still suffers. Why are we attracted to certain men? Clever men. Talented men. Why does it hurt so much when they're gone?"

When Alex should have been her most clear-headed, Astrid's words were distracting her, poking at her insides. *Loss, loss, loss,* her gut was screaming. *Make her shut up,* a voice cried inside her. *Run! Give all this up and get away!*

Astrid nodded wisely. "You can't win here, can you? It's simply a matter of who, among the candidates, you'd be less tormented to catch. And you can't leave it alone, can you? Your own demons are driving you." She stood again and went to the hutch, this time retrieving a business card. "But you won't stop. Here's a little lead. I'm not sure if it'll help, but as they say, leave no log unturned."

"Stone," Alex offered.

"Excuse me?"

"It's 'Leave no stone unturned.'"

Astrid shrugged. "I am still a little inaccurate with your American clichés." She handed Alex the business card.

"Here's the realtor in Santa Rosa who helped us find the place in Healdsburg. He and Mark used to go off together without me and do some male bonding. Maybe Mark told him something."

Alex wasn't feeling very well. She'd eaten too much All-Bran for breakfast. Her intestines were gurgling. No doubt about it, she was feeling lousy. No sleep, bloated large intestine and inner demons whispering from the depths of the soul. On the other hand, the realtor had agreed to see her. She'd falsified her motives, but that was her life now. Deception, coffee and indigestion.

Steve Cochrane worked for Century 21, commercial division. He had a nice office in a five-story building on E Street in Santa Rosa, a successful-looking office with a big mahogany desk and pictures of a pretty wife and well-fed children. He was slick, but his expression was warm.

"You said you were interested in renting space for a manicure establishment?" Steve asked.

Alex held up her bitten cuticles. "I lied, Mr. Cochrane."

The realtor burst out laughing. "Oh, no! Call me Steve. What is it? You really want to open an adult bookstore? A greasy doughnut shop? Don't worry. I've seen it all."

"Actually, I just had a few questions," she said.

She bet Steve Cochrane was a great salesman. He obviously went with the flow with his potential clients, which would be everyone unless proven otherwise.

"I have a feeling," he said, "that you don't mean real-estate questions."

"Not literally, no." She handed Astrid's restaurant drawing to Steve.

"Who gave this to you?" he asked.

"Astrid. She also gave me your name and your relationship to her. And to Mark Heller."

Steve let go of the paper. It curled itself up on his desk. "Now that was an ugly bit of business, wasn't it?" He blinked. "Hey, wait a minute. I know who you are. I saw your picture on television. What's all this about? Is this something I should be telling the police? I'm in business in this community. I can't be tarnishing my reputation."

Alex had to take this carefully. "Right now, it probably wouldn't do any good to tell the police. They think they have the killer."

He narrowed his eyes at her. "So, then what are *you* up to?"

"I'm helping the wife. I don't think she did it. I need to look at all the angles. You understand."

Steve grinned. "I watch all the crime shows. I love that one about the ex-FBI agent. What a woman!"

"Then what do you see here?" Alex asked.

"The guy was . . . how can I put it?" Steve said, "Um, arrogant. Especially for a dude not putting in any of the cash himself. And he and his partner were pulling a bit of a nasty desertion." He paused. "I know what you want to ask me."

Alex nodded. "So?"

"No, ask me. I need to feel reluctant and then need to feel repentant for telling you."

"I can see you've been watching a lot of crime shows," she said with a chuckle.

"I always wanted to be a cop," Steve said, grinning. "But I don't like to get my hairdo mussed up. Look at me. They'd never let a cop look this styled and slick."

Alex laughed. She liked people who could make fun of themselves.

"All right. Here goes. Astrid told me that you and Mark used to go out together without her. Did he mention anything about someone wanting to hurt him, or get rid of him?"

"As a matter of fact, he bragged about how much a lot of people would like to get rid of him." Steve Cochrane's lips curled with distaste. "He was a type. Look, I like to see the good side of people. It helps me deal with this crazy business. But his type, it's hard. Well, you knew him. Do I have to go into details?"

Alex shook her head.

"I didn't think so. But aside from the bragging and the paranoia, I can't think of anything significant he said. I've gone over it in my head, believe me, but I honestly don't think he said anything that would help you. Or the police."

"Let me ask you this, then," Alex prompted. "Did you tell anyone about this upcoming deal? You were sworn to secrecy."

Now it was Cochrane's turn to look guilty and suspicious, an almost imperceptible display that he quickly hid. But Alex was getting good. She felt a brief twinge of ego at her recent skill-building. *Alex Pope, Profiler.* It felt good, like the first time a woman from one of her classes defended herself successfully. Now to work on her persuasion skills.

She glanced at the photos on the desk. "What a great-looking family."

"Don't go there." Steve winked at her. "Okay, Ms. Profiler, I was going to tell you anyway." He cleared his throat. "As a matter of fact, I did blab it out. Big mouth. I was out for a few martinis with an old friend of the family, another realtor. I'm not a big drinker. And so on and so on. No excuses, really. I made him swear to secrecy too."

"And it was—" Alex prodded.

"Fred Gurkey," Steve told her. "Know him?"

Mary Szabo called at 6:00 p.m. Alex, inspired by the martini story, had stopped off at Beverages and More on her way home from Santa Rosa. She'd bought a bottle of Hendrick's gin; another of dry vermouth, the French kind; a jar of olives with pimento; and a nice martini glass. She used a quart jar to shake her drink, on which she was sipping, sprawled in her armchair, when the phone rang.

She wasn't sure, when she'd bought the implements of snooty inebriation, if she was celebrating or grieving. Now, after two, it hardly mattered.

"Alex, are you all right? You sound sick," Mary asked after she and Alex had exchanged a few words.

"Don't be polite. I'm slurring my words. I'm drunk. I'm alone and drunk."

A silence followed on the other end of the line.

"Do you think I'm pathetic?" Alex asked drunkenly.

"No, I think you're trying very hard to get by in a difficult situation. Do you want to talk tomorrow?"

Alex's stomach lurched. She *was* pathetic. She was going through a drunken moment of self-loathing. She wanted to hang up and crawl into bed and really feel sorry for herself. But she had to at least find out what happened.

"Did you get the continuance?" she asked.

"No."

"No?" Why was she surprised? Because, she realized, she admired Mary Szabo, thought of her as capable of anything. "What happened?"

The judge practically laughed in my face, even with the D.A. standing next to me. I don't blame her. Subpoenaed witnesses on Monday, et cetera. I burbled and hedged and generally made a fool of myself. It was a farce, really. I had so little to work with."

"I can't imagine you making a fool of yourself."

"Then you don't know me that well yet," Mary said.

"It's my fault. I made you go out and look like a fool."

"I can be a fool very effectively on my own, thank you. Don't blame yourself. You're mistaking windmills for giants, but you're a real trooper."

Alex knew she was drunk now, if she'd needed further evidence. She felt a swelling of affection for Mary and her literary allusion. Drunken tenderness.

"I like you," she burst out.

There was a silence on the other end. "Wait," Mary said finally.

Alex sensed that Mary was moving to another room.

"My girlfriend is teasing me about you," Mary said after about a minute. "Once, many years ago, when we were first together, I had a one-night fling with a bisexual physical therapist at a conference in Hawaii. Kim won't let me live it down."

"Well," Alex slurred, "I'd be honored if you had a crush on me." She immediately regretted her words.

"Oh, no!" Mary cried. "I didn't mean that."

"I didn't mean anything—"

"I am very sorry," Mary said. Her voice was cool. "I was being extremely unprofessional."

"I have to go!" *Oh, no.* Complete nausea overwhelmed her. Absorbed gin began exploding, lava-like. She dropped the phone and raced to the bathroom.

When she returned, mortified, and tried to call Mary back, the answering machine at the Szabo residence asked her for a message. She hung up.

THIRTY

Alex figured she had two choices. One, descend into a melodramatic remake of *The Lost Weekend*. Or two, get on with the investigation, no matter what she found.

On Saturday, she assumed Fred Gurkey was either with clients or possibly at Stumps, so she showered and dressed and headed into Guerneville.

Fred was at the counter at Stumps, seated next to Owen Lasky, the owner of Ol' Man River, the memorabilia shop on Church Street. A guarded look passed over Fred's face as she approached, which he quickly transformed into his realtor persona.

"Morning," he said. "Nice to see the sun for a change."

It *was* a beautiful day. Even Alex, driven to get on with her person-hunt, had been awed by the intensity of the sun-drenched colors as she drove along the river and into town, passing through the dappled sunlight and shade of the towering redwood trees.

But now, she had to focus.

"Can I talk to you alone for a couple of minutes?" she asked Fred.

Fred stood. "Let's go over to my office."

Alex followed Fred down Main Street, shielding her eyes from the blinding sun. Blessedly, the river had dropped before flooding into town. Fred led her into his office and shut the door. He waved her into a seat in front of his desk and took the worn executive chair behind it. His office was just as large as Steve Cochrane's, but much shabbier. His requisite family pictures looked faded.

Fred picked up some unopened mail and thumbed through it. "What's all this about?" he asked, eyes still on the mail.

"I talked to Steve Cochrane yesterday," she said.

Fred Gurkey winced.

"Good man," he said, regaining his composure. "I wish I had his business. He's a Platinum Club member."

"He told me you and he went out for drinks a while back," she said.

"His father was a realtor," Fred said. "I've known the whole family for at least thirty years. I don't see Steve as much since his father died, but we like to get together occasionally and catch up."

Alex nodded. Fred squirmed.

No use dragging it out. The poor man was starting to sweat, sending out waves of intense manly antiperspirant, the spicy scent.

"Steve Cochrane told you about Mark Heller and Astrid Sorenson opening a restaurant together in Healdsburg."

Fred's intercom buzzed. He picked up the phone receiver, clearly relieved at the interruption. "Tell them I'll be out momentarily. Is it the couple from Marin County? Offer them some espresso and the latest MLS listings for properties over a million. Wait." He jumped up, grabbing a thick sheet of papers from his desk. "My ten-thirty clients," he said to Alex. "I don't usually get these types. I'll be right back."

She'd hardly had time to study the worn photos on his desk when he'd returned. He caught her fingering a picture in a small silver frame.

"I stopped taking pictures after the divorce," Fred said. "But I can't remove the ones I have. I cling to the past. I don't recommend it as a practice, though."

It was Alex's turn to squirm. She was thinking she was going to have to redirect the conversation when Fred spoke up, moving right back to where they'd been when the intercom buzzed.

"Yes, Steve told me about the deal. I promised him I'd keep my mouth shut about it."

"Did you keep that promise?"

"I told one person. I felt it was something I needed to do. Sometimes loyalty is more important than confidentiality."

"Who did you tell?" Alex asked. But she knew.

"I told Jack," Fred said.

The intercom buzzed again. He stood.

"The clients are from Marin. They don't like to be kept waiting and a commission like this would help me out more than you can know." He reached out and shook her hand. "I know how you feel about Jack. I know you'll do the right thing."

She was certain that Fred believed he'd done the right thing. She wasn't so sure about herself and what she'd done so far. Or about what she intended to do next.

THIRTY-ONE

Tattoo You was at the far northern end of town just across the street from a gay resort called Twisted Vines. Alex parked in the front of the ramshackle converted cottage, contemplating the three Harleys parked in the lot.

When she entered the tattoo shop, two middle-aged men in black leather looked up from their magazines. One was bald, the other one had a gray ponytail. In a strange turn of synchronicity, she realized they were the two biker dudes she'd encountered at the gas station on the afternoon of her arrival to Sonoma County in November.

The men looked puzzled, trying to place her. Giving up in unison, they inspected her tattooless surface and smiled condescendingly at her. *Novice*, their looks read.

Well, people had tattoos in all sorts of places, didn't they? Who knew what she might have hidden under her jeans and Mills College sweatshirt? What tattoo snobs, in any case. The both of them were like murals. Whoever said more is better? Them, obviously.

"I'm looking for Ivy," Alex said.

The bald biker shrugged. "There ain't no Ivy, far as I know. The tattoo artist's name is Nick."

"Is he around?"

"He's doing someone," the ponytailed one offered. He flexed a forearm, causing a green snake to boogie sensuously on his forearm. "We're just waiting. We got plenty of scenery—enough for two old guys."

Before Alex could reply, a third biker came out from the back area wiping tears from his eyes. "That fucking hurts," he said, sniffling. He was a kid, maybe eighteen. His biker leathers hung loosely on his scrawny chest and spindly legs.

The bald biker stood and slapped the boy on the shoulder. "Suck it up, dude."

Just behind the boy, a young man in a smock spoke up. "Make sure he follows the instructions." He handed a sheet of paper to the bald biker, who appeared, now that Alex had studied them, to be the boy's father.

The biker with the ponytail slung his arm around the young boy's skinny shoulders. "You're coming to Uncle Mike's house and he's got some nice chicken soup with matzo balls waiting for you." He turned to Alex and pumped his arm in the air. "Man, I make the best matzo balls west of Rockaway Beach."

Alex waited until the biker family had left, then turned to the man in the smock.

"Your first time?" he asked. He pointed at a stack of books on the table near the waiting couch. "We have designs, or of course I can do whatever you want, as long as you understand the limitations."

"No Sistine Chapel?"

"The Sistine Chapel I can do," he said. "I don't do excessive violence or hate things about women or minorities, that's what I meant. I'm Nick. You're kidding about the Sistine Chapel, aren't you?"

"Of course. Could that be serious?"

"You'd be surprised."

"Actually, I didn't come for a tattoo," she said. "I'm looking for Ivy."

"Are you a cop?"

"No. My name is Alex—"

"Alex?" Nick interrupted. "The self-defense teacher? Cool! Ivy is, like, in love with you. Platonic, although I don't care. We're not monogamous or hung up on gender rules." He pointed behind him. "She's out in the garage. Rebuilding a 'sixty-eight MG hatchback for some rich guy from Calistoga."

The garage was easy to find. Alex was greeted by a blaring Indigo Girls CD and a pair of legs jutting out from underneath a blue sports car carcass. The Red Wing steel-toe boots on the feet twitched in time to the music. Alex went over to the CD player and lowered the volume.

Ivy scooted out from underneath the car. She wore baggy coveralls and a knit cap. "Alex!" she cried, jumping up. "I'd hug you, but I'm a mess."

"Nice to see you," Alex replied, involuntarily stepping back. Ivy reeked of rancid car grease.

"Wait," Ivy said. She went over to a chair with a pile of clothing. She slipped off the Red Wings and Dickey coveralls, revealing, Alex had to admit, a very attractive body wrapped in a skimpy camisole and lacy underwear. The pretty body was covered in tattoos—mostly vegetation of various sorts, including flowers and a horn of plenty spilling over with luscious fruits and vegetables.

"Good enough to eat," Alex said. Ivy's jaw dropped and Alex felt her own face redden with embarrassment. "I was joking. I'm so sorry. I think you look great. I've been so depressed and out of touch with any feelings like that for anyone and I really like you and it just popped out of my mouth and—"

"Alex, it's okay." Ivy slipped on a pair of jeans and a dreadful imitation Seventies gold sweater that bared her midriff. She went over to a sink and slathered grease remover over all her exposed parts. "Actually I'm sort of thrilled you noticed me that way." When she was done buffing herself with paper towels, she ran over to Alex and engulfed her in a tight hug. "I've missed you," she said. "I miss everyone, but you and Jack most of all."

Alex allowed herself to be engulfed in the hug for a few moments, feeling Ivy's nice firm body pressed against her. She wasn't gay but she'd learned over time that the division lines of sexuality were not all that black and white, at least for a lot of people. Ivy felt good and it was a complex and painful relief to feel again. She pulled away and nodded at the MG suspended on its jacks. "Looks like you're keeping busy with other projects."

Ivy reached out and adjusted the hood strings on Alex's sweatshirt, which had gotten twisted during the hug. "I make more money doing this, but I miss the Overlook. What's happening? I tried Jack and Marge, but they haven't returned my calls." She stepped back and squinted at Alex. "Someone told me you're running around town asking everybody questions. I was wondering when you'd get to me. If it was anyone else but you, I'd tell them to buzz off. Let's go in the house. I have a tofu-nut casserole I made last night. Nick baked some bread."

The mention of food evoked a deep growling in Alex's stomach. Even the suggestion of tofu, not Alex's favorite food product, sounded enticing. She followed Ivy the short distance to a cottage with peeling white paint and a rickety front porch.

The interior was less shabby and smelled like baked bread. The furniture was worn but clean. The walls were covered with political posters and organic-food photographs.

Ivy cut a thick slice of her casserole and brought it over with buttered whole-wheat bread. It was all surprisingly good.

Ivy watched her eat, smiling with pleasure at Alex's obvious appreciation. Then she frowned. "If it wasn't Jean who killed Mark, it probably wasn't a stranger either, was it?"

Alex wiped her mouth on a woven Guatemalan napkin. "No."

"It wasn't me," Ivy said. "I almost could have. I hated him. But you know, even though I took your class, I don't believe in killing. I don't even want to believe in hating, but I have to because I'm not dumb enough to ignore human nature."

"I do have a few questions to ask you," Alex said, skirting the philosophical issues.

"Can I be honest? I want the whole thing to be over."

"So do I. But I made a promise to Jean."

Ivy shrugged. "More bread?"

"No, thanks. Some coffee would be nice."

"We don't drink coffee," Ivy said. "We have a nice grain substitute and soy milk."

"That's okay," Alex said, trying not to grimace.

"Green tea?" Ivy asked. "It's loaded with caffeine."

"That'd be great."

Alex waited until Ivy returned with a steaming cup that smelled like hayfields. The tea was good, but the atmosphere was turning edgy. Ivy took a seat on a chair the farthest distance from where Alex was seated. Fortunately, it was a tiny room.

"Ivy, when we first met, you mentioned your grandfather and Jack were good buddies," Alex said. "How did they know each other?"

Ivy's eyes widened. "You don't think *Jack* killed him?"

"I think I need to explore every angle."

"It wasn't him."

"You said they've always acted secretive, Jack and your grandfather," Alex prompted.

"My granddad was always wigging out about things, but he wouldn't explain why. That's all I know."

"I was wondering if I could talk to your grandfather," Alex said.

"Oh, Alex." Ivy sighed. "He's a stubborn angry man."

"Could you talk to him? Ask him to speak with me?"

"You're not going to let go of this, are you?"

"No, I'm not."

"I didn't think so." Ivy stood. "I'll call him. Wait. I'm going to use the phone in the bedroom."

While she waited, Alex went into the kitchen and sliced another large chunk of bread. She buttered it and took it back to her seat at the funky Formica table. She didn't think Ivy would mind. She sipped at the tea. It tasted like it smelled, of hayfields. And it was loaded with caffeine. She was considering going back for another slice of the casserole when Ivy returned.

"Okay," Ivy said.

"He'll talk to me?"

"He'll let you come by, but he says he has nothing to say. You know, I think you'd better jam on over there or he might change his mind." She wrote directions on a scrap of paper and handed them to Alex. "It wasn't Jack. I'd rather confess and go to prison than have him locked up." She took Alex's arm. "I mean it. I'll confess. No, I won't, but I won't forgive you if you get him arrested. And you won't forgive yourself."

Alex had to admit Ivy was probably right. But that wasn't going to placate Pandora or close her box.

THIRTY-TWO

Ernie Lightfoot's welding shop, Rising Phoenix, was on 116 toward Sebastopol, about three miles out of Guerneville. Alex walked up a path surrounded by metal piled in heaps and stacks across the front yard. The sign on the door said CLOSED. Alex went around to the back.

Behind the shop, a man in a welding suit was joining two sections of metal rod together, sparks flying from his torch in a spray of light, like a comet shower. He was bent away from her, his face shielded in thick plastic. The piece he was working on was huge, nearly eight feet tall, and consisted of thin rods and circles joined to make a humanoid figure in a posture suggesting flight.

The yard was filled with welded figures—demons and animals and human beings in motion. Alex was struck with a blast from the past. Her father's substantial stone sculptures had littered their backyard, looming over the rustic landscape like lawn ornaments gone archetypal. She recognized the labor of concentration in Ernie Lightfoot's posture. She came around, placing herself in the welder's line of sight. He shut off his torch, then removed his face shield and gloves.

"Mr. Lightfoot?" she asked.

"Ernie," he said, approaching her. Ivy had mentioned her grandfather was Native American. Alex studied his dark, high-cheeked face framed in blue-black hair. His lined face suggested he was Jack's age, but his hair had no gray. Meanwhile, he studied her too, with piercing dark eyes.

"These are incredible," Alex said, gesturing around the yard.

"I do this on the weekends. During the week, I repair other people's radiators and shit like that. Let's go inside."

Ernie led her to a cramped office. He sat behind the desk and indicated the ratty beige couch for her. Prominently displayed on the wall above his head was a large calendar featuring nearly nude ladies, apparently a promotional gift from a welding supply company.

Ernie glanced behind him and turned to her, shrugging. "Ivy yells at me every time she comes here, but I have to know the date, don't I?"

"Thanks for seeing me," Alex said. She wasn't about to get into a discussion of pin-up calendars. Enjoying a nice touch of silent irony, however, she noticed that the current month's scantily clad girl resembled Ivy in her camisole. "I'm sorry to take you away from your sculpting." She smiled. "I can see where Ivy gets her mechanical and artistic skills."

"She's something else," Ernie said with a mix of fondness and exasperation. "Mind of her own, that's for sure. But she's come around. She was hell on wheels when she first came up here, let me tell you. I couldn't handle her and her crazy behavior. I have Jack and Marge to thank for their help, taking her on and so on." He paused. "But then, Jack and I go back a long ways. A long ways and a lot of history."

"That's why I came to talk to you."

"And that's why I refused to talk to *you*. But Ivy got on my case. So I agreed to let you come over. But I didn't agree to say anything about Jack."

"I understand."

He picked up a petite mass of intertwined metal. "This is the smallest thing I've ever done. Can you tell what it is?"

"It looks like a representation of a psychic wound," she said.

Ernie's eyes narrowed. "Say more."

"A knot of twisted emotions that are metallic, that is to say, entrenched and tensile."

Ernie ran a stubby, calloused finger along the entwined wires. "You get it."

"I've been around a lot of sculpture."

"So you understand," he said, "feelings so deep and confusing that you've gotta protect those around you from them? Like a damned prison guard of yourself. Your life gets devoted to keeping demons shut up inside you."

"Yes," she said, "I think I do."

"I don't think you do," he said. "Or you wouldn't be poking around where you shouldn't."

"What if the demons escaped?" Alex asked. "What if, despite all your best efforts, things happened and suddenly your demons became more powerful than your guard? A person would need help then."

He frowned. "The cure can be worse than the sickness."

"The sickness, if it spreads and hurts other people, is always worse than the cure. Sometimes the cure is also a sacrifice, to allow others to survive."

"Theories and intellectual crap." Ernie closed his eyes and took a deep breath. An eternity of one minute passed. Ernie opened his eyes. "What do you want to know?"

"Tell me about Jack."

"Tell you what?"

"What you think is important."

"Jack is a hero." Ernie picked up his sculpture and stroked it. "To me, a hero is a man who sacrifices himself physically or emotionally for the greater good. Jack and I were together for two tours of duty in 'Nam. He was the most respected man around, because he always thought of others first, he worked for the good of the team. You see how he is now? He's one of the most loyal men on earth. He understands about survival and working together. He learned that from his training and his team."

"The team?"

"In Special Forces, we're deployed in teams."

"You and Jack were in *Special Forces*?"

"We met in training, got to be friends, stuck it out together and got assigned together."

"I can't begin to imagine Jack as a commando in Special Forces."

"Because he's not an egotistical and macho John Wayne type?" Ernie snorted. "That's all bullshit. Sure, there were a lot of tough guys, but some of the best, you'd think they were Quakers. I always said, watch out for the quiet, gentle-seeming ones. Jack was like a cat, light on his feet and quick, no theatrics. He was especially good at hand-to-hand combat. He had incredible reflexes. He liked the empty-hands martial arts."

A bell rung. *Of course.* "He knew martial arts? Then he'd know how to kill someone with his hands."

Ernie glared at her. "I just told you. But I won't say any more about that topic, so don't ask."

Alex decided to come from another angle. "When were you there?"

"Where?"

"Vietnam."

"I didn't say we were in Vietnam," Ernie said.

Alex sat back, frustrated. "You did."

"If you try to find out when we were there," Ernie said quietly, "you won't get anywhere, because we were somewhere we shouldn't have been at a time when we shouldn't have been there. It was too early in the conflict for anyone to be where we were, you get my meaning? So we weren't there and we didn't do anything. There's no record *you'll* ever have access to that says otherwise. And if you ask anyone else who was on the team, you'll get nowhere. You're lucky you're getting this from me."

"Something happened with Jack, didn't it?"

Ernie's face was clearly struggling. "Things happen that most people don't even have nightmares about."

"What did Jack do? What happened to him?" The moment the words were out of her mouth, she realized her mistake.

Ernie slammed his sculpture on the desk and stood up. "I can't say. I said too much already."

She'd spoken too fast. She wanted to go back, like a tape recorder, and erase her words. "Please let me help him. I need to know how to help him."

"You have to go," he said.

"Jack needs to be rescued," Alex said urgently. "Don't let him slip away. He's falling. He's going to crash. He's going to be hurt."

"Crash?" Ernie asked, looking intently at her. "That's a funny way to put it."

Alex's heart was racing. "Jack's in trouble. You wouldn't have left him on the battlefield, would you?" The room was not warm and yet she could smell the sour odor of sweat rising from her armpits.

"I wouldn't leave him to die anywhere, but this isn't the same and I don't have to say any more," Ernie said. "I am Special Forces and I will be to the day I die. We stick together with pride and honor. We are elite because we understand evil and know it can't be fought without one another." He picked up his sculpture, which had an odd dent in it now. He cradled it in his palms. "I can't tell you any more. But I'll tell you about a man who might. His name is Chuckie F."

"Chuckie F. What's his real last name?"

Ernie grimaced. "We called him Chuckie F."

"Where is he?"

"Fresno. He's a doctor in Fresno, last I heard. Pretty sure of that."

"What does he have to do with Jack?"

Ernie walked over to the door and held it open. "You're the detective. You find out." As she passed, he sniffed in the air. "You don't smell so good, girl. Smell like some recruits I've known who just got shot at for the first time." He glanced knowingly at her. "Maybe some of us should be chasing our own demons instead of other people's."

THIRTY-THREE

Alex drove quickly to the tiny Guerneville library, hoping it wasn't closed yet. With the help of the bored transsexual research librarian, Toni, she located a Dr. Charles Finley, an emergency medicine physician at the Fresno Medical Center.

Armed with the hospital's number, Alex headed back to her place, her heart racing. As she half-expected, she was told that Dr. Finley was unavailable. She left a number on his pager and was amazed when he returned her call almost immediately. Her temples were throbbing and her voice shook when she spoke. "I understand you know Jack Campbell."

There was a silence on the other end of the line. Then he said, "I knew a man named Jack Campbell at one time. I haven't been in touch with him for a few years. Who are you?"

"A friend of his. I'm looking for some important information about him."

The voice on the other end of the line was gruff and suspicious. "Then why aren't you asking him?"

"Doctor, I think Jack may need help. He's been having some serious troubles lately. Let me come talk to you."

During another long pause, Alex could hear the wail of an ambulance in the background.

"Where are you?" Dr. Finley asked, still gruff, but his tone had softened slightly.

"Sonoma County."

"That's over four hours away."

"It doesn't matter."

The wail of the ambulance was replaced by a flurry of urgent voices, muffled in the background. "Something's come up here," Dr. Finley said. "Let me call you back. We can make an appointment for next week."

"I was thinking tomorrow. Anytime, anyplace, at your convenience."

"Tomorrow? I'm on a thirty-six-hour rotation. It's been crazy here, what with the weather."

"It's urgent."

"You'll have to come to the hospital. You may have to wait."

"I'll head down in the morning." Her breath quickened. She was getting close now. She could feel it.

Alex had intended to leave early. Much to her dismay, she slept like a person who'd been drugged, a dreamless emptiness lasting a frightening eleven hours.

It was nearly 9:00 a.m. when she opened her eyes, but it was more like arising from a near-death experience than just waking up. She felt a surge of relief mixed with panic. Driven by competing inner demons—some of them capable of psycho-drugging her, apparently—she struggled out of the sheets that had twisted around her like restraining cords and leaped from the bed in a manner that would have horrified any chiropractor.

For the briefest moment, she wished she could go back to the coma state. The next best alternative might be to give up this obsessive chase, to let it all go and let the preliminary hearing just happen.

That considered, Alex showered, dressed, made a thermos of coffee and went down to her car more or less prepared for the long trip to Fresno.

She had plenty of time to think on the drive. Traffic was light on a late Sunday morning and the weather was dry and fine for driving, despite a sky thickly overcast with menacing black clouds.

She thought mainly about Jack. It was entirely possible he killed Mark. If she could have chosen one of the last people she'd want to implicate, it was him.

But she was tired of messing up. She'd messed up in a variety of ways throughout her life, in both big ways and little. She wasn't going to mess up now. She had to complete this, no matter how painful the results.

Four hours later, the clerk at the emergency room desk took her name and paged Dr. Finley. Then an eight-car accident resulting in sixteen victims with gruesome injuries turned the entire facility into a madhouse of organized chaos.

Alex wound up sitting in a hard plastic green chair next to an adolescent girl with a runny-nosed child. The harried-looking mother looked barely out of childhood herself. The child coughed wetly without covering his mouth. In fact, the entire waiting area was filled with coughers and spitters and grumblers killing time while the horrific wounded were being pumped and tubed and patched together.

A man with a gunshot wound screeched by on a gurney. He was shouting obscenities and was trailed by two uniformed police officers. As far as she could tell, the lesser emergencies were being seen at the rate of about two per hour. At that rate, she figured she could be there until next Tuesday.

Eternity passed. She ate a truly frightening turkey and Swiss cheese sandwich from the vending machine. She bought the snotty-nosed little boy a sandwich, which inspired his child-woman mother to recount her entire life history of gut-wrenching injustice that, under other circumstances, would have completely broken Alex's heart. But now her own obsessions were filtering out any major outpouring of compassion. She leafed through battered copies of *Good Housekeeping* and *People* and lamented about Tom Cruise with the adolescent mother. They dissected a recipe for taco casserole. Alex wished she'd remembered the latest Laurie King mystery that was lying on her bedside table. She continued to wait.

It was six thirty in the evening. She'd had a frightening tuna sandwich in addition to the turkey, several cups of something brackish resembling coffee and a package of Grandma's oatmeal cookies.

The young mother and son were gone. They'd disappeared with a doctor who looked younger than the mother. They were replaced by a rank-smelling man dressed in rags who was preoccupied with the voices in his head. The man's rambling diatribe was actually interesting, but the smell was terrible, so Alex went back to the reception desk and threatened to develop a real emergency if the clerk didn't page Dr. Finley once again. In fifteen minutes, he appeared. He approached her, already looking at his watch and surveying the room. He was a thin and wiry distance-runner type, with wiry brown hair and sharp, hawk-like features. He walked, Alex noticed, with urgency, radiating energy.

"Ms. Pope?"

"Alex."

"Let's go to the cafeteria. Are you hungry? How long've you been waiting?"

"As to the waiting, a long time. I'm not very hungry, though. I've been eating from the vending machines."

Dr. Finley groaned. "I'm something of a health nut. Whole grains, limited animal protein, fibers, fruits and vegetables. You can imagine what I can eat around here."

The doctor made a salad from the cafeteria salad bar and ordered her to do the same. He supplemented his salad with a container of yogurt, an apple, a banana and a package of Fig Newtons, silently inspecting the available items and placing his choices on his plastic tray.

In the end, he filled a large paper cup to the brim with black coffee. "This," he explained, "is my drug of choice and necessity."

Alex got a small cup, considering the caffeine flow already induced by the vending machine swill.

When they'd found a place to sit, Dr. Finley carefully organized his food items into a neat, accessible pattern and covered his lap with a paper napkin.

"Speak quickly," he warned. He cut his banana in half and unpeeled one of the halves, which he sliced into his yogurt. He held the other half up to her.

"No, thanks." She sipped at her coffee. "Ernie Lightfoot told me about you. He said you could tell me something about Jack Campbell."

Dr. Finley took a delicate bite of his salad, chewed thoughtfully and swallowed. "I considered, after you'd phoned, what you wanted from me. There wasn't much to consider. What I did have to ponder is whether I should tell you anything." He poked at his lettuce. "Give me a reason to talk to you. A very good one."

"Something's happened to Jack." Alex could hear the cosmic clock ticking and plowed ahead quickly. "He's not well. I'm pretty sure it'll get worse if he isn't treated. I need to know what's behind all this before I can help."

Dr. Finley nodded. "He was doing okay, at least five years ago. I lost touch with him after my divorce. The wife always sent the Christmas and birthday cards."

"Yes, he was fine. Then—" Alex hesitated. "There was some stress. Actually, a lot of stress."

"Elaborate," Dr. Finley ordered. He was clearly used to giving orders and expected quick, cogent answers.

"He's losing control of his world," she said. "He's struggling to keep his life together and his choices are conflicting."

"Yes," Dr. Finley murmured. "That would do it." He looked sharply at her, his face resolved. "I haven't told anyone about Jack, ever. He swore me to secrecy and I respected that. But I suspect from what you're telling me that he's in trouble, like you say. And you're right. It'll get worse if he doesn't get help."

Just then, Dr. Finley's pager buzzed. Alex's heart sank.

"I'll be right back," Dr. Finley said.

He went to a hospital phone, while Alex faced the possibility of another everlasting wait. And she'd damn well wait for an eternity if she had to. She wasn't going anywhere until she'd heard what Finley had to say.

The doctor hustled back and settled back into his chair. "You're lucky. It was a consult. Don't look so pleased. I don't think you're going to like what I have to say." He took a leisurely bite of yogurt.

Get on with it! Hurry! She wanted to scream. She waited while he swallowed.

"I met Jack at the VA hospital in Palo Alto in 'sixty-four. We were roommates, both wound up there on nearly the same day, both a mess. Me, I had a concussion, broken arm and two broken ribs. Took a fall exiting a helicopter in a bad situation. I was a medic. Jack, he'd been shot twice, once in the shoulder, the other just missing his heart." Dr. Finley hesitated. "But that wasn't the worst. The worst was his state of mind." He glanced around with the glazed look of a person recalling a terrible memory. "We got to be friends. I had a way of getting his spirits up, when he wouldn't talk to anyone else." He pointed his yogurt spoon at her. "He *is* a great guy, no matter what."

"I know," Alex said firmly. She hoped Finley believed it, because she meant it with every fiber of her being. *Oh, God.* She felt like a modern-day female Benjamin Arnold.

"Jack was Special Forces," Dr. Finley said. "Before America's official entry into Vietnam, elite Special Forces units were sent on highly secret unofficial tours of duty. You've probably heard about that. It's public knowledge now. They were there to teach the native troops, supposedly, but they saw action, of course. They did things we'll never know about. We've heard about some of it, but it's the tip of the iceberg."

Finley took another bite of yogurt. He stared into space, organizing his thoughts as he had his food on the tray.

"Those guys, they shared two things, no matter what their personalities were otherwise. First, a determination to get the job done and not dwell on the means to get it done. Second, a fanatical loyalty to one another."

Get on with it! Alex thought. *What if your pager goes off again?* But Finley was a methodical man. He was getting there, in his own way.

"You have to understand, we were awake at night in the hospital sometimes, not able to sleep. In the dark, Jack told me things he wasn't supposed to."

Finley's pager went off again. Alex thought she might undergo a highly visible nervous breakdown. She took a deep breath while Finley watched her, looking both pained and amused.

"Don't worry," he said. "I'm going to finish, because I don't have much else to say." He sighed. "Jack did something bad." He stood. "Wait a minute. Maybe it's just another consult."

While she waited, Alex found a clean spoon and stole a few bites of yogurt from Finley's container. She wasn't even remotely hungry.

Finley returned, frowning. "I have to go in a couple of minutes." He sat down, pushing away his tray of half-eaten food. He took a gulp of lukewarm coffee. "Have you been eating my yogurt?"

"Yes," she admitted with shame.

Finley grinned and held the container out to her. "Want to finish it?"

"I want you to finish about Jack!"

His grin disappeared. "You've heard of post-traumatic stress syndrome?"

"Yes," Alex said. "I used to work with abused women, teaching self-defense."

A look of respect passed over Finley's face. "Good for you." He shook his head sadly. "You may know about a post-traumatic type that we call delayed PTSD. A person can be fine for many years after a traumatic incident and then stress later in life can trigger a powerful reaction. If you don't know about it, look it up. You can find out more about it on the Internet these days than I could ever tell you."

When he'd left, she pocketed the doctor's apple and the unopened package of Fig Newtons. No use wasting them. She'd need something to stimulate the digestive enzymes on the long drive back to Sonoma.

While she was in the hospital, a cold, hard rain had started to fall in huge drops. The windshield wipers swiped with increasing futility as the drive wore on. She could barely see a car's length ahead, but she felt compelled to forge her way back to the lodge. Outside of Merced, a three-car crash held up traffic for almost an hour. By 11:30 p.m., she was feeling exhausted but had reached the Sonoma County border. Just past Petaluma, her cell phone rang.

"Where are you? I was asleep and I had a terrible dream about you and I felt like I had to call. Then, to top it off, you weren't answering your home phone or your cell. I left five messages, each one more desperate than the other."

"Jeffrey? I was in a hospital and had to turn the cell off. I just remembered to turn it on again a few miles back and I didn't listen to the messages."

"A hospital? Oh, my God, are you all right?"

"I'm fine."

"A few miles back from where?"

"Fresno. Meeting with someone who used to know Jack."

"I take it this has something to do with your Nancy Drew personality disorder."

"No sarcasm. I think I know who killed Mark."

"I don't like this. Call me as soon as you get close to home. I'm coming over."

"I'll call you but don't come over." Alex snapped the phone shut. She had to grip the steering wheel with both hands to contain the trembling. *Breathe.* She did her deep breathing. She surrounded herself in her orange cone of light.

When she reached her place at the Overlook an hour and a half later, she immediately picked up the phone and dialed.

"Who is it? What's the matter?" the voice on the end of the line cried.

"It's Alex. No emergency."

A pause. "No emergency? Alex, you nearly gave me a heart attack, the phone ringing at this hour."

"I need to ask you something."

"I must admit, I'm surprised . . . wait . . ."

Alex could tell Arlene was holding the phone away from her mouth, but Alex could still hear her mother speak.

"No, she's all right . . . Go back to bed . . . there's no emergency . . ." Arlene came back on the line. "I was talking to your father. He almost had a heart attack, too."

"I'm sorry."

"As I started to say, I'm surprised you're calling me for personal advice."

The notion of asking her mother for personal advice almost made Alex laugh aloud, but she knew that would be mean. She had sworn to herself that she would never be mean to her parents. She knew they loved her, or at least the image they had of her, which would have to be, for eternity, good enough. "Not advice. I need information. Expert opinion. About delayed post-traumatic stress disorder."

"Well, in your case, I would hardly call it delayed. Of course you've had a tragedy—"

"I told you, it's not about me."

"You know, so many people phrase their questions as though it's about someone else—"

"It is about someone else. Someone who was in Vietnam, someone who did something terrible. Then he came home and lived a normal life until just recently and then he—well, he did something bad."

Another pause. Alex could imagine her mother's acute mind gathering together information. "Yes," Arlene said thoughtfully. "It's becoming a problem, these vets who are getting older, starting to retire or are experiencing the death of a loved one. Major life events are triggering a delayed PTSD reaction in some of these former soldiers."

"What are the symptoms?" Alex asked.

"Diverse," her mother answered. "Guilt, sleeplessness, flashbacks and, often, odd behavior associated with something they might have done in the past." She cleared her throat. "I'm afraid I'm going to have to be insistent now. Are you in trouble? I don't like what's been going on up where you are. Jeffrey's told me—"

"I don't like feeling like you have Jeffrey spying on me. I'm fine. I just need to finish up some business, that's all."

"I know that's not all. But you have your ways and you've always been stubborn. Maybe we gave you too much independence when you were little—"

"No psychoanalyzing. Remember, you promised." It was a compromise Alex and her mother had worked out when Alex left home for college. If they were to stay on speaking terms, Arlene would have to stop offering analytical opinions about Alex's motivations and potential routes to transformation.

"I wasn't going to psychoanalyze."

"Okay, then. I'll let you get back to sleep. I know you've been busy. Tell Arthur I'm proud of him for that lifetime achievement award he got from the International Sculpture Center."

"Alex—"

"It's late. Can it wait?"

"Your father and I are getting older. I know you don't believe this, but we can change. Give us a chance. Don't shut us out."

"It's very late."

"Don't do anything dangerous."

"I won't," Alex lied.

"You will." Her mother sighed. "You have a wild side, I don't know where you got it from. But you always seem to pull out okay. Anyway, please think about what I said. About us, your parents. Let us change and maybe you can change, too. Can you consider what I'm saying?"

"I can," Alex said. This time, she wasn't lying. It was something she could consider after all this other mess was finished. At least it was something she could consider in theory. How much did people change? She didn't want to be a cynic. She really didn't.

THIRTY-FOUR

Marge's face was a study in complicity masked as guilelessness. Standing in the doorway of the Campbell residence, she was wearing a frayed yellow bathrobe over a white cotton nightgown with lacy trim.

Alex could hear the pugs yapping from the back of the house. "I need to see Jack." When she had arrived back at her place at 1:00 a.m., there was a note from Jack tacked to the door. I NEED TO TALK TO YOU, it said. Jack had printed out his name below the request, also in block letters. FROM JACK CAMPBELL. After speaking with her mother, she went to the Campbells and banged on the door. Now she was facing Marge, who was trying to look puzzled and clueless.

"He's not here," Marge said.

Alex studied her face.

"I'm not lying," Marge said, her voice strained. "He really isn't." Tears began to stream down Marge's cheeks. Whatever else she had done, her anguish didn't seem like an act unless she was some kind of specially gifted amateur actress, a psychopathic everyday Meryl Streep.

"Where is he?"

"I don't know," Marge whispered. She gestured toward the outdoors. "Somewhere out there." She backed up. "I can't make you stop, can I? You're relentless. You might as well come in."

Alex followed her to the plaid couch. They sat a few feet away from each other. The pugs yapped pathetically from the bedroom.

Marge grimaced at her. "Can I let them out?"

"Sure." She waited until Marge and the pugs returned, Marge gloomy, the pugs happy to be free and alive. They bounded up to Alex, licking at her legs and wheezing through their flattened noses.

"Go lie down," Marge ordered. The pugs skulked to their dog beds, lying so they could watch the people on the couch endure the curse of higher awareness.

"What's he doing?" Alex asked.

"He's wandering the property. He says he's protecting the borders."

"How long has this been going on? How long has he been protecting the borders?"

Marge stared down at her hands. "Since I started taking the pills."

Alex nodded. "At first, you didn't know because the pills knocked you out."

"Yes," Marge said.

"So, if Jack went out in the night, you'd never know."

"No, I wouldn't."

"And you told the detectives something different. That you'd know if he was gone in the night."

"I did. I told them he was with me the night of the murder. I assumed he was with me. I didn't have any reason to think otherwise."

"Then what?"

"Then," Marge said, "I stopped taking the pills. I hate them. They make me groggy all day. I didn't tell Jack. He worries about me getting my sleep."

"And?" Alex asked.

"I pretended to sleep," Marge said. "He got up, after he thought the pills had started working. Finally, I had to tell him the truth. He was suspicious anyway. He always knows when I'm hiding something. That's when he explained to me what he's doing. Guarding the perimeters from threats to his family."

One of the pugs whined. Alex glanced over. It was probably her imagination, but they both looked worried. Why not, she thought. Who said humans had a lock on awareness? Look what good it did them, anyway. She turned back to Marge. "I feel very sad. I think you know why."

The tears started streaming down Marge's face again.

"We could escape," Marge said, voice choking. "We said we'd go and retire. You could just let us run away."

Alex's heart was being squeezed by an uncompromising fist. "I can't." How low, she wondered, would one have to go in the evolutionary chain of being, to not feel so conflicted?

Marge's face tightened. "He didn't do anything. Let them try and prove he did." She glared at Alex. "You can't prove anything."

Alex stood. "I'm going to the main lodge. Can I get the key?"

Marge's eyes widened. "Don't go."

"The only one out there is Jack. You said he didn't do anything. Then I have no reason to be afraid, do I?"

Marge went to a side table and removed a ring of keys from a drawer. But she held them in a tight fist, refusing to hand them over.

"Do you really want to live this way?" Alex asked. "Do you think Jack really wants to live this way?"

"We got used to living with secrets." Marge's body sagged like a deflating balloon. "And we suffered for it." She brought over the ring of keys and handed them to Alex.

"I hope you believe me. I don't want this. I hate it," Alex said.

Marge stood frozen, hands clutched together, as Alex turned to leave. "But not enough to stop and live with a secret," Marge called after her. "Not enough to stop hurting us."

Her cries fell on deaf ears. Alex let the cliché ring in her head as she picked up the flashlight she had stored in the trunk of her car. *Let the chips fall where they may.*

THIRTY-FIVE

Alex crept through the lobby swinging the flashlight in an arc, avoiding shadowy obstacles. She made her way through the dining room—still not turning on any lights, not wanting to illuminate any reminders of what these rooms meant to her. It was eerily quiet. Every square inch of her body and mind was on alert. But she didn't expect any confrontations. Not yet.

She pushed through the swinging door to the kitchen, feeling every fiber of her being alert to her surroundings. The kitchen went from black to fluorescent brilliance with the flick of a switch. For a moment, she was blinded by the sudden light. When her eyes had adjusted, she shivered at the crime scene's scrubbed-clean blandness. She walked over to Mark's office cubby and peered in. She wasn't expecting to see anything new. She was simply waiting. It wasn't a long wait.

"Alex."

He had come in silently from behind her, but she wasn't startled. Jack stood near the entrance to the dining room with a black knit cap pulled over his scalp. He wore thin black gloves over his hands, black pants and a black pullover shirt.

He held out his empty hands. "No guns. No knives. But then, we don't need them, do we? They make things easier, but they're not absolutely necessary. We know how to hurt with our hands and feet. Our elbows and knees. Our bodies are our weapons." He started toward her.

Alex adjusted her center of gravity and raised her hands. "Stay back." She felt light on her feet. She could feel time slowing down.

Jack halted, let his arms rest at his sides. He surveyed the kitchen. "Do you believe in evil?"

"I believe there are very bad people in the world," she replied. "Some of them are so bad, I would call them evil. But I think most bad people are just foolishly, clumsily, pathetically bad."

"Mark was a bad man," Jack said. "Maybe not evil, according to your definition." The tone of his voice was mild, emotionless, distant. "He was a selfish tormentor. He reminded me of a lieutenant on my first tour of duty. That man caused the death of two of the best guys on my team through cowardice and selfishness." Jack frowned. "He didn't last long."

"He was murdered?"

"Let's just say he wasn't protected by the rest of us in dangerous circumstances. When he realized his situation, he got himself transferred to a different unit. Nobody had to kill him." He looked intently at her, his eyes refocusing. "I didn't intend to kill Mark. He tried to come between my son and me, he abused women, he abused his subordinates, but I didn't come in to this kitchen intending to kill him."

"What *were* you intending?"

"I was watching," Jack explained. "I was surveying the situation. I observed him with Jean. I observed him with Wesley. When they both left, I made a stupid mistake. I went in to talk to him. I should have known better. You don't talk to people like that. They bring out the worst in you." He raised his right hand, formed it into a weapon-like shape.

Alex sank deeper into her stance and let her vision widen. It was just a subtle refinement of readiness.

Jack winked at her, clearly aware of the minute correction. "You would make a very good team member." Then his tone grew dark. "That lousy egomaniac insinuated my own son was against me. He was like a rabid dog—nasty and infected and needing to be put to sleep. It isn't fair, you know. They train us to kill quickly and efficiently, then you come home and are supposed to forget it all. That's war. Making regular men into emotional cripples." He snapped his hand out in a blindingly fast karate chop. "I made sure he was instantly unconscious. I fractured his vertebral arches—they protect the vertebral artery."

"Yes," she said. "The autopsy report said that."

"He didn't suffer. I made sure he was dead and dragged him into the freezer." He smiled grimly. "One big bully ice cube."

Suddenly, a loud scrabble came from nearby, sending both Alex and Jack back into defensive, alert postures. A fat, scruffy rat ran across the floor. Alex couldn't help smiling. "False alarm," she said, relaxing her stance a little.

"You see?" Jack replied, smiling back. "Training."

He was right, of course. The muscles and fibers of her body were imprinted with the ability to act quickly. But she liked to believe she'd never kill anyone. *Unless?*

"Why did they come back after all that time?" she asked. "The symptoms. The depression, the flashbacks. Stalking people, stalking the Overlook."

Jack's face became guarded.

"Was it the retirement?" Alex prompted. "Oh, and Fred Gurkey told you about Mark and Astrid's plans to leave the Overlook. Was it that?"

"Before that," Jack said. His hands balled into fists at his sides.

"Was it Shayne Elliot invading your property and threatening your family?"

"No," he replied.

"Tell me," Alex persisted.

"You don't want to know."

"I do."

He looked her straight in the eyes. "It was you."

Alex took a step back, taking in a quick gasp.

Jack took a step toward her. "It was you that started it all."

"Stay back," she warned.

He halted, clearly struggling. "On my second tour, I went out on a mission to capture a prisoner. We weren't officially doing things like that, but then we weren't officially there anyway. The target was a high-ranking guy and we found him in a hut with some of his personnel. One of his aides was a woman—a pretty but tough-looking lady with quick reflexes and training, like you. I don't want to get into details, but she took out my buddy, so I took her out. I had never killed a woman before. And it wasn't easy. She was a fighter. It was awful, horrible." He was trembling. "Nothing was the same after that. I lost something. I knew I wouldn't be safe to work with anymore. I let myself get shot." Jack looked intently at her. "Do you understand that?"

"I think I do," Alex said. At least she understood feeling so bad you wanted to be punished by circumstances.

"I thought you might. When I first met you, that night outside my house, the way you reacted, your strength. You reminded me of that woman. It was a weird association that wouldn't go away. The nightmares started again. I hadn't had them for a number of years, not since Chris was little."

Something deep inside her was clenching, throbbing. *My fault again. Why is everything my fault?*

Jack took another step toward her, putting his arm out. "Forgive me. It was me, not you."

"No," she said. "Don't come any closer."

"It wasn't your fault," Jack said, moving slowly toward her.

"Stop," she cried, but he kept coming.

My fault. My fault. Her world was shrinking and expanding at the same time. Maybe she deserved to be overpowered.

"Don't blame yourself," Jack soothed. "You caught me. Isn't that good enough?"

"You have to stop moving," Alex said in a thick voice.

"I'd never hurt you. I'm not going to hurt you," he said, advancing. "You're like a daughter to me. My little girl."

She raised her hands, got in her stance. He came closer, moving slowly and gracefully. She took a step back. It was like a dance through stretched-out time. One step, two steps. Then Jack moved swiftly, closing the distance. When he was within striking distance, she watched her arms raise. In the next moment, when she should have been most in control, she found herself watching her fingers reaching out as if they had a life of their own. Jack's fingers floated toward her and their fingertips touched.

When Chris found them, twenty minutes later, they were huddled next to one another, sobbing, on the cold cement floor.

THIRTY-SIX

"Get up!" Chris cried, his face red. "What's wrong with you two?" He turned to Alex. "What did you do to him? Ever since you came here, there's been trouble. Now what?"

"It's not her fault." Jack got to his feet and held his hand out, helping Alex to hers. "We need to call the sheriff now."

"You didn't do anything," Chris said.

"Don't bother, son," Jack said.

"Who else knows?" Chris asked. "Besides her?"

"It's too late." He indicated the phone on the wall. "Do I have to call to get myself arrested?"

"Why don't you let the traitorous bitch call?" Chris and Alex glared at each other.

"Now, now," Jack said, taking on a tone of parental admonishment. "We're in for some tough times. I want you to promise me you won't fight. That you'll work as a family while I'm away."

"That's absurd. I can't believe you and your irrational bullshit about families," Chris said bitterly. "She tracked you down, for God's sake."

"Did a helluva job," Jack said. "Of course, there were clues."

"What garbage." Chris moaned and reached up to rub his eyes.

Alex stared at him. His face was almost purple. He looked as though he might asphyxiate on the spot.

"You can't do this," he said to Jack. "I won't let you."

"Let justice be done," Jack replied calmly. "Then get on with your life and make this lodge something to be proud of."

"Oh, yeah," Chris said witheringly. "Jack Campbell, the sacrificial lamb and everyone's hero."

Jack turned to Alex, who was simply frozen, staring at the two men. "I did it. It's that simple."

"He did not!" Chris whined childishly. "I did it. I killed Mark. I know all about karate chops. My father showed me."

"Chris, be quiet," Jack said.

Chris turned to Alex. "My father here made the mistake of telling me that Mark and Astrid were planning on screwing us over with their restaurant plans. I went back to the kitchen after the closing party to confront the bastard. Somebody had already hit him, it looked like a couple of times maybe, but he was still abusive and mean—only not real steady on his feet. Made him an easy target."

"Be quiet," Jack said urgently.

Chris ignored him. "I'll give this to Mark. Never met a man who could find the heart of your insecurities and taunt you with them as well as he could. He could make anyone feel like a piece of shit. He started up and I just lost it." Here, Chris made a little bow to her. "I helped Leslie with her self-defense practice and reviewed my technique in the process." Now he turned to Jack. "I was good, wasn't I? You were watching. Stalking around, monitoring your borders or whatever the hell has gotten into you." Chris chopped into the air with an impressive speed. "My father watched me kill a man. I killed a man. It's so weird. It's not that hard and somehow your normal feelings are gone. And they stay gone until the nightmares come." He turned to his father. "That's where yours came from, huh?"

Jack nodded.

"I'll bet you didn't like it that Jean was going to take the rap, did you? But if you got her off, then I might be suspected. What a dilemma."

Poor Jack, Alex thought. His incredible pain was clearly written on his face. She herself could almost consider a nice chop to Chris's neck for his derisive attitude.

Chris wasn't done. He pointed at Alex. "Then this busybody got nosy. Your adorable little adopted daughter. Aren't you glad you welcomed her with open arms?"

Jack stared at the floor. "Enough," he said. "Please, Chris, enough."

"Okay, okay." Chris sighed. "Call the sheriff," he said to Alex.

It wasn't necessary. The wail of a siren grew louder, then tires screeched, and a stampede of feet ended in a clump of deputies with their guns drawn. Among them was Pete Szabo.

"Freeze!" Pete cried, but it was ridiculous given the relatively placid scene the deputies had come upon.

"It's all right, Pete," Jack said. "I'm the one. I killed Mark Heller."

"Screw you!" Chris yelled. "I'm not grateful for this, Dad. I won't let you do it." He turned to the deputies. "Leave him alone. He didn't do it."

Pete sighed. "Now what?"

"I did," Chris said. "I killed Mark Heller."

"He's trying to cover up for me," Jack interjected.

"It won't work," Chris said. "You will not do this. I won't be grateful and I won't get on with my life. You'll have failed in everything you're trying to do." Chris turned to Pete Szabo. "Arrest me. I did it."

Pete looked back and forth between father and son. Jack, in his all-black outfit, had crumpled and shrunk into himself. He looked like a damaged crow. "I'm going to arrest your son," Pete said.

Alex thought her heart would break at Jack's silent pain.

Pete shrugged and went over to Chris, took him by the elbow. "I don't have to use the cuffs, do I, Chris?"

Chris shrugged. "I don't want him alone when he tells my mother."

"Alex will go with me," Jack said, glancing up at her.

Alex, who had become like a statue, unable to do anything but watch the Oedipal drama unfold, woke up. "Of course," she said.

"*Of course*," Chris repeated. "Now she gets you all to herself, doesn't she?" His lips curled. "You really know how to mess up people's lives, don't you, Alex?"

"Chris," Jack intoned, "we're all in this together."

Chris turned his back on his father. "Three cheers for family values."

EPILOGUE

Kim answered the door. She looked pretty good. Better than the picture on Mary's desk. A fuzzy growth of hair on her bumpy scalp. Better color. But her welcoming smile seemed a bit forced. She was holding a glass of wine and, from the slur of her words, hadn't waited for the guests to start imbibing with gusto.

"Mary's in the kitchen unpacking the cartons," Kim said. "I hope you like Chinese take-out. We're terrible cooks."

"Love it," Alex said. "I'm Jewish by heritage. We have a genetic predisposition to Chinese food, especially take-out."

"I hope you got some plain things," Pete grumbled.

"Pork fried rice for you, dude," Kim said. "And beer."

"All right," Pete said. He took Alex's elbow as if to guide her into the house. Alex gently removed herself from his grasp. *Really.*

"What a gentleman," Kim said, observing the gesture and Alex's refusal to encourage chivalry.

Pete blushed a deep crimson.

"Leave him alone, Kim. He's such an easy target." Mary Szabo entered the living room from the kitchen. Like Kim, she was holding a glass of wine. "Alex, wine or beer? We have a couple of six-packs of Lagunitas India Pale Ale."

"Oh, wow. The IPA sounds good," Alex said. "Finest beer around."

"Glass?"

"No, thanks. I like drinking out of the bottle."

"Are you sure you're not a lesbian?" Mary asked.

"Mary!" Pete reprimanded her.

Mary shrugged. "If she's going to be around us, she's going to have to endure teasing, just like everyone else. We're Czech. It's in our genetic predisposition."

This was the most at ease Alex had seen Mary Szabo. She hoped it wasn't just the wine. Mary was very compelling when she relaxed.

A cheer rose from the television.

"What's happening?" Pete asked.

"The Kings were up three over the Lakers, but it's just the first quarter."

TV trays had been set up by the couch and chairs, which had been positioned to face the game.

"Sit," Mary said. "I'll get the drinks."

It was, all in all, a safe way to approach the evening. Stir-fry from paper cartons and little greasy ribs and plenty of alcohol and a fierce NBA rivalry. That limited conversation to the commercial breaks.

It was Wednesday evening. Chris had officially confessed in the wee hours of Monday, at the sheriff's substation in Guerneville. He was being held, pending arraignment, at the Sonoma County Main Detention Center—the same place from which Jean Heller had been released on Tuesday afternoon. Mary Szabo was off the case.

"How did the conversation with your father-in-law go?" Mary asked Alex. They'd spent the first commercial break mostly chitchatting, although with intent, reviewing what had happened in the last few weeks. Now came the difficult part.

Alex took a swig of ale. "One of the hardest things I've ever done. I had to make some compromises."

"Regarding the lawsuit?" Mary asked.

"Mary," Kim interrupted, "maybe she doesn't want to get personal."

"No, it's all right," Alex said. "Yes. I've promised to be a good girl. To fully cooperate in the lawsuit—even if it means getting a manicure and dressing like Jackie Kennedy. But it was worth it. Now Chris will have the best defense possible." She grimaced suddenly. "Oh," she said, looking at Mary, "I didn't mean anything about you. I think you're incredible."

"Look," Mary said, "let's be real. I'm a public defender. If you convinced your father-in-law to get some hotshot for Chris, that's great. Who is it?"

"Rufus O'Malley," Alex said.

Mary whistled. "No kidding?"

"No kidding. My father-in-law got O'Malley to take the case for a reduced fee. Apparently O'Malley owes him a big favor. And, to top it off, O'Malley also served in Vietnam. He was a Navy SEAL."

"He got that socialite Priscilla Blake off last month and she was guilty as hell, as far as I'm concerned," Pete said, helping himself to another serving of pork fried rice. "This rice ain't bad."

"Finish it," Kim said. "We got it for you."

He sighed and heaped the rest of the carton onto his plate. "Gotta watch my waistline. Maybe I'll finish this and start watching tomorrow."

"What waistline?" Mary turned to Alex. "He's built like a male underwear model. You should see him in a swimsuit. Wait until the summer."

"I look forward to it," Alex said, while Pete turned an interesting shade of reddish purple.

"So." Pete picked at the label on his bottle, refusing to look up. "Think you'll stick around here until the summer?"

Alex sighed. "I don't know. I love it up here."

"Surely they don't want you at the Overlook, do they?" Kim asked, causing both Mary and Pete to look horrified. Kim shrugged. "Sorry. I'm too blunt sometimes. Especially after three glasses of wine."

If her observations were correct, Kim's alcohol consumption was more likely in the six-glass territory. "No, it's all right," Alex said. "I don't know. Nobody knows. Jack insists we work together. It's a strange world, isn't it? Mary, I was rude to you because you gave Shayne Elliot the best defense you could. Now, with Chris, I want to see him get the best defense he can."

"Do you think he did it?" Kim asked.

Alex shrugged. "You mean, is he covering up for Jack? I don't think so. He doesn't seem like a martyr or a hero to me. I believe he's the one. But I don't think anyone will really ever know for sure, though. Does it matter?"

"Don't go too far into left field," Pete said. "There's still right and wrong."

"Spoken like a cop. It's a complex world that we try to fit those concepts onto," Mary said.

"Spoken like a lawyer," Pete retorted. "Truth is the most important thing." He turned to Alex. "Isn't it, Alex?"

Before Alex could reply, Kim interrupted. "Game's back on. Time-out on the ethical debate. Hey, maybe we can just skip it tonight altogether."

"Sounds good to me," Alex said. She knew there was plenty of time in the future to pursue that particular discussion.

Publications from Spinsters Ink

P.O. Box 242
Midway, Florida 32343
Phone: 800-301-6860
www.spinstersink.com

A POEM FOR WHAT'S HER NAME by Dani O'Connor. Professor Dani O'Connor had pretty much resigned herself to the fact that there was no such thing as a complete woman. Then out of nowhere, along comes a woman who blows Dani's theory right out of the water.   ISBN: 1-883523-78-8 $14.95

WOMEN'S STUDIES by Julia Watts. With humor and heart, Women's Studies follows one school year in the lives of these three young women and shows than in college, one's extracurricular activities are often much more educational that what goes on in the classroom.   ISBN: 1-883523-75-3 $14.95

THE SECRET KEEPING by Francine Saint Marie. The Secret Keeping is a high stakes, girl-gets-girl romance, where the moral of the story is that money can buy you love if it's invested wisely.
                    ISBN: 1-883523-77-X $14.95

DISORDERLY ATTACHMENTS by Jennifer L. Jordan. 5th Kristin Ashe Mystery. Kris investigates whether a mansion someone wants to convert into condos is haunted.   ISBN 1-883523-74-5 $14.95

VERA'S STILL POINT by Ruth Perkinson. Vera is reminded of exactly what it is that she has been missing in life.
                    ISBN 1-883523-73-7 $14.95

OUTRAGEOUS by Sheila Ortiz-Taylor. Arden Benbow, a motor-cycle riding, lesbian Latina poet from LA is hired to teach poetry in a small liberal arts college in northwest Florida.
ISBN 1-883523-72-9 $14.95

UNBREAKABLE by Blayne Cooper. The bonds of love and friend-ship can be as strong as steel. But are they unbreakable?
ISBN 1-883523-76-1 $14.95

ALL BETS OFF by Jaime Clevenger. Bette Lawrence is about to find out how hard life can be for someone of low society standing in the 1900s.
ISBN 1-883523-71-0 $14.95

UNBEARABLE LOSSES by Jennifer L. Jordan. 4th in the Kristin Ashe Mystery series. Two elderly sisters have hired Kris to discover who is pilfering from their award-winning holiday display.
ISBN 1-883523-68-0 $14.95

FRENCH POSTCARDS by Jane Merchant. When Elinor moves to France with her husband and two children, she never expects that her life is about to be changed forever.
ISBN 1-883523-67-2 $14.95

EXISTING SOLUTIONS by Jennifer L. Jordan. 2nd book in the Kristin Ashe Mystery series. When Kris is hired to find an activist's biological father, things get complicated when she finds herself fall-ing for her client.
ISBN 1-883523-69-9 $14.95

A SAFE PLACE TO SLEEP by Jennifer L. Jordan. 1st in the Kris-tin Ashe Mystery series. Kris is approached by well-known lesbian Destiny Greaves with an unusual request. One that will lead Kris to hunt for her own missing childhood pieces.
ISBN 1-883523-70-2 $14.95

Visit

Spinsters Ink

at

SpinstersInk.com

or call our toll-free number

1-800-301-6860